STONEHILL
BOOK ONE

the road leads back

This is a work of fiction. Names, characters, businesses, places, events, locales, and incidents are either the products of the author's imagination or used in a fictitious manner. Any resemblance to actual persons, living or dead, or actual events is purely coincidental.

Cover design by Okay Creations
Book layout by Lori Colbeck

ISBN-13: 978-1-950348-00-8

STONEHILL
BOOK ONE

the road leads back

MARCI
BOLDEN

PINK SAND
PRESS

Thank you to everyone who has been on this journey with me. Your support and encouraging words have pushed me through every time I wanted to give up on my dreams. I sincerely appreciate you.

CHAPTER ONE

Kara Martinson squeezed her way toward the crowded bar, nudging between two kids she couldn't quite believe were old enough to be legally drinking in public. They should have been funneling cheap beer in a college dorm somewhere. Or sneaking shots from Daddy's liquor cabinet.

Art gallery openings used to be much more sophisticated than this. When she was a young artist, openings were about appreciating the art and the artist, not the free booze.

Shit.

Had she really gone there? Kara shook her head at her bitter thoughts.

The bartender, a walking tattoo with spiked black hair, leaned over the counter. "What'll it be?"

She realized all she wanted was wine. And quiet. The kids around her were acting more like preteens jacked up on sugar than art aficionados. One made a face, squished and reddened, as he held up an empty shot glass as proof of his triumph.

Kara wondered when she had gotten so damned old. She never used to snub her nose at a good drink. Actually, she completely understood what her problem was, and it had nothing to do with age. She'd conformed. She'd fallen in line. She'd done what she was supposed to do.

Agent? *Check.* Gallery opening? *Check.* Interviews with all the fancy-pants art magazines? *Check.*

But this wasn't her. None of this was her.

Frowning, she leaned toward the bartender to make sure he heard her over the jeering kids. "Tequila."

Within seconds he set a glass in front of her and filled it with amber liquid. He started to walk away, but she held up one hand and lifted the glass with the other. She downed the drink, slammed the glass onto the counter, and gestured for another. One shot wouldn't be nearly enough to numb the misery of this evening. She motioned for him to fill the glass again.

The young man raised his brows and smirked as he poured. "I can't do this all night, lady."

"One more."

"Some of the crap in here costs more than my car. No puking. Got it?"

Kara chuckled. Clearly he didn't recognize her as the artist responsible for the crap. "Honey, I was doing tequila shots before your daddy dropped his pants and made you."

The barkeep threw his head back, laughed, then filled her glass one more time. "Nice one, babe."

Babe? Kara snorted, the shot almost to her lips, when someone squeezed her shoulder.

"Kara?" asked a deep, smooth voice, as if the man wasn't certain.

She turned and her eyes bulged as she looked into the intense, dark gaze she hadn't seen since the night she'd lost her virginity.

The music had been loud, the beer lukewarm, and everybody who was anybody—and several nobodies like Kara and Harry—in their senior class of Stonehill High was at the graduation party. The only person she had cared about, though, didn't care about her. Or so she'd thought. Until she somehow ended up on Shannon Blake's disgustingly pink and ruffle-covered bed with Harry Canton, book club president and algebra superstar, who clumsily removed her clothes and left slobbery kisses in their wake.

Kara swallowed hard as the flash of a memory faded and the man standing before her, looking as shocked as she felt, came back into view.

She downed the liquor, slammed the glass against the bar, and sighed before she announced, "I've been looking for you for twenty-seven years."

He sank onto the vacant stool next to her and lifted his hands as if he were at a loss for words. Something that appeared to be guilt filled his eyes and made his full lips sag into a frown. She'd be damned if temptation didn't hit her as hard as it had when she was a hormonal teen.

"I wanted to tell you I was leaving," he said, "but I didn't know how."

"You should have tried something like, 'Kara, I'm leaving.'"

"You're right. But I was a kid. I didn't have a lot of common sense. All I could think about was how I finally had my freedom."

She tilted her head and narrowed her eyes at him. "You had your freedom? You selfish prick."

His eyes widened. "Well, that might be a little harsh. I was just a kid, Kara. Yes, I should have told you I had no intention of staying with you, but I was a little overwhelmed by what had happened. I'm sorry."

"You're sorry?"

Harry's shoulders slumped, as if he had given up justifying sneaking out on her in the middle of the night. "Look, I saw a flier for your gallery opening, and I wanted to say hello. I thought maybe... I don't know what I was thinking." He sounded hurt—dejected, even. "I didn't mean to upset you."

Harry stood and Kara put her hand to his chest and shoved him back onto the barstool. The move instantly reminded of her their one night together. All of seventeen and totally inexperienced, she'd fancied herself a seductress and pushed him onto the bed before straddling his hips like she had a clue what she was doing.

As she touched his chest now, warmth radiated through her entire body.

She glared, pulling her hand away and squeezing her fingers into a fist. "Do you live in Seattle?"

He shook his head. "I had a conference in town. There were fliers at the hotel. As soon as I saw your picture, I knew I had to come." His smile returned and excitement lit his face. "I can't believe you have a gallery opening. This is amazing, Kare."

She wasn't nearly as thrilled by her accomplishment as he seemed to be. She felt like she was selling her soul instead of her art. She'd always preferred the indie route, but that crap agent had cornered her at a particularly vulnerable moment and convinced her she needed him...just like he'd convinced her she needed to be in a gallery. Although, now she was glad she'd conceded on the open bar.

The tequila swirled through her, making her muscles tingle and preventing her from fully engaging the nearly three decades of anger she'd been harboring. She had spent an awfully long time wanting to give Harry Canton a piece of her mind.

Even so, hearing him say she'd done something amazing warmed her in a way very little ever had. If he had come looking for another one-night stand, she hated to admit that she would consider reliving that night again—only this time with more sexual experience and less expectation of him sticking around.

He might be almost three decades older, but his face was still handsome and his brown eyes were just as inviting as they had been when he was a high school prodigy and she was a wallflower.

She smirked at a realization: he was in a suit, probably

having just left a corporate meeting, while she was wearing a red sari-inspired dress at her gallery opening.

He was still the straight arrow. She was still the eccentric artist.

"Did you hear what I said, Harry? About looking for you for the last twenty-seven years."

His shoulders sagged. "I never meant to sleep with you that night. I mean"—he quickly lifted his hands—"I was leaving and should have told you before taking you upstairs. I shouldn't have just left like that, but I didn't think you wanted to see me again anyway. If it's any consolation," he said, giving her a smile that softened the rough edges of her anger, "I'd been working up the courage to kiss you since junior year when you squeezed a tube of red paint in Mitch Friedman's hair after he made jokes about Frida Kahlo's eyebrows in art class."

Kara frowned at him. That hadn't been her finest hour. Then again, neither was waking up thinking she was starting a new life as a high school graduate and the girlfriend of the cutest boy she'd ever met, only to find the other side of the homecoming queen's bed empty. "There's nothing wrong with a woman embracing her natural beauty."

His smile faded quickly. "I'm sorry," he said, sounding sincere. "I shouldn't have left you like I did. I hope you believe that I regret it. Not being with you," he amended, "but leaving without explaining."

He'd had that same nervous habit in high school. He'd say what was on his mind and then instantly try to recover, afraid his words had come out wrong. Usually they had. For as awkward as she'd been, at least she'd always been able to say what she meant and stand behind it. Of course, that ability got her in trouble more often than not.

She'd told herself a million times that Harry didn't owe her an explanation. They hadn't been in any kind of relationship. She'd drooled over him from afar, but he'd barely acknowledged her existence in high school. Even if he hadn't gone off to start his Ivy League college career the day after graduation, he likely never would have looked at her again. Well, at least not until she could no longer hide the truth of their one-night stand from the world.

"I expected so much more from you, Harry," she said sadly, the sting of what he'd done back then numbed slightly by the tequila.

"I know."

"Why didn't you ever write me back?" She thought her voice sounded hurt and pathetic. She was surprised that after so many years of being angry, there was still pain hiding beneath her fury. "I must have sent you a hundred letters."

He creased his brow. "Letters? I didn't get any letters."

Kara searched his eyes.

He looked genuinely confused.

"I sent them to..." Her words faded. Suddenly the tequila-induced haze wasn't so welcome. "Your mother said if I wrote to you..."

"My mother? I never got any letters."

"But you sent money."

Harry shook his head slightly. "What the hell are you talking about? Why would I send you money?"

She stared at him as realization started to weave its way through her oncoming buzz. He hadn't responded to her letters because he hadn't received her letters. And if he hadn't received the letters, he hadn't sent her money. And if he hadn't sent her money, he hadn't known that she needed it. Sighing, she let some of her decades-old anger slip. Her head spun, either from the alcohol or the blurry dots she was trying to mentally connect. Leaning onto the bar, she exhaled slowly. "They never told you, did they?"

"Who? Told me what? What are you talking about?"

Kara couldn't speak. Her words wouldn't form.

Someone wrapped an arm around Kara's shoulder, startling her and making her gasp quietly. She turned and blinked several times at the man who had just slid next to her.

"Sorry to interrupt," he said, "but I need to get home." Leaning in, he kissed her head. "Congratulations on the opening, Mom. It was great."

"Um..." She swallowed, desperate to find her voice. "Thank you, sweetheart." She flicked her gaze at the man sitting next to her. The longer Harry looked at her son, the wider Harry's eyes became.

Phil cast a disapproving glance at Harry, the way he always did when assessing a man who might distract her from her responsibilities, and then focused on her again. "Don't forget that

Jess is expecting you to make pancakes in the morning. You promised."

"I haven't forgotten." Kara returned her attention to Harry. His jaw was slack and his cheeks had grown pale.

Phil nodded at Harry, as if he were satisfied that he'd made the point that his mother didn't need to stay out all night, and walked away. Harry watched him leave while Kara waved down the bartender and pointed at her glass. The tattooed kid hesitated, likely debating the ethics of giving her another shot. She pointed again, cocking a brow for emphasis, and he finally filled her glass.

"Kara..." Harry's voice was breathless, like he'd been kicked in the gut. "Was...was that my...son?"

No. His mother definitely hadn't given him the letters Kara had written. She lifted her shot, toasting him. "Congratulations, Harry. It's a boy."

Harry couldn't deny Phil was his if he tried. The picture on Kara's phone might as well have been a picture of himself from twenty years ago. The man had Harry's dark—almost black—hair and his dark brown eyes. He had the same oval face and long nose. Phil had Kara's smile, though. Wide and inviting. Or at least that's how Harry remembered it. She hadn't exactly smiled at him since he surprised her.

When he walked into the gallery and saw her, she'd looked

as beautiful as she had back in high school. His heart had nearly exploded. Her long, strawberry blond hair hung in waves down her back, and when she'd turned to him, he could easily make out the spatter of freckles across her nose he remembered from so many years ago. The lines caressing her mouth reminded him how he'd once traced his thumbs over her cheeks before delving in for their first kiss. He'd seen that in a movie and had played it over and over in his mind, imagining Kara instead of Molly Ringwald.

If only he'd stuck around to give Kara a happy ending like the movies promised.

Almost thirty years may have passed, but he felt like he was instantly transformed back into that awkward teenager who wanted nothing more than to profess his undying love and promise her forever—if only she'd want him, too. She never had. Whenever he'd smiled at her in the hallways at school, she'd always looked away. He'd tried talking to her several times in art class. She'd blown him off each time, muttering responses, too focused on her work to give him the time of day.

But he wasn't that awkward teenager anymore. He was confident and successful. He took life by the balls and dragged it where he wanted it to go, not the other way around. Not anymore. So when he'd spotted her as he walked toward the bar, he had taken a breath and headed straight for her.

He'd expected her to be a little miffed by his disappearing act all those years ago, but he'd thought they'd talk it out and move on. He'd even had a little light of hope that she'd forgive him.

He'd wanted to ask her to dinner, catch up on her life, find out if she was as fascinating to him now as she'd been all those years ago.

What he hadn't expected was for his life to be turned on its ear.

He had a son. He was a father. A real father. Not a stepfather who had never been quite good enough for his ex-wife's kids.

He had a kid. His own kid.

Not that Phil was a child anymore.

"I still can't believe this," Harry said.

Now, sitting in a diner down the street from the gallery, Kara ate pecan waffles and drank coffee, while Harry stared at the picture of his son. The sounds of her coffee cup and silverware clinked in the empty diner as they put together the pieces of how their parents had sealed their fates.

Kara's parents had kicked her out without a second thought. She had run to Harry's house, desperate for help. His mother had assured her all would be well. She fed Kara and tucked her away in Harry's bedroom while discussing the issue with Harry's father. Then, Elaine sent Kara away with false promises and never, not once in twenty-seven years, said so much as a word to him about his child.

While Harry was in college, Kara had lived in a community that not only supported but embraced girls like her—single mothers with no one else in the world. They'd both lived lives they'd seemed destined for—Harry with corporate friends and family and Kara with likeminded artsy types who embraced a bohemian lifestyle.

Harry had married the woman he was supposed to, and Kara had moved from place to place with Phil in tow. She'd lived all along the West Coast, only settling in Seattle after Phil had asked for help raising his daughter. Harry had returned to Iowa after college and took over his father's marketing firm. Kara hadn't set foot in her home state since the day she left it.

"Phil?" he asked. "Why Phil?"

"Why not?"

Harry wasn't sure if her clipped tone was from sarcasm or frustration or something in between—she never had been black and white like that—but her meaning was clear. He had no business questioning decisions she'd had to make without him.

He lowered her phone. He didn't blame her for being angry, but he couldn't help that his mother had deceived him.

If anyone other than their respective parents knew that Phil existed, they had kept it a tight-lipped secret. In all the years since Harry had come home from college, his mother never even hinted that she had a grandson. How many times had he told her how disappointed he was that his ex-wife hadn't wanted children with him? How many times had he said he wanted a family of his own? Elaine could have given him the one thing he'd been missing all his adult life. Instead, she had stolen his one chance to be a father.

He was angry, too, damn it.

He clenched his jaw. "I was robbed of my son as much as he was of a father. I would have stood by you, Kara."

She narrowed her eyes. "The only standing by me you ever did, Harrison, was to sneak out while I was sleeping."

"I'm not proud of that, but if I'd known about our son, I would have been there."

She looked out the window at the deserted street. "Your mother was so sweet when I went to her. So understanding. She let me stay at your house that night. The next morning she fixed me breakfast. She said she'd talked to you and you wanted to finish school, which was the most logical thing because you couldn't support a family without a job. She said she'd help me out until you could. I was so relieved. I remember wishing I knew her well enough to hug her because I'd been so scared she'd turn me away, too. And then she put me on a bus, and I never heard from her again. Other than receiving a check once a month."

"I'm sorry," he whispered.

She blinked, but the sheen of unshed tears in her eyes caught the light as she focused on him again. "I sent you letters every week. Stupid, stupid letters, thinking you were reading them. That you cared about us. But you never responded. Finally, I stopped writing. It took five years," she said with a bitter laugh, "but I finally caught on that you weren't coming for us. Even so, I felt obligated to let you know where we were. Every time we moved, I'd send a note with nothing but an address inside. I kept you...*your mother* up to date on our whereabouts until about seven years ago."

"What happened seven years ago?"

She hesitated, as if she didn't want to share the next bit of information. "Phil became a father himself. I figured at that point, if you hadn't opted to be a part of our life, I wasn't going to invite you to be a part of hers."

Harry's heart leaped in his chest, and he sat a bit taller. "I'm a grandpa?"

Kara actually smiled, and it was as dazzling as he remembered. "Her name is Jessica. Scroll through the photos. There are plenty on there. She, um..."

Harry paused on a picture, and his smile dropped a bit. The girl had Phil's dark hair and dark brown eyes. Her eyes, however, were set wide apart and slanted, and her face was flat and broad.

"She has Down syndrome," Kara said.

Harry stared at the photo. The girl wore a long sundress and yellow rain boots. A pink bandanna kept her braids away from her face and she held up dirty hands. He looked at the next photo and the one after that. Jessica was smiling in all of them. Not just smiling. Beaming.

"Is she always this happy?"

"No." Kara laughed. "She's as moody as any other seven-year-old girl. But I don't take pictures of sulking."

Harry chuckled. "She's beautiful." He looked up and saw doubt playing on Kara's face. "She's beautiful," he said more firmly.

"Yes, she is," she whispered. "Do you, um... Do you remember what song was playing when we were together?"

He creased his brow as he thought back. It may have been a lifetime ago, but he still had a clear memory of that night. He'd wanted to be alone with her, to tell her what he'd been wanting to say for two years—that he thought she was amazing. Wonderful. That he wished he'd been braver and had asked her out. That he was sorry he'd blown their high school years being a chicken shit.

While everyone else was getting drunk, he'd taken her hand and led her upstairs so they could talk. It turned out the only empty room they could find was Shannon Blake's bedroom. He hadn't planned to have sex with Kara that night, but before he could work up the nerve to say anything, her curious gray eyes lured him in. He kissed her—his first real kiss. And then somehow they were on the bed, and he was pulling at her clothes. In true virgin nerd fashion, he was inside her and both of their first sexual experiences ended before they even knew what they were doing. Their time together couldn't have lasted more than five minutes, but being with Kara had changed everything for him. From that moment forward, every woman in his life was judged on his own personal Kara scale. And none of them had ever measured up to the memory he'd cherished, and probably embellished, over the years.

He could remember that. All of that. But he couldn't recall any music playing.

"'One More Night,'" she said. "Phil Collins."

Harry stared at her for a moment before he finally realized why she was telling him this. He had asked why she'd named his son Phil. "You named our son after the artist singing the song he was conceived to?"

She shrugged. "I had asked for permission to name him after you, but you didn't answer my letter. I didn't want to name him after my father. He'd disowned me. I was at a loss. Phil was all I had."

"What's his middle name?"

Kara gawked, as if he'd just asked the dumbest question she'd ever heard. "Collins."

He let her admission process for a moment before he laughed outright. She threw a wadded-up napkin at him.

"I'm sorry, but...Phil Collins Canton?"

"Martinson," she corrected. "He has my name."

His smile faded at the sting in his heart. His only son didn't have his name? But why would he? Harry hadn't been there. He hadn't married her. He hadn't raised his son. "Right. Of course he has your name."

Tension rolled between them for a moment before she grinned. "If you'd been able to figure out how to get me out of my clothes faster, I would have had to name him Starship."

Harry laughed, but it wasn't as heartfelt. "That's better than calling him Mr. Mister, I suppose."

"Oh, I considered it."

He chuckled as he scanned the diner, not really seeing the booths and bored waitresses. He couldn't fully grasp how the night had turned out like this. The one girl he'd never been able to get out of his head was sitting across from him, and she was the mother of his child.

"You said you've been looking for me for twenty-seven years." He scoffed. "You couldn't have looked very hard, Kara. I moved home after I graduated college. I never left. I'm on social media. I own a business. I'm not exactly living under a rock. And my mother still lives in the same house. If you sent me letters back then, you knew how to find me."

"Yeah. 'Looking' might have been a stretch. Like I said, I stopped writing to you on Phil's fifth birthday. I always kept you —or so I thought—up-to-date on where we were living. I figured if you were so inclined, you'd reach out to us."

Harry frowned. "I know it doesn't mean anything now, but I would have been there. I would have given up everything to be there."

"I guess your mother knew that, huh?"

He nodded. "I guess."

"I've never been back." She focused on her coffee mug, but before she looked away he glimpsed the hurt she must have felt at being shunned by her family. "Not for class reunions or birthdays or Christmas. I don't even know if my parents are still alive. I've thought about contacting them, but…what would I say? What could they say? Sorry doesn't cover it. And I don't know if I could forgive them. Every time I think about how they threw me out, I just get so angry. I could never be so cold to Phil."

Guilt tugged at him. She shouldn't have had to face that alone.

"The last time I saw my father, he was shutting the door behind him after shoving me out. He told me I was never welcome in his home again." She worked her lip between her teeth as she blinked rapidly. The sheen of tears returned. "I sat on the swing for what seemed like hours, thinking they'd calm down and let me back in, but they didn't. I didn't know where else to go. I didn't exactly have friends back then. So I went to the closest phone booth and looked up your address. Thankfully you were named after your father. It made narrowing down which Canton household to go to much easier."

Harry lowered his face as her voice quivered. He figured these were memories she didn't dredge up too often. "This place that my mother sent you. What was it like?"

"It was nice, actually. I don't think she could have found a better place. There were women there who had been through similar situations. When Phil was born, they taught me how to change diapers and nurse him and all those things that...that my mother should have shown me. They taught me how to garden and sew and barter for the things I couldn't make. We left there when Phil was five and landed in another place like that. It kind of started a trend. I moved a lot, learning and growing. Phil resents not having a regular childhood, but we saw so much and did so much. I think he'll appreciate it someday."

"I bet you were—are—a great mother."

She scoffed, and Harry thought the pain in her eyes

deepened. "He's like you, Harry. He's just like you. He needed a stability that I couldn't provide for him. I couldn't stand to be in one place for too long. I still can't. Whenever roots start to grow, I get twitchy. I need to keep moving. I've only stayed in Seattle this long because of Jess."

"Running," he offered.

She looked offended, but he suspected he was more right than wrong. She was still hurting from her parents' rejection. She was still angry over raising a son on her own. She was still feeling alone, even if she had Phil and Jessica.

"It's called *running,*" he said. "And I hope you'll stop now, Kara."

She held his gaze. "But I so enjoy it, Harry," she responded with the sarcastic bite she'd had since he'd met her.

He was tempted to call her on it, but they had more pressing matters to discuss. "I'd like to meet them. My son and my granddaughter."

She frowned and drew a slow breath. "Well, I'm sure they'd like to meet you, too."

CHAPTER TWO

Kara smacked at Phil's hand as he tugged his tie. "Stop it," she snapped. "You're making me crazy." She tugged the knot loose only to retighten it at the base of his neck. "You don't even need this, you know. He's your dad, for crying out loud."

"I want this night to be perfect."

"It is going to be perfect. Now stop fidgeting."

He skimmed his gaze over her outfit—a green and gold tunic over matching pants. "Is that what you're wearing?"

"What's wrong with what I'm wearing?"

"It's very…"

"What?"

"Buddhist. Are you Buddhist now?"

Kara stopped straightening his jacket and cocked a brow at him.

"For the better part of my life, I thought you were Janis Joplin reincarnate. Lately you look more like...Maya Devi."

"Mrs. Prasad brought these for me from India. They were made by—"

"Single mothers trying to survive the caste system. I know." He grinned at her frown. "Mom, I appreciate you being here tonight, but can you please tone down the eccentricities? Just for one night?"

"I have no need to impress your father, Phil. I already know him. *Intimately*."

He furrowed his brows. "I don't want to hear about anything you know intimately. I just want things to go smoothly tonight."

"And my clothes are going to cause waves? I'm not naked."

"Mom. Please."

"Fine." She sighed. "I'll put on something more Eleanor Roosevelt."

He widened his eyes. "Please, for the love of all that is good and holy, Mother, do not talk politics, feminism, sex, religion, Indian caste, or any other topic that could possibly be construed as controversial."

"Don't call me Mother. I hate that. It sounds so chastising. And do you really think I don't have enough common sense to get through one evening with your sperm donor? Just because I shirk the conventional doesn't mean I don't know how to act like one of them."

He moaned. "I don't know why I thought having you around would make tonight easier."

She laughed as he walked away, readjusting his suit coat. She'd never understand how she ended up with a conformist for a son. She'd never colored within the lines, but Phil was born that way. While she'd lived life wandering and changing from day to day, he'd clung to normalcy like it could save him.

And maybe it had.

If he hadn't gone to college like society told him he should, he wouldn't have married and had Jess. Even if the marriage had failed miserably, he was left with the most amazing daughter who gave him a reason to be stable, which was what he'd longed for all his life. He definitely was Harrison Canton's son. In this particular battle of nature versus nurture, nature had won tenfold.

Less than twenty minutes later, dressed in black slacks and a white blouse with her long hair swept into a loose bun, Kara bowed before Phil. "Better?"

"You look perfect. Thank you."

Kara crossed her eyes and stuck out her tongue at Jess.

She giggled. "You look so normal, Grandma."

"That's what I was afraid of." Winking, she poked the girl's stomach. "Aren't you supposed to be in bed?"

"She's headed that way now," Phil said.

Jess stuck her lip out in a pout. "I want to stay up."

"Not tonight, Punky." Phil swooped his daughter up and kissed her head as he hugged her tight. "It's a school night. You need to get to bed."

Jess's face melted a bit. "But, Daddy..."

"Hey, it's already past bedtime. Now, go brush your teeth and wash up. I'll be right up to tuck you in."

The girl wriggled down and hugged Kara around the waist. "Good night, Grandma."

Kara ran her hand over Jess's head. "Good night, love. I'll see you in the morning."

"You said you're going to teach me to paint horses, remember?"

"I remember."

Jess grinned and darted off.

Once her footfalls were far enough away that she couldn't hear, Kara asked, "Why aren't you letting her meet him?"

"I want to meet him first." He stopped messing with his cuffs and met her gaze. "No, it's not because I'm hiding her."

"I didn't say you were."

"You were thinking it."

She smirked. "Since when can you read minds?"

"You aren't exactly difficult to understand, Mother."

She opened her mouth to challenge him, but he continued.

"There's no point in my hiding her, even if I wanted to—which I don't. You already told Harry Jess has Down syndrome." Leaning over, Phil kissed her cheek. "I know you feel like you have to protect her from the world, but you don't have to save her from me. I'm her dad, remember?"

Kara exhaled as a sense of shame caused her cheeks to heat. She was fiercely overprotective of her grandbaby. She couldn't help herself. People had a tendency to feel uncomfortable around

Jess. Other people's bad reactions to a perfectly normal little girl pissed Kara off.

"Yes, I remember."

"I just don't want her to get excited at the thought of having a grandfather, only to have him disappear for another twenty-seven years. That wouldn't be fair to her. She wouldn't understand."

"You're right." She nodded. "Of course you're right. But I don't think he'll disappear again. He honestly didn't know about you."

Phil returned his focus to tugging his sleeves down. "I can't believe his mother sent you away like that."

She smiled slightly. Phil rarely came to her defense. "Well. At least she found a place for us and sent money every month. Mine just washed her hands of us. We were better off anyway."

"Easy for you to say," he muttered. "You enjoyed living in a commune."

"Yes, I know." Her sentimental feeling deflated as his lifelong resentment spilled from his mouth. "Your childhood was filled with *so much* disappointment."

He stopped fussing over his jacket and looked at her. "All I wanted was to go to a normal school and have a normal life like normal kids."

The doorbell rang, and Kara lifted her brows. "Oh, shoot." Her voice oozed with sarcasm. "I was so enjoying this conversation." Her smirk softened when Phil's shoulders sank and his dark eyes, so much like his father's, widened.

"He's here," he managed to say.

Kara waited, but Phil didn't move. She couldn't blame him. Her nerves were wound so tight she felt a little queasy herself. Undoubtedly, Phil was a thousand times more anxious. She squeezed his arm, giving him a supportive smile, and stepped around him. Taking several breaths as she crossed the small living room, she opened the front door. Her heart tripped when she found Harry looking nearly as fearful as his son had moments before. Kara gave him that same weak smile she'd given Phil—a silent offering of support in a moment that was far too stressful for all of them. Stepping aside, she gestured for Harry to enter. He didn't move from the doorstep.

"I didn't know you'd be here. Not that it's a problem," he quickly amended.

"Phil's a little bit nervous."

Harry grinned. "Yeah. Me, too." He looked down at the teddy bear in his hand. "I didn't know what...but I thought..." He thrust the stuffed animal at Kara. "For Jessica."

She took the gift. "She's already in bed, but I'm sure she'll love it. Would you like to come in?"

He blinked several times, as if surprised that he was still standing outside. He crossed the threshold and looked around the small home. Kara couldn't afford much on her artist's wage, but it was enough. She taught classes and some one-on-one lessons, but her income was iffy most times. She was much better at bartering for her needs than earning money. Unfortunately, the utility companies didn't trade services.

Phil had been laid off four months before and moved in with Kara to save money, making the tiny home seem even smaller. She didn't mind, though. She loved having Jess there day and night. It had taken some time getting used to having Phil under her roof again, however. He didn't appreciate her carefree life any more now than he had as a teenager.

Harry stopped in front of a painting of the sun setting over the ocean and smiled. "Is this yours?"

"Yeah. I tried my hand at landscapes for a while. It didn't stick."

"Why not? It's great, Kare."

He turned his smile on her, and she had to look away. He made her stomach tighten and her heart trip over itself even now. He always had, but she wasn't a stupid girl anymore. She refused to swoon just because he gave her a compliment.

"I always envied your talent," he said.

"Oh, yeah? Well, I always envied your..."

He grinned at her. "My ability to avoid getting my ass kicked by the cool kids?"

She snorted. He could talk his way out of any situation then, and she suspected he still could. Whereas she would resort to sarcastic commentary that got her in more trouble than not, Harry could always soothe the most ruffled of feathers. The day she'd squirted paint all over the most popular boy in school, Harry convinced Mitch Friedman not to retaliate even as he aimed tubes of paint in her direction.

"Yeah." Kara pushed the memory aside. "Something like

that."

He focused on her painting again. She realized he was stalling.

"Are you ready to meet your son? He's in the next room."

He looked at her, and the fear in his eyes made her heart ache for him.

"Is he angry?" Harry whispered.

"No. I told him you didn't know."

"I'm sorry. For everything you both went through."

She frowned at the misery in his voice. "It wasn't so bad. We had a good support system."

"You should have had me." Guilt tinted his eyes.

She drew a deep breath. "Harry—"

"I didn't sleep at all last night. I just kept thinking back on how selfish I was to leave like I did. How idiotic it was of me to never even call you and tell you why. I know we were just kids, but I hate that I was so scared of my parents, of you...of everything."

She creased her brow. "Me? Why the hell were you scared of me?"

He stared at her for a moment. "Because I was a nerdy boy and you were a beautiful girl."

"Right."

"I wasn't lying last night," he said softly. "It took me two years to work up the courage to kiss you graduation night."

She laughed. "I hate to remind you, buddy, but you did a little more than just kiss me."

He grinned. "The rest was just icing on the cake."

"It was something," she muttered. Taking a breath, she wiped the smile from her face and nodded her head toward the other room. "He's in there. And he's just as terrified as you."

Harry exhaled harshly. "I doubt that."

"Come on."

She nudged him toward the living room. After a moment, he took a few hesitant steps toward the doorway. Phil stared at them, his mouth open slightly and his eyes wide.

"Phil," she said when the men remained silent. "Say hello to your father."

8h

Harry looked across the room at this man who was his son. He wanted to laugh and cry and hug him all at once, but he was frozen. He thought the look on Phil's face—one of shock and confusion—must have mirrored his own. Yesterday he woke up without a family, other than his mother. In what seemed like the blink of an eye, he had a son. A granddaughter. He hadn't even said a word to Phil, hadn't seen Jessica, but somehow his world seemed fuller, more complete.

Kara was standing at his side, but she seemed miles away. His son was a younger version of himself staring back at him. Phil was a full-grown man with short-cut hair and a close-shaved face. He was wearing a suit and tie. There was nothing about his son that was a child anymore.

As quickly as Harry felt joy, remorse took its place. He'd missed Phil's life. He'd missed everything. Every milestone, every chance to teach his son how to throw a ball, every scraped knee, every birthday, every Christmas, every Halloween.

He'd missed his entire life. Almost.

A sob choked out of him, and Kara put her hand on his arm, snapping him back to reality.

"I'm sorry," he said. "I, uh..."

Phil stepped forward, closing the gap between them. "It's-It's good to...meet you..."

Harry looked at the hand being held out and bypassed it. He pulled his son to him and hugged Phil like he was a kid. Harry was hugging his son. How the hell had that happened?

After a long time, Harry leaned back and put his hands on Phil's face. Harry blinked away the tears blurring his vision. He didn't know why he was crying. He wasn't a crier, damn it. But he couldn't seem to control whatever it was that was rolling through him.

He already felt so much love for this stranger that the sensation was overwhelming him. He searched Phil's eyes, wishing he could have seen them look up at him like he'd seen so many other little boys looking at their fathers.

"Please, Dad." He imagined his child saying the words. "Just one more..." One more book, candy, ball toss... One more whatever it was that was so important.

He'd never hear those words from Phil. He'd never run down the street holding the back of a bicycle seat shouting encouraging words to his son. He'd never read him a bedtime story or ground him for staying out too late. He'd never fight with him about doing his homework or make up with him by taking him fishing. He'd never build him a tree house or help with a science fair.

That damn sob welled in his chest again, but he swallowed it down this time. "I would have been there," he managed to say around the brick of emotion in his chest. "I wouldn't have abandoned you or your mother."

Phil nodded. "I believe you."

Harry felt a bit of the restriction around him ease. He had worried all day that Phil would hate him, blame him. But his son's eyes were sincere and welcoming. He didn't seem to have the same underlying grudge that Kara had. Harry had a long way to go to make things right with her, but relief surged through him with the first indication that Phil was giving him a level playing field. He could never get back all the moments of his son's childhood, but he could be there now and without the resentment he saw when Kara looked at him.

She may have understood that it wasn't his fault he hadn't been there for her, but she still harbored anger. And he didn't blame her. He just hoped they could move beyond it. He already felt more optimistic about Phil.

"I'd better check on Jess," Kara said.

She left them alone, and Harry finally released his hold on Phil.

Harry took a deep breath and let it out slowly. "I apologize for being emotional."

Phil shook his head and gestured toward the couch. "No. It's good. It's… I wasn't sure how you'd feel about having a kid you never knew."

"How do you feel about having a father who never knew about you?"

He gave a lopsided smile. "It's better than thinking you didn't care about us."

Harry sighed. "I'm sorry you thought that."

"Mom always said you were just working far away. She never said you didn't care, but as I grew up I kinda came to that conclusion. When I was younger, I'd ask where you were. She'd tell me stories about what she thought you were doing. When I was convinced I'd grow up to be an astronaut, she pointed to the moon one night and said, 'I bet your dad is up there building the first city in space. Maybe we'll live on the moon someday.' I talked to the moon every night until I was eight and one of my friends told me how stupid that was. When I asked her if she really thought you were on the moon, she said probably not. She thought you were probably in New York, working at a top-secret pizza factory. I think we had some form of pizza for dinner every night after that for months."

Harry laughed gently, but his amusement faded quickly as he imagined a young Kara lying to protect her little boy from the truth. He could see it in his mind as clearly as if he had been there. He pictured her putting a hand on Phil's small head, smiling that warm smile that had won Harry over the first time she'd offered it to him, and using that soft, soothing voice to reassure Phil that his father—who had never acknowledged his existence—was out in the world doing something wonderful. The fake memory tugged at his heart and made breathing difficult.

Harry had clearly seen the blame and resentment in Kara's eyes the night before. Yet, she'd risen above painting an ugly portrait of Harry to his son—a son she presumed he had abandoned. He'd have to thank her for that. She could have easily twisted Phil around and made him hate his father. It seemed that despite her own feelings, she'd never said a negative word about Harry.

Looking down at his hands, he rubbed his palms roughly together in an attempt to stop the emotions from surging through him again, but he couldn't stop shame from settling in his gut. He could hardly look Phil in the eye. "I wish…I wish she wouldn't have had to do that. She shouldn't have had to lie to protect you. I should have been there."

"Well," Phil said, shrugging slightly, "like you said. You would have been. If you'd known." Phil gestured to the books on the coffee table. "Um, Mom thought you might want to look at pictures."

"Yeah. That'd be great."

"She has about a million," he said, moving to the sofa. "Some guy gave her a camera before I was born. She was obsessed with taking pictures. She still takes photos for people sometimes, but mostly she paints and sculpts." He reached for an old tattered album. "Start with this one, I think. Yeah," he confirmed after flipping the cover back. "This one."

Harry hesitated before moving to the couch. He nearly laughed. He was about to sit down and go through his son's baby pictures. Easing down next to Phil, he sighed when he looked at a picture of Kara pulling a shirt tight against her stomach. She was wearing clothes that were obviously homemade, and guilt tugged at him again. She hadn't even had proper maternity clothes.

Harry pushed the sense of responsibly from his shoulders and focused on the image. Her heart-shaped face was the same as he remembered. Her hair was different, though. Instead of the feathered look she had sported in high school, it was un-styled save for the braids that kept the front from hanging in her face. Her stomach was bulging to the point that it looked like she could topple over at any moment.

Though she wasn't much older than she had been the last time he'd seen her—sleeping soundly in Shannon Blake's bed—she somehow looked wiser and more aware of life. She looked like a woman in the photo, like someone who had realized that the world wasn't as cut and dry as teenagers tended to believe.

She'd matured. It showed in the shadows in her eyes.

Harry imagined if he looked at a photo of himself taken at the same time, he'd still look like a kid. He'd been carrying on in college, not exactly living it up, but he certainly hadn't been facing the hard truths that Kara had.

There were several photos of her showing off her stomach,

but on the next page, she had an infant in her arms. The blanket he was in was old and ragged, definitely used, but Kara was smiling brightly. However, Harry was certain he saw fear in her eyes. He traced his finger on her face, trying to imagine how terrifying it must have been. She'd given birth to their son without him. She'd pushed and screamed and cried as Phil came into the world, and Harry was hundreds of miles away, living his life as though it was just another day.

In one photo, a woman with dark hair leaned in close to Kara. She looked protective of the new mother and child, but that did little to ease the ache growing in Harry's chest. As he once again skimmed the first photo of Kara holding a newborn, he noticed more than her pale face and timid smile. The sheets had a paint spatter scheme, something that was on trend back in the day. The room around her was a far cry from a clinical hospital setting.

Harry tried to age the image, but it was clear this was taken right after Phil had been born. He was still red and wrinkled. Kara still had a sheen of sweat on her cheeks. "What hospital were you born in?"

"Hospital? This is Mom we're talking about. I was born in a birthing pool at some midwife's house. Mom tilled and seeded her garden that spring to repay her. There are a few pictures of her gardening with me on her back."

Harry frowned. He never would have allowed his baby to be born in a pool.

There were two pages of photos of newborn Phil. Most of

the photos showed women supporting Kara. In some, girls not much older than Kara held Phil in well-worn blankets. In others, a woman held Kara's hand, looking as though she were doling out motherly advice.

Page by page, Phil grew. First, he was a tiny red bundle tied to Kara's back by a long wrap of material while she peeled a huge pile of potatoes. Then a chunky little boy grinned up from the same papoose-type wrap while she leaned on a hoe, apparently taking a break from tearing up the ground. That must have been the midwife's garden. Harry chuckled as he looked at a close-up of Phil's face. His cheeks were round and full. He hadn't wanted for food as a baby, that was for sure.

Kara, however, lost the pregnancy weight fast. She was thin, possibly thinner than she'd been in school. Her simple handmade clothes never seemed to fit properly.

As Phil grew bigger, Kara's hair grew longer and more ragged. Sometimes she wore long skirts and baggy shirts or bohemian sundresses with her long, wavy hair in braids or pulled back. He smiled at one picture of a tiny Phil sticking flowers in her hair. She was smiling in all the photos, even the candid ones, though in the close-ups Harry thought her eyes reflected buried pain. The setting around them changed constantly—farms, deserts, the ocean, mountains. They must have moved more frequently than Harry had imagined.

"She said you guys had a good life," Harry commented, more an observation than an expectation at conversation.

Phil scoffed. "She had a good life."

Harry stopped looking at the album and turned to his son. "What do you mean?"

Phil shrugged. "I just wanted to be in one place, have a house, go to school. Mom moved us around a lot. She's never held down a real job. She was always bartering for things. She'd paint murals on someone's wall, and they'd let us crash there for a while. She'd tend to someone's garden, and they'd give us food. We never stayed anywhere long."

Harry remembered Kara's off-the-cuff comment about Phil resenting his childhood. "Sounds like an adventure," he offered.

"I was in eighth grade before I convinced her to put me in public school. She'd homeschooled me all that time. Sometimes with other kids. That bartering thing again. 'I'll teach your kid if you feed mine.'"

"Well, that sounds like a job to me."

Phil ignored Harry's defense of Kara. "I was thirteen when we finally settled in a little town on the Oregon coast. She got an apartment, an actual apartment." He smiled. "It was the first time I had a bedroom I didn't have to share with her or other people's kids. I still remember what it looked like. Mom convinced the manager to let her paint the rest of the apartment, but I refused to let her touch my room. For the first time in my life, I finally had plain white walls. We stayed there until I graduated high school, but as soon as I left for college, Mom was off again. She didn't settle down until Jess came along. She wanted to be close to help out—and it's a good thing she did. My ex-wife left when Jess was just a baby. We've been in Seattle since."

Harry looked around the living room. It was the color of rust. The entryway had been a lemongrass color. He had not seen a single white wall, not that he'd ventured far into the house. "You got over your dislike of colors, huh?"

Phil glanced at him. "Oh, no. This is Mom's house. Jess and I moved in a few months ago. The marketing firm I was working for merged with another company. They laid off most of us from the business that got swallowed. I haven't found a new job yet, and I didn't want to blow through my savings. Jess and I moved in here to save money while I get back on my feet."

Harry heard all of what Phil had said, but he was hung up on two words: marketing firm. "What did you do? At the firm?"

"I designed print ads, banners, things like that."

"I own a marketing firm, Phil." Harry's son eyed him suspiciously. "The Canton Company. Not very original, I know, but my father started it when I was just a kid. He was content with it being local, but I've been working on gaining some national accounts. I was out here for a convention, hoping to network. I took a lot of résumés, but if you need a job, you've got one."

Phil stared at him for several heartbeats. "Really?"

"Yeah. Insurance. 401k. Paid vacation. The works."

"What's the catch?"

Harrison shrugged. "No catch. I mean, not really. You'd have to relocate to Iowa, but you guys can stay with me."

"The hell they will." Kara stood in the doorway, her eyes narrowed angrily as she glared at Harry.

CHAPTER THREE

Kara tried to calm her fury, tried to bite her tongue, but she'd never been good at impulse control. "I leave you alone with my son for ten minutes, and you're already trying to convince him to leave?"

"Mom," Phil warned.

She ignored her son. "What the hell gives you the right to try to take my family from me?"

Harry sighed. "I'm not trying to take anyone away from you."

She cocked a brow. She'd heard enough to know otherwise.

"I own a marketing firm," Harry said. "It just so happens my son works in marketing."

"Isn't that beautiful? Must have been all the time you spent with him when he was a kid."

"Mother!"

Harry lowered his face, and Kara mentally kicked herself. She wanted to apologize, but the anger she felt ran too deep. Phil and

Jess were all she had. Sure, she'd made friends over the years. Sure, she'd been in Seattle for the last seven years. Sure, Phil was an adult with his own mind and his own life to think about, but Harry had no right to drop in out of nowhere and try to be Father of the Goddamned Year.

Phil stood and walked around the coffee table. He stopped in front of Kara, giving her the disapproving look that came so naturally to him. "He's offering to help me. In case you forgot, I'm unemployed at the moment."

"You don't need to go to..." She poked her head around him. "Where are you living these days, Hare?"

"I'm still in Stonehill, but the office is in Des Moines."

She refocused on her son. "You don't have to go to Iowa for a job, Phil. This is Seattle. You will find a job here, like you planned. You just have to keep looking."

"Do you know how many résumés I've submitted?"

"Four months ago, when you were laid off and I suggested moving, you had a laundry list of reasons why we couldn't relocate. It was important to keep Jess in her school, keep her where she is familiar and comfortable. What about that?"

"Christ, Mother," he seethed. "He didn't even finish offering me a position. I haven't had a chance to think about it, let alone accept. But you know what? Maybe you were right, for once. Maybe Jess will adjust. Maybe it would be good for her to try something new and meet new people. Maybe I should expand her world and show her different things."

His words took the wind from her. When she'd argued the

logic of relocating, it was just the three of them. She'd pictured them living in a small town like the ones that she and Phil had passed through during the years Phil was growing up.

Kara had tossed out the idea, the logic, the hope of relocating, but not to the Midwest. Not to Iowa. And definitely not Stonehill.

"I have a big house. More than I need. You could stay with me." Harry walked to where Phil was staring down Kara. "All of you could. If you wanted."

Kara's heart dropped to her stomach. She turned and stepped nose-to-nose with Harry. "How dare you show up after thirty years and try to turn my life upside down all over again!"

"Goddamn it." Harry raked his hand through his hair. "I would have been there. I wouldn't have left you alone."

"But you did," she spat. "You got to live your life while I was sent away like some kind of leper."

"I didn't know you were pregnant!"

"Of course you didn't, Harry! How could you when you barely took the time to pull your dick from between my legs before abandoning me?"

"Jesus," Phil said, reminding his parents he was in the room. "I did *not* need to hear that."

Both Kara and Harry sagged a bit. Tears bit at her eyes. *Damn it.* She didn't want to cry. She refused to cry.

"Look," Harry said gently. "I'm not trying to take them away from you, but this is my son. My granddaughter. And I deserve to know them. I deserve to be in their lives as much as you do. I didn't choose to leave them. I know," he cut in before she could speak, "I walked away from you, and I sincerely apologize for that. But I didn't leave Phil. I want to know my son. I want to know his daughter."

"Then come *here*." Kara hated how her voice trembled with a crazy mix of anger, fear, and desperation.

"I can't. I have a business to run, and I can't do that from here. Phil needs a job. He needs insurance and security for his daughter. I can give that to him. For the first time in his life, I can give him something. I can take care of him. But I can't do that with him here." He turned to Phil. "Come to Iowa. Bring Jessica." He focused on Kara again. "You can come as well. Des Moines has changed so much. You can find a place to show your art there."

Returning to Iowa was not an option. Going home had never been an option. It was never going to be an option. She had been forced to leave, and she'd never looked back. She would *never* look back.

Heavy silence hung in the air until Harry said, "You don't have to decide now, Phil. You can come whenever you want. The offer is open-ended. If you choose to stay here, I'll help out as much as I can. It shouldn't all be on your mom. And I'll visit, if that's okay. I'd like us to have a relationship, even if it is long distance."

Phil smiled, and Kara despised the way he looked at Harry. Like Harry was so wonderful, so wise, so parental. She didn't think she'd seen that expression on Phil's face since he was six years old. Phil's clear admiration for Harrison tore at her heart, and she wanted to cry and scream and take back the moment she'd admitted they were father and son.

"Thanks, Harry," Phil said. "I'll think about it."

Harry shifted when Kara rotated her jaw and turned away. "Do you think I could talk to your mom for a few minutes?"

Phil lifted his brows at Kara, and she completely understood what he was trying to convey to her.

Be nice.

"I was thinking a beer sounded good. Would anyone else like one?" Phil didn't actually wait for anyone to answer. He stepped around his parents and left the room.

Kara rolled her head back and exhaled. "You are unbelievable," she whispered.

"Because I want to know my son?"

"He doesn't need you to fix things for him, Harrison."

"This isn't about fixing things, Kara. Damn it. That's my kid. He's an adult now. A father. He's twenty-six years old. He's been married and divorced. He's graduated high school and college. I missed all that. I didn't get to help him with any of that, but I can help him now. And I do have a right. I'm his father."

"You don't even know him."

"That wasn't my choice. I wasn't given a choice." He lowered his voice. "Look…"

She knew that trick from his teenage days. On one hand, it pissed her off even more. On the other, she couldn't help but be soothed a bit.

"We both got screwed over, okay? But we're here now. All of us. Together. I'm not trying to take Phil and Jess away from you. But they're my family, too, and I want my chance."

He put his hand over his heart, and hers broke a little.

"I want to get close to him," Harry said. "I want him to see me as his father. Not because I had unprotected sex with his mother when we were both stupid kids but because I *am* his father. A father who is there, who he can rely on. Who *you* can rely on when you need someone to help you out. I want to make this up to you as much as I do to him. I know we aren't technically a family, but you're the mother of my child—my only child. That makes us family in my eyes, Kara. And I need a second chance with my family. All of my family."

She sighed and looked away. "I can't go back there. I can't. Not there."

"I can't leave. Not when my business is growing. And it isn't just my business anymore. It's Phil's, too. It's his future. His and Jess's."

"I can't."

He put his hands on her shoulders and held her gaze when she looked at him. "I know it hurts. I have to face my mother, too. I'm terrified. I'm furious with her. Part of me wants to cut her off, never speak to her again. But I have to know why. I have to know if she and my father even cared that their grandson was out there, growing up without me. I have to face the past, Kara. And so do you."

She couldn't breathe. Could barely hear his voice over the

pounding of her heart as the truth she'd been ignoring for almost thirty years crashed down on her.

She had wanted to confront her parents so many times. She wanted to demand an apology. She wanted to shame them the way they shamed her when she told them she was pregnant.

But more than anything, she wanted to know why they hadn't loved her enough to help her when she needed them most.

The thought of following through, however, was worse than any other fear she'd ever faced over the years. "Harry...I can't."

He caressed her cheeks, reminding her of the way he'd touched her that night. "Yes, you can. I'll help you. It's time to stop running, Kara."

CHAPTER FOUR

Sometime during breakfast Harry realized Kara and Phil acted more like bickering siblings than mother and son. He took a bite of the rainbow pancakes he'd ordered to impress Jess as Phil talked about how he'd learned to play the guitar before he'd learned to add.

"Mom thought music was more important than math." Phil didn't even attempt to hide his displeasure with her decision.

"Would you like me to remind you how many times that guitar earned you enough cash to pay a bill or two?" She glanced at Harry. "He's made ends meet by playing in coffee shops plenty of times."

Phil shook his head but didn't verbally disagree.

Harry wondered if they had always teetered on such precarious edges. Phil clearly hadn't approved of his upbringing, but he was independent and intelligent. He'd gone to college.

And he was patient with his daughter. He'd had a promising career until fate stepped in, but he was young, and losing a job to downsizing wasn't a reflection on Phil's skills.

Even so, one wrong word seemed capable of tipping the two into uneasy territory. They didn't fight exactly but disagreed—passionately—about what their lives had been. Kara had been just eighteen when she'd had Phil. Not quite mature enough to raise a child on her own. Even if she'd had her hippie support group, at the end of the day, she had been alone.

But Harry was determined to put an end to her single parenthood.

Clearing his throat, he sat forward. "Phil, I know you need time to think, but I'd like to send you some information on the company. If that's okay."

Kara stiffened beside him.

Instead of treading lightly, he looked at her. "I'm going to send you some information as well. Like I said, Des Moines is growing."

"Like I said, I'm not going to Des Moines."

"Are you going to send me something, Harry?" Jess asked.

Harry grinned at his granddaughter. "As a matter of fact, I am."

Her eyes widened but not as much as her smile. "What?"

"Well, you did such a great job painting this pony"—he gestured to the artwork she'd brought for him— "I thought I'd send you some special paints. How about that?"

As she smiled, Harry's heart melted. Time passed quickly, though, and before long, they left to take him to the airport.

Kara drove with Harry in the passenger seat. While Phil and Jess chatted in the back, Harry considered how he could convince them all to come to Iowa. He was certain with the right information on schools and housing, he could convince Phil that relocating was the logical choice. Kara, however, was going to take a bit more coaxing.

"Stop it," Kara said, pulling Harry from his thoughts.

He looked at her. "Stop what?"

"Cooking up your evil plan. You still get that same glazed-over look you did in high school."

He smirked at her. "How do know my plan was evil?"

She scoffed but didn't answer.

"I'm not looking forward to this," he said after a few moments.

"What?"

"Facing my mother."

Her scowl softened. "I'm sorry."

"For what?"

She shrugged. "It can't be easy to realize you were lied to most of your life."

"You were, too, weren't you?"

"She isn't *my* mother."

That was the kicker, wasn't it? Elaine had lied to Kara, deceived her, and betrayed her. But Kara didn't know Elaine. In a strange sense, he'd always trusted that his mother's overbearing behavior was for his own good. How could she explain this?

Glancing over his shoulder at Phil, he sighed.

There was no explanation.

Their goodbyes were a bit awkward. Phil and Jessica hugged him willingly, but Kara leaned away as soon as he reached for her, so he simply promised to be in touch.

The flight back to Iowa was probably the longest of his life. He stared out the window, focused on what he was going to say to his mother.

Harry couldn't think of a time in his life when he was more nervous than when he drove from the airport to Elaine's home.

Kara had a lot of anger, and Harry didn't have a clue how to help her through it. Part of that was because he had his own anger to sort out. He'd been a victim to his parents' lies, too. He had lost twenty-six years with his son and with the woman he would have married had he known she was carrying his child.

"Who the hell knows how that would have turned out," he muttered.

Pulling up in front of the house he grew up in, he sat for a long time, imagining a teenage Kara knocking on the door. How had that conversation gone? What had she said?

Finally, he turned off the ignition and faced the hot Iowa summer. He opened the front door to Elaine's house and sighed with frustration. He tested the door every time he arrived, and almost every time it was unlocked. He'd told her a hundred times the least she could do was turn the damn deadbolt and make burglarizing her home a bit more of a challenge.

"Hello?" He closed the door and flipped the lock behind him.

"In the kitchen! You're just in time for dinner."

His stomach tightened as he took the first step toward confronting his mother.

In all his life, he'd never looked her in the eye and called her on her bullshit. As a teenager, he'd simply cowered to her imperious nature.

He had never intended to come back. It wasn't until his father had died of a heart attack weeks before he finished his final semester of school that his plans changed. He took over the family business with the support of its long-term employees. He'd never left.

Stepping into the kitchen, he watched her reaching for a second plate. In that moment, he pictured how she looked when he was in high school. Her light brown hair was always perfect. Her clothes always looked pressed. Her dark eyes were sharp, never missing a thing, and she never hesitated to call Harry out on whatever she thought was wrong. Not that she'd been a horrible mother. She'd just been strict. She'd never been the mom who baked cookies for the class or encouraged Harry to go out and play with the other boys.

Not much had changed over the years, really. She'd never tolerated messes. Apparently that wasn't limited to grass-stained jeans. She'd always liked things neat and tidy—hated the unpredictable—and went to great lengths to keep things in order.

Watching her now, he wondered if she regretted the life she'd had. Did she miss how things could have been if she'd just let him live a little? Make mistakes? Get dirty? Take responsibility for a certain night that had happened so long ago?

She glanced over her shoulder and smiled at him. "How was your trip?"

His stomach turned over once again. "Interesting."

"Interesting good or interesting bad?" She set the plate on the counter.

"Both, I guess." He sat at the table and watched her dish out two servings of pasta.

"Did you find some good connections for the company?"

He scoffed. "Oh, I found something all right."

She glanced back, and it was clear she hadn't heard him.

Harry swallowed his bitter retort. "I offered a job to someone. He hasn't taken me up on it yet, though."

"Well, that's unexpected. Not even so much as an official interview, huh?"

"He doesn't need an interview."

"My, he must be impressive."

His heart raced as he focused on his mother grating fresh parmesan over noodles. "I went to school with his mother. You may remember her. Kara Martinson." Elaine froze as Harry continued as casually as if he were discussing the weather. "She's an artist in Seattle now. I saw a flier for her gallery opening. I decided to go and catch up on old times. Imagine my surprise when she scolded me for never responding to a single letter she sent me."

The grater and cheese shook in his mother's hands until she set them on the counter.

"Of course, that was nothing compared to my surprise when I met her son. He has my eyes, my hair. He even has my nose. As a matter of fact, you'd almost think he was *my* son." He tilted his head and narrowed his eyes, no longer able to hide his fury. "But he couldn't be mine. *Could he, Mother?*" he asked through clenched teeth.

She turned slowly to face him. Her jaw was set tight, but her cheeks had lost all color, betraying the calm she was trying to convey.

Her reaction killed any last hope he had that his mother was somehow innocent in this deception.

"She came to you, and you sent her away with a promise to tell me all about the baby she was carrying, but you never said a word."

"Harrison—"

He jabbed a finger into his chest. "I have a son. And you knew." He turned the finger that he'd aimed at himself and pointed it to her. "You stole him from me. You stole my child."

"No! No, Harrison." She took a ragged breath. "Your father and I…we wanted to protect you."

"From what? My responsibility?"

"She would have ruined your future."

"What about *her* future?"

"We took care of her, Harry. We sent her money."

"Money? She was alone and scared! She didn't have anyone to help her raise her son. My son!" He shook his head, warning her when she opened her mouth. "I didn't come to hear your excuses. I can't deal with that right now. The only thing I want to know is if you still have the letters she sent."

Her mouth opened again, but she didn't speak.

He slammed his fist into the table. "Do you have the letters? Do you have the pictures of my boy?"

Elaine put her hand to her chest, and her lip trembled until she clenched her jaw. She stood up straight, as if digging her heels in. "Your father and I—"

"You know what, Mom? Dad died when I was still in college. Don't you put this off on him. You've had almost thirty years to come clean, but you didn't. Not once. Not in all these years. You knew I wanted a family."

"You had a family with Laura."

"Laura's kids resented me from the day I married her until the day she left. I wanted my own kids, and you knew I had one. You had a grandson. How could you… Never mind. Just give me the letters. I want them."

She stared at him for several breaths.

"Now!" Harry demanded.

She darted from the room.

Running a hand over his hair, he tried to wrap his head around what was happening. The last few days had been so surreal. Standing here, demanding letters from thirty years ago, was surreal.

Elaine reappeared several minutes later. The box shook in her hands.

Harry scoffed. He had seen the old fabric-covered container in her closet more than once but had never given it a second thought. He had no idea it held such a dark secret.

He snatched the box from her. It seemed to weigh a thousand pounds. He flipped the top back and realized Kara hadn't been exaggerating. There likely were a hundred letters in there. And all of the envelopes were torn.

He glared at Elaine. "You opened them?"

"I just—I wanted to make sure they were okay."

He shook his head, pulled one of the letters out, and then dropped the box onto the table. He tugged the yellowed paper free and unfolded it. A photograph fell onto the placemat, and he picked it up. His heart broke at the little face grinning back at him.

"'Dear Harry,'" he read aloud. "'I hope school is going okay. Phil is going to be six months old next week and is growing so fast. He will be crawling soon. He babbles all the time. I'm not sure where he gets that from. I don't think either of us ever talked that much. I sold my first painting yesterday. Well, not sold exactly. I traded it for some new cloth diapers.'"

Harry lowered the letter and glared at Elaine. "She was bartering for diapers, and you thought she was doing okay? How could you do this? To her? To me? To your grandson?"

"She was okay. I sent money."

He focused on the paper again, scoffing when he got to the end. "'I've been saving the money you sent. I have enough to get a bus ticket home as soon as you tell me you're ready for us.'" His anger deepened. "She wanted to come home? And you left her there?"

"She was okay," she whispered.

Harry shook his head as he put the letter back inside the box, which he tucked under his arm. "Don't call me. Don't come to me. I'll come to you when I can talk to you about this without wanting to choke you."

The sound of her calling his name followed him through the house, but he was unmoved. Slamming his car door, he set the box in the passenger seat and sighed heavily. He hadn't planned on walking out. He had a million questions, a thousand things to say, but nothing he said now would solve anything. Screaming and yelling and blaming his mother would do nothing. Instead, he backed out, trying to determine what he needed to do next.

sh

Kara knew the guilt trip was coming, so she wasn't surprised when Phil walked into her makeshift studio—which was really the back corner of her mudroom—with a steaming coffee mug. He looked so much like Harrison it made her heart ache.

Before he left, Harry had looked terrified to face his mother. Phil seemed to have that same fear in his eyes.

He held the mug out to her. "I made you some tea."

Kara frowned as she looked at the blank canvas that had been staring at her all afternoon. She exhaled and accepted the cup. "You want to go to Iowa."

He sat on the stool that Jess usually occupied and clasped his hands between his knees. "It makes sense, Mom. And not just for the job. I want to know my father. I know we can call and e-mail and all that, but it's not the same."

"I know."

"I want you to come with us."

Her heart started pounding just at the mention of going home. "I can't do that, Phil."

"I know your parents hurt you," he said softly, "but Harry cares about you. He wants to make things better. For all of us."

She looked at him and scoffed. "Are they so bad now, Phil? Really? Jess is happy. She's settled. We have a nice little life, don't you think?"

He nodded. "For now. But reality will crash in on us sometime. When I was a kid, all I needed was food and shelter. Jess needs medicines and special care that you can't get in exchange for a mural, Mom. I have to put her first, and if that means taking a job where I'll have insurance and job security, then I need to do that. Besides all that, I spent my entire life fantasizing about my father. I have the real thing now, and he seems like a good guy."

She focused on putting her brush down. "He is a good guy. He always was."

"He was just a kid, but I think he would have done what he said and given up school to be there for us. Don't you?"

"Yes. I think he would have. And I think he would have grown to resent me for holding him back. I think he would have tried to squeeze me into a mold, and I would have started to hate him. I think we would have had a miserable marriage, an ugly divorce, and you still would have grown up blaming me for not having the life you wanted."

Phil sighed. "I don't... Okay, I do blame you, but I also know you did the best you could given the circumstances. But the circumstances have changed now, and Harry deserves the opportunity that was taken from him. He wants to help us out. I think we should let him. Now is the perfect time. Jess is on summer break. She'll have time to adjust before school starts. We'll *all* have time to adjust." Leaning forward, he put a kiss on her head and handed her an envelope. "He asked me to give this to you."

He left her sitting in her little room, holding a coffee mug and staring at her name scrawled in black ink. Setting her mug down, she gently tore the envelope open and pulled out several folded sheets of notepad-sized paper with a hotel logo at the top.

Dear Kara,

I cannot begin to express how sorry I am for not responding to your letters sooner. Though I can't make up for the years you spent waiting, I hope you will accept this delayed reply as the answer you were hoping for.

Since you told me about our son, I have been trying to imagine what your life must have been like. I wish I had been there to help ease the pain of your parents' rejection. Even more than that, I wish had been there to stop my parents' deception. I know you must have felt incredibly alone raising a child on your own. While I was at college thinking my life was difficult because I had tests to study for and papers to write, you were providing all of life's necessities to Phil, nurturing him and teaching him things he should have learned from me.

The last twenty-seven years of my life seem incredibly selfish and shallow in comparison to yours. I spent my time growing a business, catering to strangers, while you created an amazing man and became a grandmother to a wonderful little girl.

I wish I could have been there to see Phil grow and to help carry your burden. The fact that my mother sent you money every month eases my guilt somewhat, but I know nothing can ever make up for how abandoned you had to have felt by everyone involved in this situation.

I can't change the past, Kara, but I hope, more than anything I have ever hoped for in my life, that we can move forward. We had twenty-seven years taken away from us without our consent. I don't want to lose another moment.

~Harry

Kara read the letter a second and a third time, letting his words sink in. Finally, she pushed herself up and walked through the house until she found Phil on the couch with Jess. The girl was bouncing up and down as he showed her something on his laptop.

"Look how big the backyard is, Punky," he said. "I bet Harry will let us put up a swing set."

Jess noticed Kara in the door and waved her over. "Grandma, look. Look at the pictures Harry sent."

Easing onto the sofa, Kara laughed quietly. The house couldn't look any more conventional if Harry had built it himself. White siding, black shutters, two stories, and a white-picket fence to round it all out. It was so traditional, so perfect, so…so Harrison Canton.

"This is where we are going to stay when we go to Harry's," Jess said.

Kara nodded. "It's lovely."

Jess took her hand. "You're going, too, right, Grandma? Harry says there are only three bedrooms but that we can make it work. You can sleep in my room if you want. Maybe we can put rainbows and unicorns on the walls."

"Maybe we can." Kara hugged Jess closer and looked at Phil. She sighed and nodded.

Yes. Fine. She would go. She would give Phil the house, the yard, the fence...the life he'd always wanted. She would forgive Harry's unintentional neglect, put the resentment and anger behind her, and yes, damn it, they would move on.

Somehow.

CHAPTER FIVE

Kara's heart pounded so fiercely she feared she may not survive. Harry hadn't been lying. Des Moines had grown and changed so much since she'd been gone, she barely recognized the area she grew up in. She did, however, start to remember older houses and buildings as Phil drove them deeper into the suburb where she and Harry had been raised. She turned in her seat as they passed an old malt shop where kids—not Kara and Harry but the more popular ones—would hang out on the weekends. Kara glanced at the GPS and sighed. One more turn and they would be at his house. Their new house.

What the hell was she getting herself into?

"Wow! Look at that," Jess said from the back seat when Phil pulled into the driveway.

He laughed. "I see, Punky."

The house—a perfect representation of her suburban childhood and all that had betrayed her—made Kara cringe.

Harry opened the front door just as Jess climbed from the car. She bounded up the driveway, through the bright green grass, and hurled herself at Harry as if she'd known him her entire life.

Kara turned her gaze away as Harry hugged Jess back. Something about seeing grandfather and granddaughter together made her stomach tighten. She wasn't prone to jealousy, but she'd been the only grandparent Jessica had ever known. She wasn't sure how she felt about sharing that coveted position.

Jessica was talking so fast her words were running together, but Harry seemed to keep up for the most part. Finally, he convinced her to go inside the house and find her room—the one with the walls painted the exact shade of sunset pink she had requested. It was ready for Grandma to add unicorns and rainbows.

Once Jess skipped her way inside, Phil hugged Harry. Kara watched, her sense of dread growing, as they warmly greeted each other. Another pang of jealousy struck her. She couldn't recall the last time Phil had been that happy to see her. Had he ever?

"Take your stuff upstairs. First door on the right," Harry said.

He disappeared through the same door Jess had, and Harry turned his dark eyes to Kara. She leaned against the car, crossed her ankles casually, and stared up at his home with a smirk.

"Wow, Harry. Did you get this house from a How to Fit In with Society kit?"

He shoved his hands into the pockets of his jeans and grinned at her. "I bought this place when I got married. When she left, she said I could keep the house and all that was in it. So I did."

Kara looked at him through her dark-tinted John Lennon sunglasses. "Why did she leave such suburban paradise? Isn't this what Stepford wives live for?"

He tilted his head and grinned at her teasing. "She said I wasn't exciting enough for her. Maybe she should have stuck around. Having you here will certainly shake things up."

Kara chuckled and stood upright. "I'm not sure any wife, even a bored one, would appreciate you inviting the irresponsible mother of your only known child to live with you."

"Who says you're irresponsible?"

"Your son." She opened the back door, but before she could start unpacking, Harrison stepped in her way and reached for the tattered duffel bag that had sat in her closet for the last seven years. He pulled it out, and she took it from him.

"I emptied out my home office. I thought it'd make a great bedroom, art studio combination." He pulled out several boxes marked as hers and hefted them up. "Come on. I'll show you."

She let out a low whistle as they walked inside. The foyer was open to the second story, creating an elegant entrance. Dark woodwork that matched the floor accented the doorframes. The walls were almond color and plain except for a few perfectly hung knickknacks. It looked like a model home from the late nineties. And that wasn't a compliment.

Kara suspected his ex-wife had been in charge of décor and

Harry hadn't changed a thing since they'd moved in. "How long have you been divorced?"

"Um, about six years, I guess."

"You haven't so much as moved a vase, have you?"

He chuckled. "You want to redecorate?"

"Be careful," Phil warned, coming down the wooden staircase. "You'll have life-sized nudes on every wall before you know it."

"I haven't painted nudes since 2005," Kara deadpanned.

Harry shrugged. "It's just paint. I can go over anything I don't like."

Kara smiled at Phil. "I've been telling you that all your life, haven't I? Now that the sperm donor has said it, maybe you'll listen."

Harry flinched. "Sperm donor sounds so callous."

Kara hummed thoughtfully for a moment. "Now that the guy-who-knocked-me-up-and-left-without-so-much-as-a-word has said it, maybe you'll listen."

Harry canted his head. "Sperm donor it is."

Phil rolled his eyes and disappeared through the front door as Kara laughed and put her hand to Harry's back, urging him on. As soon as he pushed a paned-glass door open, her breath left her. The walls were the same almond color as the rest of the walls she'd seen, but it worked in this room because there were so many windows. Sunlight streamed in, brightening it more than any colors could. A full-size bed sat along one wall and a dresser along another, but for the most part the room was empty.

Her gaze fell on an easel in the corner. She turned her attention to Harry, questioning him with her eyes.

"Phil said you left yours behind because it wouldn't fit in the car."

"I could have replaced it on my own."

He lifted one shoulder and let it fall. "I wanted to get you one. Think of it as a thank you gift."

"For what?"

"For coming."

"Harry," she called when he turned toward the door. "I don't know what arrangements you've made with Phil—"

He furrowed his brow. "Arrangements?"

"You know, to pay you for letting us stay here."

"There's no payment necessary, Kara."

"I just mean, usually when we crash with someone, I plant a garden or—"

"Teach their kids or paint their house. Yeah, Phil told me. You don't owe me anything. I'm the one who owes you, so there was no arrangement made and none will be made. You're welcome to stay here as long as you want."

Not pulling her weight didn't sit well with her. "Well...I'll cook and clean. Mostly because I saw what you ordered at the restaurant in Seattle, and I don't want to eat like that."

He grinned. "Fair enough."

With that, he left her to settle into the space that was hers for the time being. It had been a long time since Kara had to unpack her bag, knowing her accommodations were temporary —she couldn't live with Harry forever—but she easily fell into the routine.

As she put her clothes away, he delivered several boxes and deposited them inside without a word. She pulled the tape back and unloaded her art supplies, several pieces that weren't yet finished, and a few that were ready to be sold or traded.

She unwrapped some sculptures and set them on the window ledge, desperately trying to make this space feel like home.

Harry slowed as he entered the kitchen. The counters were stacked high with containers of food. "What are you doing?"

Kara pulled a half-empty gallon of milk from his fridge. "You can't keep eating like this, Harrison. You'll have a heart attack or cancer by the time you retire."

He lifted a can of soup off the counter and looked at it. "It's reduced sodium."

She took it from his hand and set it back in the pile. "It's filled with chemicals. Help me pack this up, and then we'll go to the store." She paused. "You don't happen to know any farmers, do you?"

He lifted his brows and smirked. "No. Not off the top of my head. What are you going to do with all this?"

"Find a place that takes food donations."

"So it's okay to give the needy heart attacks and cancer?" He did his best to wipe his grin away when she stopped what she was doing and cocked a brow at him. He failed miserably and let a small laugh escape. Phil often gave her that same look, and Harry had to wonder if she even realized she doled it out just as frequently. He doubted either Kara or Phil realized how alike they were. "I'll go grab a box."

"I told you it wasn't a good idea to have me move in," she said when he returned from the garage.

He started putting the cans from his pantry into the box. "This actually proves it was a terrific idea. I clearly need you to save me from myself."

"You'll regret it soon enough. Hurry up. We have to go find some decent food for dinner before Phil takes Jess out to some horrid fast food place and fills her up with deep-fried pink goo."

"That's a myth, you know," he said. She gave him that look again, and he smiled. "I checked on them before coming downstairs. They are passed out in Jess's room."

Kara nodded slightly. "So I have to go find some decent food."

"I'll go with you," he offered.

Her desire to argue was plainly written on her face.

"I obviously need to learn how to grocery shop correctly," he justified.

She didn't counter his logic.

After dropping off their donation at a church not far from

Harry's, she filled him in on the hazards of ingesting processed foods. He, in turn, promised to improve his eating habits. She chastised him for placating her, and he tried to hide his amused smile.

He'd never spent so much time in a grocery store as he did with Kara explaining what to buy and what to avoid. She told him she'd find a farmer in the area to get eggs and dairy.

"What about meat?" he asked.

Her frown let him know his diet was going to be missing more than cans of processed soup.

"Okay, look," he said. "I can agree to cutting canned goods and frozen dinners. I'll even stop buying milk from the store. But I have to draw the line somewhere, Kara."

She patted his shoulder. "You'll be fine, big guy."

"Who is placating now?" He looked at the pack of tofu in her hand. "I'm not going to eat that."

She chuckled. "I'll buy meat from a farmer who doesn't use hormones and chemicals on his animals. I'll start looking for one tomorrow. I promise, by the end of the week you'll have some kind of meat on your plate. What do you like to eat?" She dropped the mashed soybean curd into the cart.

"Meat."

She reached for a bundle of spinach. "Hmm. What else?"

"Chicken. I had buffalo at this restaurant in Seattle. It was delicious. I could eat that again."

"Stop with the dead animals, Harry. What do you like? Chinese? Mexican? Spicy? Mild? What flavors to you enjoy?"

"Meat is a flavor. I'm sure of it."

She sighed. "You and Phil are so much alike it frightens me."

He smiled. "Oh, yeah?"

"Yeah. You can sneak cheeseburgers when I'm not around. He does." She stopped scanning the vegetables and eyed him. "I will not feed people I care about processed foods and mistreated animals."

Harry tilted his head. "So you care about me, huh?"

She sighed and walked away. He caught up to her and leaned on the cart while she started assessing the apples.

"Does Jess have a special diet?"

Kara stopped examining a Fuji and looked at him. "You mean because she has Down?"

"In part."

"And the other part?"

He shrugged. "Because sometimes kids have special diets. If I want to take her out for pizza or ice cream, I should know if she can't have something. Shouldn't I?"

Kara hesitated, as if judging his sincerity, and then focused on the apples again. "She was born with a heart condition, but she had surgery to correct it. She's perfectly normal in every way except her chromosomes. She likes painting, dancing, and playing games just like other little girls. She may not run as fast or catch on to math as quickly, but she can hold her own with her classmates."

"I wasn't insulting her, Kara."

"I know. But in a few months' time, you're going to

understand why I get defensive. People treat her differently, and she's old enough now to recognize it."

"Unfortunately, it's something we all have to learn to deal with. Jess especially."

"She shouldn't have to."

"No, she shouldn't. But you and Phil shouldn't have been taken away from me either." He stood upright as she turned and faced him. "You shouldn't have been a single mother. He shouldn't have grown up wondering where his dad was. There are a lot of things in our lives that we shouldn't have to deal with, but we do. I'm going to need your help in not being one of those people who treat her differently and helping me connect with Phil."

She scoffed. "He already thinks the world of you."

"For now, but we both know the newness won't last forever. I want to be the kind of father to him now that I should have been back then."

"Yeah, well...the next time he needs his diaper changed, it's on you."

He smiled. "Smartass. Gather up some of that hippie grub and let's go. I'm starving."

"Apples." She held the organic red orb out to him. "These are called apples."

CHAPTER SIX

Kara glared across the table at her son. Harry's suggestion of unwinding from the long day with a bottle of wine had sounded great right up until Phil started in on how horrible his childhood had been.

"We may not have had a big house, but you grew up in loving communities surrounded by people who cared about you," she reminded him.

"They were communes, Mom."

"They weren't cults, Phil. Nobody made you drink poisoned Kool-Aid."

"Might as well have."

"We were taken care of because we took care of others. That's how it worked when you lived with a group of single mothers who were tossed out on their asses."

He shook his head.

"We were a part of something wonderful. No, we didn't have a lot of material things, but we had food and we always had a roof over our heads."

"Yeah, but never one that belonged to us."

"Golly, that must have been tough on you," she said with faux sympathy.

She pushed herself up and briskly left the room, empty wineglass in hand. She was loading the dishwasher when Harrison walked in and put his empty glass in the sink. He leaned against the counter and rested his palms on the tile, watching her. She hated how heavy his gaze felt on her. She wanted him to leave. Leave her to the dishes and her anger.

"He's got quite a bit of resentment about not having a stable home, huh?"

"Oh, you noticed."

"I reminded him that's on me. Not you."

"Don't come to my rescue. I don't need it."

"You don't need him giving you a hard time over things that happened thirty years ago, either."

She slammed the dishwasher door shut and faced him. "I did my best, but it has never been enough for him, and you know what? I'm sick of hearing how hard his life was because of me. I'm the one who was tossed aside. I'm the one who lost everything. I'm the one who had to make a life for us out of nothing. He acts like that's what I wanted. Like I had a choice. I didn't have a choice. I didn't have anything."

"I know."

"No, Harry. You don't know. Because you weren't there."

She brushed past him and walked the short hallway to what was now her bedroom. She wanted to slam the door with her frustration, but she suspected the glass panes wouldn't withstand the force. Instead, she closed it gently and leaned against it, wondering why Phil's comments had hit her so hard. It was nothing he hadn't said before, but tonight his criticism felt like he was cutting her off at the knees.

Actually, she didn't have to wonder why his words hurt so much. Harry had suddenly appeared with his perfect life and perfect home and everything she had never been able to give to Phil. This was the life Phil had wanted, even as a kid, and there Harry stood after being missing in action for almost thirty years, offering it up on a silver platter. And there Kara was with nothing to give to her son. As always.

"Must be nice to be so fucking wonderful," she muttered to herself.

Pushing herself from the door, she crossed the room and looked out the big window. The stars were shining brightly. She could almost pretend she was back home—home being anywhere along the West Coast and as far from Iowa as she could get. Though the city was close, they were far enough that the lights didn't drown out the beauty of the sky. She glanced back at the bed and decided to move it under the window so she could fall asleep admiring nature. She'd once stayed with a friend who had put skylights in every room in his house. She would spend hours curled up in bed staring at the stars.

She moved the easel and some of the boxes she had yet to unpack and started tugging at the bed. She'd only moved it about eighteen inches when it suddenly started shifting with ease. She nearly fell on her ass from the surprise. She gasped when she noticed Harry moving the foot of the bed as if the frame and mattresses weighed nothing. "Really?"

"I'm sorry. I didn't mean to enter without knocking, but I saw you struggling."

"I guess I'll be making curtains tomorrow."

He ignored her. "Where do you want this?"

"Over there."

"The window can be a bit drafty. It won't bother you now, but come winter, having the bed there may be too cold."

"It's the first week of August, Harry. How long do you plan on me sleeping in your office?"

Instead of answering, he pushed the bed to where she had pointed and left her side. She glanced back, wondering where he'd gone. Clearly he hadn't peered in her door just to see if she needed help moving the bed.

He scooped up a box he'd left on the chair next to the door and then sat on her bed, apparently waiting for her to join him. She hesitated but finally did. He lifted the top off, and she recognized her penmanship scrawled across several envelopes.

He pulled one out and ran his fingers over her writing as if it were some great treasure. "I've read them all. Thirty years too late, but I finally read them. You were a great mom, Kara. I can tell in the way you wrote about him. The things you guys did… I wish I'd been there."

Her shoulders sagged as he pulled out a photo. Toddler-aged Phil was laughing as a wave crashed against his back. She took the picture from Harry and sighed. "When he was ten, he was fascinated by the ocean. By everything about it. I agreed to clean this guy's fish, whatever he caught, if he'd take Phil and me out with him. Phil loved every minute we spent on that stupid boat, so the guy offered to keep taking us. Every Tuesday for months, I scaled fish so Phil could learn firsthand what the ocean was about. He can tell you the best bait, the best time of day, the best locations off the Oregon coast to fish. He can tell you about currents and temperatures and name just about any fish in the Northwest Pacific." She handed the picture back to Harry. "But do you think he ever tells anyone he learned that because of the sacrifice I made?"

"He's got his own issues to resolve. You and I weren't the only ones impacted by what happened here."

"I know that, but he isn't a kid anymore, Harry. He's old enough to have processed some of that."

"So are you, but you're still pretty damn bitter that I wasn't there."

She frowned. He was right.

"We all have to work through the anger of not having the life we wanted," he said. "He blames you. You blame me. I blame my mother. And we're all pissed off at the world in our own way right now. But we're in this together, and we have to stop being so hard on each other so we can figure out how to have the life we lost."

"I know. It's just... He never tells people that I decorated our bedroom like a zoo when he wanted to be a zoologist, or a jungle when he wanted to be Tarzan, or a doctor's office when he wanted to practice medicine. He just tells them that we had to share a room because we didn't have our own house. He doesn't even give me credit for stepping up to help him with Jess the minute he asked me to. His wife left him with an infant, and I was there, without question or hesitation, taking care of his baby so he could finish school. Once, just one time, I'd like to hear him share a story where I wasn't screwing everything up."

"He has." He looked out the window, up at the night sky. "You once told him I was probably on the moon, building a city for us."

Kara smiled at the memory. Phil's eyes had grown wide as he hung on her every word.

"And then you told him I was perfecting pizza crust."

"I really regretted that one. He wouldn't eat anything but pizza for weeks."

"And you let him because what he needed to believe was important. You could have told him I was a worthless jerk who disappeared on you. You could have told him that you wrote letters and tried to make me be his dad until you got so disappointed and angry that you finally gave up on me. You could have told him I didn't want him. But you didn't. You never threw me under the bus. That wasn't for my sake, Kara."

She hated the burn in her eyes but couldn't stop the tears from filling her eyes. "He always thought you were a better parent than me, and you weren't even there."

"If I'd been with you, he would have resented me, too. All kids do."

"This runs a bit deeper than teen angst, Harry. He really hates the life I gave him."

Harry sighed as he brushed a hand over her head. "I'm sure it was tough on him to never have the things that some of the other kids did, but I promise you, once he works through some of this anger, he's going to realize he had so much more, and he's going to understand you gave him that."

She swiped at her cheek. "Don't hold your breath. He's never been shy about pointing out how I failed him. Somehow it never got to me because I was at peace with the fact that I had done my best. Now..."

"Now I'm here shoving your nose in all you couldn't give him."

Her frustration returned. "Maybe I could have given him that life if I hadn't been sent away."

"But you were. And I was lied to. And Phil will come to terms with all this in his own time."

"He's twenty-six."

"He's a twenty-six-year-old single dad with an almost-eight-year-old child who has Down syndrome. He's never had a chance to resolve his own issues. Jessica is great," he said before she could get defensive, "but as much as you and Phil want to insist it isn't any harder having a child with special needs, you know that's a lie. Not because of Jessica but because she has had health problems and because she needs you more. You've both buried yourselves in caring for her and never dealt with the familial problems that everybody has. You think you're the only mother out there with a kid who thinks he got a raw deal?"

She shook her head. "You don't get it, Harry. I've always known that if he could choose between living with you and staying with me, he'd choose you. From the time he could talk, he wanted you." She shrugged. "And the moment you showed up, I lost him."

"You didn't lose him, Kara."

"Not like that." She sighed. "I don't mean he'd walk away and never look back. I just mean…any little bit of respect he had for what I gave to him is gone because you've already given him more than I ever did."

He put his arm around her shoulder. "No, I haven't, Kara. I could never come close to giving him what you have. He's just always had you, so he doesn't see what has been right in front of him. That's all. He loves you."

"I know that."

"But he doesn't appreciate you."

"It sounds selfish when you say it like that."

"Wanting our sacrifices recognized isn't being selfish."

"It's more than that," she whispered. "This isn't where I belong. He fits here. You fit here. I don't. I never will."

"You're right, you never did fit in here. If you had, I wouldn't have noticed you. Every girl in school was trying so hard to be like Shannon Blake. But you didn't care about that. You were passionate about your art, about music, about everything. I admired you so much."

She shook her head, not believing him.

"I wanted to ask you to prom our junior year. I had this whole speech planned out. Do you remember how I used to stand by your easel in art class until you would finally snap at me to go away?"

She chuckled.

"I couldn't get the words out. I was terrified. So, I decided I would take you to the Valentine's dance. When that didn't happen, I decided I'd take you to homecoming senior year. And then Valentine's again. Then senior prom. I never worked up the nerve, but I never stopped wanting you to notice me."

"I noticed you. As I'm sure you realized graduation night."

"Yeah. I was still standing in the corner, waiting for some surge of courage to kick in. Then all of a sudden you were standing in front of me."

"And then I was pregnant."

He laughed. "Yeah. Then that happened." He wrapped his arm farther around her. "The point is I wouldn't ask you to change, Kare. I don't expect you to try to fit in. I just want our family to have the chance that was taken from us so long ago. We can't have that if we tear each other down from the inside."

She nodded. As usual, Harry was right. She ran her fingers over the letters in the box he was still holding. "I'm glad Elaine didn't throw them away."

"Me, too. I feel more connected to you both now. Like I was there, at least on the outside, while he was growing up."

"Have you talked to her?"

"Not since I took these."

"Are you going to?"

He exhaled heavily. "I have to sometime. I just haven't figured out what to say or how to say it without wrapping my hands around her throat."

"Are you going to be able to forgive her?"

"I don't know. This isn't like the time she took my dog to the pound and told me he ran away. She stole my family from me. She lied to me for years. I missed so much that I will never be able to get back. I don't even think the enormity of what I lost has hit me yet."

Kara frowned. "Look, Harry, you and Phil can make your own decisions, but Elaine has no place in our lives as far as I'm concerned. I know that's my own selfish view, but I don't want to have anything to do with someone capable of doing what she did. And I don't want you trying to make me feel bad for that. Okay?"

"I wouldn't. I won't push you either, Kara. But, having said that, I looked into your parents. They still live in the same house. You do what you want with that information."

She shook her head. "They hurt me, too."

"You know," he said softly, "my mother's reaction to your pregnancy was ongoing. Deliberately carried out for years. But your parents never had a chance to take back what they did. Maybe if you'd gone to them a week later, they would have opened their arms to you."

Her anger sparked again. "Maybe I could have if your mother hadn't sent me to the other side of the country with no way home."

She stared at him with hard eyes for a long moment before regret kicked in. She couldn't blame him for trying to make things right. That's what he did. He'd always done that. Whenever there was a confrontation in class or someone aiming paint tubes at her, for God's sake, it was Harry who stepped in and negotiated peace.

"I'm sorry," she whispered, lowering her face. "I guess that's one of those things I need to work through, huh?"

"Yeah. So is your resentment toward your parents."

She held his gaze. "I know it was a long time ago, Harry, but finding out your parents sent me away to be rid of me instead of help me has churned up an awful lot of the hurt I felt back then. I came to terms with what my parents did, with how they didn't want me. But your mother led me to believe she was taking care of me, and even if it was foolish, I believed her. I thought she wanted me, in her own way at least. Finding out she only wanted me to go away...it hurts."

"Well, I want to take care of you now." He gave her a crooked, uncertain smile. "Better late than never, right?"

She laughed softly. "Right. But I don't need you now, Harry."

"I think you do. I think you need me more than Phil and Jessica combined. Funny thing is, I need you, too."

With that, he pushed himself up and, carrying the box of her letters, left her exhausted in the wake of their conversation.

CHAPTER SEVEN

Harry exhaled as he sat on the couch next to Phil. One emotionally exhausting conversation down, one more to go. It left him wondering if family was always this difficult, but then he realized he didn't care. He had his family now—that was all that mattered. And if he were honest, he could think back on his teenage years and remember his father being the peacemaker between Harry and his mother.

"I didn't mean to upset her," Phil said before Harry could point out he had.

"You sure about that?"

Phil clicked off the television and looked at Harry. Harry couldn't decipher the look in his eyes. Maybe it was offense that Harry would think he had upset Kara on purpose or shock that Harry would confront him.

"You've been making jabs about your childhood since I showed up, Phil."

"Well, if you had to move from place to place your entire life, you'd be pretty tired of it, too. All I wanted was a normal life, Harry."

"Yeah, you've said that a time or ten. When I went to my mom and told her that I had run into Kara, she looked like she was going to faint. Her hands started trembling, and she started trying to make excuses for what she'd done. I demanded she give me the letters your mother had written to me." He opened the box and showed Phil all the envelopes inside. "For five years she wrote, bragging about all your accomplishments. Telling me how amazing you were and how she was waiting for me to bring you guys home. She wanted a house—not a big one, just enough for us to be a family. She said more than once that she was learning so many skills that she could use to make our lives easier. She asked if that would be enough of a contribution for her to be able to stay home with you."

He pulled out the last letter he'd ever gotten from Kara. He knew which envelope it was because he'd read it so many times. "The last time she wrote, she sounded so broken. She said she had finally accepted that I wasn't going to send for you guys. She finally realized that she was on her own. She told me she was going to give you an amazing life without me. And you know what, Phil? She did. How many kids got to see the things you did? Sure, you didn't get to sit in a classroom day after day and you didn't have your own room, but you rode horses and fished in the ocean. You picked grapes in Napa Valley and camped in the desert. Your mom has spent her life trying to make up for the fact that I wasn't there, and you just keep giving her a hard time for it. She gave you the ocean and the valley and the desert. All I ever would have given you is a house and a curfew. Your mom deserves your respect—not only for what she gave you but for what she has given up for you—and you damn well better learn how to give that respect to her. I'm not going to lose either one of you again. You're my family—you, Jessica, *and* Kara. I want her here. I want her happy. Just as much as I want that for you. So you're going to back down. Do you understand?"

Phil stared at him for a long moment before grinning. "You sound like such a dad."

Harry smiled. "I am your dad. But the truth is, I wasn't there. She was. If for no other reason than that, you need to go easier on her. She could have left you. She could have sent you away like she was sent away. That alone makes her a better parent than either one of us ever had."

Phil's amused smile faded as he looked at the letters in the box.

"I don't think she was as happy and free spirited as you always imagined," Harry said, sharing the conclusion he'd come to from reading her letters. "I think she's been running away from the hurt for so long, she didn't even know she was doing it. All those adventures, all the different places, I think those were just new ways not to feel the rejection that her parents, my parents, and even I showed her."

"You didn't reject her, Harry."

"She didn't know that. She didn't know that until two weeks

ago, Phil. For almost thirty years, she thought I didn't want you guys in my life. You can't tell me that didn't hurt her. I'd bet that knife twisted a little more each time you had some accomplishment she wanted to share with the family that had deserted her."

Phil was quiet for a moment. "I was about thirteen when I really started blaming her. I was finally in a normal school around normal people. I was on the basketball team, and all these dads were showing up, cheering their kids on. Mom never missed a game, but it wasn't the same. Nothing about me was ever the same as the other guys. I couldn't put that off on you, so I put it on her."

"It's a lot easier to blame what you can see, huh?"

Phil nodded. "When Jess was born, I was barely older than Mom was when she had me. I was determined my kid was going to have the life I never did. But then my wife left soon after Jess was diagnosed with a heart condition, and I was suddenly a single parent. A kid with a kid and no idea what the hell I was doing. Mom was there, without fail, every time I needed her. All that time, I just…I thought she owed me." He looked down at his hands and sighed. "She didn't tell me the truth about how you disappeared until the morning after the gallery opening. I mean, I'd already decided that you didn't want us, but I had always blamed her for that. Part of me thought that even if you had, you'd never find us because she moved us so much. When she told me that she'd run into my father and that he wanted to meet me, I felt like I'd finally won. She could run all she wanted, but you finally found me. Sounds stupid for a grown man to think like that, but it's true."

"Did you ever ask her how to find me?"

He shook his head. "No. I thought about it, especially after Jess was born, but the possibility of you shutting the door in my face was more frightening than not finding you at all. It was easier to blame her than to have to accept a reality in which maybe you really didn't want me."

"She never told you that I left her without a word?"

Phil shook his head. "She sat me down the morning after the gallery opening and told me how her parents kicked her out and yours sent her away. She said she'd written to you, thinking you were getting her letters, and how she finally gave up. Then she told me how you guys put the pieces together and that you never knew I existed. She also told me that she had kept sending address updates to you right up until Jess was born. All those years, I blamed her for not having a father, and she'd gone above and beyond to leave the door open for you."

"So maybe you should tell her that you know it wasn't her fault?"

He scoffed. "She knows—"

"No, she doesn't," Harry interjected. "She really doesn't, Phil. She doesn't think you have a very high opinion of her at all. And she's very hurt about that."

Phil exhaled loudly, and Harry handed him the box of letters.

"I want these back, but I think you should read them. Maybe your childhood wasn't quite as bad as you remember." Pushing himself up, Harry climbed the stairs and got ready for bed. Lying in the darkness, he stared at the ceiling, hoping the second day of having his family home would go much more smoothly.

Kara spent most of the night staring out the window. The stars, however, failed to bring their usual peace of mind. It was the first night she had spent in her hometown since Elaine had put her on a bus, and this night had gone just as badly. However, instead of fretting over being a homeless, unwed, pregnant teenager, Kara spent the night wondering if she should—could—face her parents. Wondering if she could find a way to forgive Elaine. Hoping that Phil would forgive her for not providing him a better childhood. Wondering what, exactly, Harry was expecting from her by incorporating her into his family. Worrying that Jessica wasn't going to find her place in this new town.

And then her mind would go back to the beginning of her worries and start over again.

She felt none of the freedom that usually came with relocating. All her adult life, finding a new place to live meant the excitement of new friends, starting fresh, and learning new things. None of that could outshine the darkness of her past. Ever since she'd run into Harry at the opening, she'd been on an emotional roller coaster that she'd managed to avoid for the better part of thirty years. She'd held on to hope for so long that when she finally let it go, she felt free. Free from her parents, free from Harry, free from the fear of disappointing everyone—everyone except Phil.

Boy, had she messed that one up.

She thought for so long that he'd learn to enjoy their adventures. She'd finally caved and found them a place when he was a teenager, deciding it wasn't fair to keep him out of public school when he so badly wanted it. That, however, seemed to have been her biggest mistake. That was when the slight crack between them had grown into a chasm she couldn't cross until Jessica was born.

Sometimes it still amazed her that he called on her to help him after he'd been left with a baby. She figured she would be the last one he'd want helping him raise his child—he seemed to oppose every parenting decision she'd ever made. Then again, who would he call? He didn't have anyone else.

Kara had no idea what time she finally started to drift off, but she hadn't gotten nearly enough sleep when the creaking of the door caused her to jerk her eyes open. She smiled as Jess tiptoed into her room.

"You awake, Grandma?" she asked in a hushed voice.

"Nope."

"You are too!" She hopped onto the bed and leaned over Kara. "Daddy said to tell you to come eat."

Kara creased her brow. "Daddy made breakfast?"

"It didn't go well," Jess said with a dramatic shake of her head.

Kara inhaled but didn't smell anything cooking. "What did he make?"

"Cereal."

"How could he go wrong with cereal?"

"Not with the cereal. With Harry's blender. It got ugly." She again gave her head a sad, theatrical shake.

Kara giggled and pulled her down for a hug. "I love you, Punk."

"Love you, Grandma. Now get out of bed! I have big plans for my room. I'm pouring rice milk on your cereal. If you aren't there in two minutes, you'll have to eat mush!"

Rolling onto her side, Kara smiled as Jessica used the threat on her that Kara had issued so many times herself. School mornings were nothing but pushing Jessica to get ready. The child was not usually a morning person.

The thought brought back Kara's worries about Jess fitting in at a new school. It wasn't easy for the girl to keep up, even with a teaching assistant. She struggled, but she did it. Her grades might be mediocre, but she managed to hold her own. Kara was terrified that would change.

"Come on already, Grandma," Jessica called from the hallway.

Kara crawled from under the covers and slipped into the half bath off the office. When she emerged, wrapped in a tattered old robe, she found Harry and Jessica at the table, happily eating their cereal. Phil stopped mopping the floor long enough to give her a half smile.

"I tried to make you a smoothie, but the blender is apparently smarter than I am."

"It's just tricky," Harry offered.

"There is coffee, though," Phil said.

Kara sat in front of a bowl as Phil put a cup of coffee in front of her. It wasn't like her son to serve her. She looked at Harry and frowned with the realization that after leaving her side last night, he'd likely gone straight to their son.

He responded to her scowl with a wink and focused on his granddaughter. "So, tell me again, what is Grandma painting on your walls?"

Jessica rambled on through breakfast, and the list of creatures Kara would paint kept growing. After putting their dishes in the sink, Jessica dragged Harry upstairs to show him where each flower, fairy, and unicorn was going to go.

Kara opened the dishwasher to load their breakfast dishes. "She's full of energy this morning."

"She's still excited about her new room. Do you remember when we were staying in Pacific City? We had that little guest house for the summer while you nannied for a doctor and his wife. What was their name?"

"Williams."

"It was the first summer you thought I was old enough to go to the beach alone. That was cool."

Kara waited. Where was the part where she did something wrong? It didn't come. Just "that was cool." After a moment, she nodded. "You learned to surf that summer. Or came close to it."

"Right. I waxed all the boards at this little shop on the beach in exchange for some lessons."

She smirked. "You mean you bartered."

He'd always said that word like it was a bad thing. Pointing out that he'd done the same things without even realizing it gave Kara a twinge of pleasure.

He hesitated and then nodded. "Yes. I bartered." He leaned on the counter, almost in the exact same place and position as Harry had been in the night before. Like father, like son. "Sometimes I felt like you were living your life the way you wanted without caring what it did to me. That pissed me off for a long time. I never stopped to think about how I got something out of it, too. I didn't know how bad you were hurting because of your parents. You should have told me."

"That was my burden, Phil. Not yours."

"But maybe I would have been more understanding if I'd known you were running instead of wandering."

She cocked a brow. "That sounds an awful lot like something Harry would say."

Phil shrugged. "He's a smart guy. Must be where I get it."

Kara gasped and playfully swatted at him.

He laughed before putting his arm around her shoulder. "I know what your parents did was shitty. Real shitty. But of all the so-called fresh starts we've had, Mom, this is the one I want to work out. For all of us. I want to focus on making a great life for my daughter, and I need my parents to do that." He grinned. "Did you hear that? I said 'my parents.'"

She smiled. "I heard."

"I'm sorry I've given you such a hard time. I didn't take into consideration what you were going through. I love you, Mom, and I'm glad we did so much of what we did when I was a kid. Even if I was a brat sometimes."

She hugged him. "I love you, too."

He kissed her head and left her with the same unsettled feeling Harry had left her with the evening before.

At some point, whether she liked it or not, she, too, was going to have to face her resentment toward her parents.

The sound of Jessica giggling was like a magnet. Harry couldn't resist the pull. He walked down the hall and peered into her bedroom. Kara was on the floor, legs crossed, while painting on the wall. Jessica was spinning, her sundress flaring out as she laughed.

He eased into the room and checked out the changes they'd made. He'd spent an evening painting the walls the color Jessica had picked out before arriving at his home, but Kara had added unicorns, flowers, fairies, and was putting the finishing touches on a flower near a rainbow.

"What do you think, Punk?" Kara asked.

Jess continued to spin until she fell onto the plush carpet. "I think I'm gonna puke."

Kara laughed, and Harry's smile widened. He imagined a hundred scenes like this had played out when Phil was a child.

Jess reached out and put her hand on Kara's back and stroked as if she were petting a cat. Now that he was really watching—observing—he realized Jessica did that frequently but only with Kara. She clung to Phil's hand, tugged to get his attention, but with Kara she tended to pet. That was the only word he could think to describe it.

"We gonna find me a school, Grandma?" she asked as she soothed her hand over Kara's back.

"I guess we have to, huh?"

Jessica continued petting Kara. "Think there will be other kids like me there?"

"You mean funny, smart, adorable girls who have their grandma wrapped around their finger? I think there will be lots of kids like that."

Harry chuckled softly when Jess sat up, swaying a bit, probably still dizzy from spinning so much.

"Kids with Down," she said.

Kara put her brush in the jar of purple water and turned to face Jess. She reached down and stroked her hand over Jessica's hair, and Harry made the connection. Jessica petted Kara because Kara petted Jessica. Their own secret way of communicating. He wondered if he'd ever make a bond so strong with his granddaughter.

"I don't know," Kara said. "Maybe."

"Think they'll be nice?"

"Yeah. I think they'll be nice."

Jessica sighed. "But there's always one, you know."

Kara chuckled. "You sound cynical like your dad."

"I don't know what that means, but it sounds serious."

"It is very serious. Cynical means you see the bad in things instead of the good."

"Like you see the bad in coming to Iowa?"

Harry lifted his brows. *Nice one, kid.*

Kara reached over and tapped Jessica's nose. "Don't try turning my words around on me, little lady."

"Harry's nice."

"Harry is very nice."

"Think he'll let us live here forever?"

"Oh, I don't know about that. I think we will stay until we can find something for ourselves."

"But we're family, right? So we should stay here forever."

"That's what I think," Harry said, finally making his presence known. Squatting on the floor next to Jess, he made a show of checking out the walls. "Holy cow, this is the best room I've ever seen."

"Grandma is a famous artist."

Kara laughed. "Hardly."

Jessica jumped up and pointed at the fairies, telling Harry their names. Then she named the unicorn and started telling him the story she imagined playing out on the wall. Kara turned from Harry, focusing again on the final touches of her painting.

He leaned back on his elbows so he could see her face. She

looked intent, just like she had in art class all those years ago. She was clearly more comfortable now, though. She handled the brush as if it were an extension of her. Even though she was no longer struggling to control the brush, she seemed off balance, and Harry didn't have to ask why.

She may have been smiling for Jessica's sake, but when she focused on her task, she looked haunted by whatever was going on in her mind. He imagined she'd spent a lot of time the last few weeks thinking back on the last time she was in Iowa—when she'd been tossed out like garbage. He was happy she was there with him, but he hated that she so obviously didn't want to be.

A frown tugged at his lips. He wanted nothing more than to reach out and hug her, to let her know that she was wanted. Maybe it was too late. Maybe it didn't make a difference now, but he did want her there. He did care about her happiness.

She glanced at him and cocked a brow as if daring him to continue to stare.

He grinned in response. "Looks nice. Want to paint my room next?"

"Sure. I'll paint a mural of Mount Rushmore with the inclusion of Kennedy."

He sat a bit higher. "They could do it. Right on the wall next to Lincoln."

She smirked. "Yes, I remember the proposition you wrote for art class."

"You remember that?"

She shrugged. "Your debate was the most logical. No one else took time to plan how their project could be done. They just tossed out ideas to be finished with the assignment." She paused in her movements, as if thinking back. "That's what got me in trouble with Mitch, wasn't it?"

"Yes. When asked what famous piece of art he'd alter, he wrote about how all Frida Kahlo's self-portraits should have two eyebrows. You took offense to that."

She chuckled and glanced at Jess to make sure she was far enough away before whispering, "He was such an ass."

"Yes, you told him that."

"And you saved me from his wrath."

"Nobody squirts paint on my girl."

Her smile faltered. "I wasn't your girl, Harry."

"You were in my mind."

"Hmm." Her attention returned to the wall. "You never said anything about that."

"I wasn't nearly as bold back then."

She leaned back so she could look him in the eye and narrowed her gaze. "Don't go getting any big ideas about me being your girl now just because I'm living in your house."

He brushed a wayward strand of hair from her face. "Wouldn't dream of it. Mitch isn't so bad now. You'd like his wife. She's sweet."

Kara's brows lifted. "You're friends with Mitch Friedman?"

"Not friends, exactly. He's a financial advisor now. He helps me with the business."

"I thought you knew everything, Harry. Why would you need a financial advisor?"

He smiled in return. "I do know everything, Kara. I just don't want to do it all by myself."

A quiet chuckle left her. "What did you say to Phil?"

"I've said a lot of things to him. It's all part of the getting-to-know-you process."

She gave him the look again, and it was his turn to laugh softly.

"I suggested he stop being angry long enough to see that your life wasn't exactly what you had expected either. I let him read your letters."

She lifted her brows. "Those were private."

"They were a real look at what you went through. I don't think anyone could ever accuse you of holding back, Kare. When you were excited, or angry, or lonely, it showed. He needs to know you went through all of those things so he can see you as a person instead of just his mother."

"Don't insert yourself into my relationship with my son, Harrison."

"I'm not inserting. I'm...refereeing." He winked as he sat up. "Hey, Jess, I'm hungry. What do you say we go out for dinner?"

"Daddy," she screamed as she darted from her room. "Harry's hungry!"

He pushed himself up and held his hand out to Kara. "Come on. I'm sure we can find something that hasn't been chemically altered or mistreated to eat."

Kara passed on Harry's invitation for a glass of wine that evening. She walked away, leaving him and Phil chatting about work. She couldn't remember the last time she'd felt stress run so deep. She'd developed a way of letting things roll off her back. So little in life could be controlled. She'd found a way to accept that a long time ago and very rarely let what she couldn't change bother her.

Being back in Iowa, however, was within her control. She could leave. But she wouldn't. Not as long as Jessica and Phil were there. And that meant she had to face a lot of things she had been ignoring most of her life.

The hurt hadn't been so raw in years, but there it was whenever she stopped moving long enough to feel. Shaking the pain off, she refused to let the feelings take root. She still had a room to finish organizing, curtains to make for her doors, and paintings to finish so she could start making plans for how to sell or trade her work. The problem seemed to be that she couldn't figure out what to focus on first.

She'd start one thing but then find herself staring off into space, recalling the way she had begged her mother to help her as her father pushed her out of the house. Or how sweet Elaine had seemed and how she now knew it had all been an act.

How had she been so gullible? Even at seventeen?

Kara dropped the material she had found to make curtains onto the sewing station she'd set up in the corner of her room. It was too late to start that project. She wasn't in the mood to finish unpacking the clothes she'd brought. She turned her attention to the half-finished painting on her easel. Sinking onto the stool, she skimmed over the work. Her paintings had always varied depending on her life, but this was a first.

Unicorns jumping stars, leaving rainbow trails in their wake. Who the hell was going to want this?

She laughed at herself, but the sound didn't hold the least bit of amusement. Phil had been telling her for years that if she could just focus on one thing, she'd be much more successful. He'd been so thrilled when she stepped in line with the crowd and signed on with that nitwit agent who set up the gallery opening. He'd been so excited, in fact, that he had done most of the marketing himself. He'd never shown an interest in her work before then—other than the frequent reminders that she couldn't build a brand for herself if she couldn't stick to one thing. Upcycling clothing, sculpting, landscapes, portraits, abstract, cubism. None of it meshing with the other. Just random bits of things that she tossed out.

He seemed far more interested in her success than she did. The only time he wanted to talk about her art was how she could make it mainstream and make more money. She just wanted to sell enough to cover the cost of living, which would be substantially less now that Harry was footing the housing bill.

And what was that about anyway?

She'd spent so much of her life thinking he was a selfish jerk, she couldn't quite wrap her mind around this guy who suddenly wanted to take care of her family without anything in return. She kept waiting for the other shoe to drop.

A knock at her door interrupted her thoughts. Harry smiled at her through the window and lifted a glass of wine, silently offering it to her. She sat for a moment, debating before gesturing for him to enter.

He opened the door and crossed the room as she focused on her painting again.

"For Jess?" he asked.

She laughed softly as she accepted the wine he held out to her. "I guess. I don't think anyone else would want this crap."

"It's not crap. It's every little girl's fantasy world."

She shook her head. "I get these ideas stuck in my brain, and they have to work themselves out. Then I just move on to the next thing. Drives Phil crazy. He tried to help me market my work, but he says it is impossible when I don't have a common thread through anything I do."

"Not impossible. Different. More difficult. But not impossible." He sat on the stool next to hers. "He said you make all of Jessica's clothes?"

"Most. Not all. It's hard to find clothes in stores that fit her. We do a lot of alterations and up-cycling."

"It's great that you can do that. Do you sell your clothes?"

She shrugged. "Some. I trade for supplies mostly."

"He said you weren't thrilled at having a gallery showing in Seattle?"

She narrowed her eyes at him. "You're quizzing our son about me?"

"Just conversation."

"Hmm." She focused on the unicorn again. "No. I wasn't happy about the showing. In fact, I was almost as unhappy as my agent was when I told him I wanted to pull out of the exhibit. He dropped me. But that saved me the trouble of breaking the contract."

"So, what do you want to do?"

Kara looked at him. "What do you mean?"

Harry shrugged. "I mean…what do you want? For yourself?"

She stared at him, uncertain what he was asking.

"In high school you wanted to work in a museum restoring art."

"You remember that?"

"Of course. I wondered if that's where you had gone. When I came home from college, no one seemed to know what had happened to you."

She leaned back. "You asked about me?"

Harry simply grinned again. "I imagined you'd gone to Europe to learn your trade."

She sighed. "Wow. That would have been amazing. Too bad your mother didn't ditch me in France."

"I'm not sure if that's funny or not."

"I'm not sure if I'm kidding or not."

"Well, since you didn't go to Europe and you aren't restoring art, what do you want to be doing?"

Back to that question. "I don't know. I mean, taking care of Phil and Jessica keeps me pretty busy, actually. Now that we are getting settled here, I expect that won't ease up anytime soon. I've got to find out which school Jess will attend and take her there a few times so she feels more comfortable. I'm going to have to find a farmer to buy eggs, milk, and meat. I actually meant to start looking today, but with painting Jessica's room—"

"Kara," he said before she could continue. "What do you want for *you?*"

She focused on the painting to avoid his drilling gaze. "Not a gallery opening. That's for sure. I don't enjoy that much scrutiny. I don't want to justify my work or be made to feel like I have to fit a mold. I'd rather fly under the radar and paint what I enjoy, not what sells." She cast him a side glance. "Why does it even matter what I want? Being a mother, a grandmother, isn't about what I want. It's about doing what is right for Phil and Jess."

"You're more than just a mother and a grandmother, you know..."

She couldn't remember the last time she felt like more than Phil's mother or Jessica's grandmother. Perhaps that was why she failed to be happy about having the gallery showing. She should have been thrilled. Honored. She knew that. Many artists strived for that one moment, yet she had wanted nothing more than to run from it. If she were honest, the only reason she ever agreed to it was to impress her son. To show him she was more than just some flighty, wafting-through-life artist. And he had been impressed. Then Harry swept in and took those two seconds of glory away from her.

Which was actually a good thing, Kara had decided. There was no way she could continually live up to the expectations she was setting. Moving to Stonehill, having to start over, those were both really good excuses not to be pursuing a new agent and gallery.

"I just want to be, Harry. I just want to do what I do without disappointing everyone around me. That's not such an easy thing for me."

"You've yet to disappoint me."

"Yeah, well, stick around. It'll happen eventually." She looked at the still-full glass of wine in her hand and sighed before handing it back to him. "It's late. You have a big day tomorrow, introducing your son to your staff. You should get some sleep."

He accepted the glass but didn't budge from the stool. "It is important to me that you find a way to be happy here, Kara."

"Why?"

Instead of answering, he drank her wine in one gulp. "You have a big day tomorrow, too. Good night."

She watched him leave, her brow creased in confusion. "Strange as he ever was," she whispered to herself before looking at the star-jumping unicorns again.

CHAPTER EIGHT

Jessica was talking a mile a minute. Harry couldn't understand a word until Phil told her to take a breath and slow down. Once she did, and quite dramatically, she told them about registering at a new school. The principal was the most beautiful woman she'd ever seen. She was dressed in a long pink sundress, and Grandma promised to make one exactly like it for Jessica. Then they went to the playground and there were kids, and they played with her, and they didn't even treat her different. She was going to love her new school, she was sure of it.

And could she pretty please get a goat? And maybe a chicken.

She followed Phil upstairs as he questioned why she wanted farm animals. As interested as Harry was in the answer, he headed to the kitchen, where he found Kara cringing as she butchered a chicken.

"Whoa. Is that meat?"

She rolled her eyes at him as he shrugged out of his suit coat and sat at the counter. While she prepared dinner, she explained how the principal's brother was an organic, free-range farmer. Kara and Jessica had gone to inspect the farm themselves before determining he was worthy of their business. He had a few birds and several dozen eggs ready to sell. She'd bought some of each so Harry could have meat on his plate. She also got some goat milk for his coffee, which Harry wasn't completely sure he appreciated, but it had to be better than the rice milk he'd been drinking since she'd gutted his fridge.

Phil and Jessica came wandering in, and he encouraged her to tell all of them more about her day. As they set the table, Kara bounced all over the kitchen fixing dinner. Harry realized this was all he had ever wanted for his life. He tried not to get too caught up in the moment, but it was impossible. These people had been in his home for a week, and he was already more at home with them than he'd ever been with his ex-wife and her kids. The boys had resented him. Hell, his wife had resented him.

But when Kara looked at him, he felt connected to her. When Phil leaned back and talked about some inconsequential thing, Harry felt like the conversation meant something. And when Jessica grabbed his hand to get his attention, he couldn't help but forget everything else around him and focus on her like she was what she'd already become—the most important thing in his life.

Sitting at the table, the four of them fell into a natural conversation. His feeling of contentment lasted even as he was helping Kara clean up dinner, chatting more about their day while Phil and Jess went to get her bath. Harry was drying a pan, laughing at the image Kara was conjuring of Jessica chasing a goat, when his phone rang. The ringtone told him who was calling without even pulling the device from his pocket.

"My mother," he said quietly.

Kara's smile fell as she looked away. "Something could be wrong," she said when he didn't answer.

He frowned and set the pan and towel down before digging the phone from his pocket. "Hello?"

"Harrison," Elaine said, sounding uncertain. "You haven't called."

"I've been busy with my family."

"Are you in Seattle?"

"No." He looked at Kara. "I asked them to stay with me. We all thought it was time we get to know each other better."

Kara's ferocious scrubbing increased, and Harry walked away.

"Har—" Elaine started and then stopped. "I'm sorry. I have no excuse for what I did to you."

"No, you don't. But it isn't just about me."

"I made sure she was in good hands."

"She has a name."

"I know. I-I made sure Kara was looked after."

"You sent her away. How the hell was that looking after her? Anything could have happened to her. To my son. They were alone. They could have been hurt. You didn't look after her. You hid her away and never gave her another thought."

"No, that's not true."

"I have a granddaughter now. Do you know what she calls me? Do you know what my son calls me? They call me by my name. Because I'm not Grandpa, and I'm not Dad. I'm just some guy who came into their lives from out of nowhere. You did that to us." He closed his eyes and exhaled as his tone took a hard edge.

Sniffling on the other end on the line let him know she'd heard it, too. His mother wasn't a crier. The act should have moved him. It didn't.

"I can't talk to you right now." He ended the call and tossed his phone carelessly onto the table.

A moment later, Kara was at his side, her eyes filled with concern as she rubbed his shoulder. "I'm sorry," she whispered.

"It's not your fault."

"The Dad and Grandpa thing will come with time."

"It isn't about that." He pulled a chair out and dropped into the seat. "I feel like I've missed so much, not just of your lives but mine, too. I did all the things I was told I should do. I came back here after Dad died. I took over his business. I took care of Mom. I married the right kind of woman. I bought the right house in the right neighborhood." He sighed heavily, and she eased into the chair next to him, silently waiting for him to continue. "A month ago, all I cared about was keeping the business alive so I could eventually sell it and retire. Now I'm a father." He looked at her, still amazed at the transition his life had made. "I'm a grandfather. But at the same time, I'm not. What if I do something wrong and I lose them?"

Kara leaned close and held his gaze. "If he hasn't walked away from me yet, he sure as hell isn't going to walk away from you. Nothing you do, Harry, could compare to what I put him through. Maybe he doesn't call you Dad, but he already thinks the world of you."

Harry frowned at her words. "Don't put yourself down to try to make me feel better."

"When he was six, I was tending a lady's garden in exchange for some of the fruits and vegetables. She had this one plant with the most divine strawberries. They were huge and sweet and juicy. Phil loved them. He sat down and ate probably a dozen of them. He woke me up that night so sick. The next day, he was fatigued and splotchy and had this hacking cough that wouldn't go away. I felt so bad for him, I just kept giving him strawberries because that was all he wanted. After the second day, I took him to a midwife I knew. Turned out he was allergic to the strawberries. The very thing I was giving to him to make him feel better was making him sick. The midwife didn't say it, but I'm sure she thought I was the dumbest broad ever for not figuring it out."

Harry smiled sadly. "Well, I didn't even know he liked strawberries, let alone that he was allergic to them."

She grinned. "My point is, you feel like you failed him by not being there, but I was there. And I failed him, too. Lots of times.

We can't walk by someone eating strawberries without him reminding me how I very nearly killed him."

Harry chuckled quietly. "At least he can't accuse you of abandonment." His amusement faded. "I don't know what to do about my mom. How do I forgive this?"

"I don't know."

"I don't think I can."

"Sometimes I wonder if they ever worried about what happened to me." She looked at her hands as she toyed with a ring on her finger. She blinked several times, but she couldn't hide the tears in her eyes that always seemed to come with speaking of her parents. "I wonder if they ever feared that I'd ended up dead in some back-alley abortion clinic somewhere, my body dumped in the woods to hide the evidence."

Harry closed his eyes and rubbed his fingertips into his forehead. "Jesus, Kara. The way your mind works sometimes."

"Do you think that didn't happen to girls who were in my position?"

His heart ached as he acknowledged that, yes, it did happen to girls like her, and yes, it could have happened to her. "I think they did worry about you," he said quietly, hoping to wipe images of her death from his mind.

"I tried to call them so many times, but I just couldn't bring myself to do it. I'd pick up the phone and look at the numbers, but I couldn't dial. Part of me was terrified they'd reject me again. Part of me wanted them to be scared, not knowing. I thought they deserved the stress of worrying. By the time I realized how childish that was, so much time had gone by, I wasn't sure they'd even want to know what became of me. I thought of sending them letters, like I'd done with you, but I didn't know what to say. I wasn't going to apologize for having Phil. I *won't* apologize."

"Would you want to know? If it was Phil out there?"

She cut her gaze to him. "I'd never throw away my son like that."

"I know you wouldn't," he soothed. "But if he disappeared, would you want to know what became of him? Would you wonder if he were okay? Want to know what he was doing with his life?"

She focused on her ring again before nodding.

"I bet they want to know, too."

One of the tears she'd been trying to hide plunged over her lashes and landed in a splatter on the table. "What if they don't?"

"Then they don't deserve the time you've given worrying about it. If you go to them and they still think you deserved to be turned out, then it's your turn to reject them because they don't deserve you or our son, and they sure as hell don't deserve our granddaughter. But if you go to them and they are repentant, ask for your forgiveness, and tell you they've worried about you for all these years, then you've managed to give even more back to Phil. And to yourself."

"What about your mother?"

He sighed. "She played a completely different role in this. She was always controlling, but I never imagined her to be some kind of manipulative mastermind. I don't know what to make of this. I need answers that only she can give me, but until I can get through some of this anger, I can't face her. I don't want to go to jail."

Kara laughed quietly, and he smiled.

He used his thumb to wipe away a tear from her cheek. "Hell of a mess we've got, huh?"

"Yeah, it is. Phil really wants this to work for Jess. He's determined to give her the stability that he never had. I want that for him. I want to be a part of that for her. But it's so hard being here."

"He's not the only one who wants this to work. We've been a broken family for too long, Kare. You asked why your happiness mattered. Senior year, you had fourth period study hall in the library."

She creased her brow, clearly confused by his jump in topics. "So did you. You sat at the table next to mine."

"I wasn't in study hall. That was my lunch period. I ate between classes so I could sit in the library and be close to you."

"Wow, Harry. How very *Fatal Attraction* of you."

He laughed softly. "I was going to have to sit alone at lunch anyway. I know we rarely spoke, but you were the closest thing I had to a friend back then. It was better to sit in there with you, even if you ignored me most of the time."

"I wasn't ignoring you. I was just as socially awkward as you were. I didn't know you liked me."

"Well, I did. A lot. You're more than just the mother of my

child, Kara. When I think of high school, every good memory I have is of you. I measured all the women in my life against you. Do you know why I even noticed my ex-wife?"

"Do I want to know?"

He grinned and ran his fingers over her hair, gently pulling a strand. "The first time I saw her, my heart leaped in my chest. She had her back to me. All I could see was this long, wavy, strawberry blond hair that reminded me of you." He smiled softly. "Of course she wasn't you. She didn't even come close. Your happiness matters to me because you are a part of me. You always have been. Even before I knew about Phil."

"Yeah, well...you've always been a part of me, too. Unfortunately, I hated you for the better part of the last three decades."

He ran his hand over her hair again. "You were my best friend back then. The girl I adored. I want you to be happy because I still adore you and I still feel like you are my friend. Only now, we are family and have to come to terms with a lot of things. We have to help each other. It's the only way to make sense of any of this."

Kara shook her head slightly. "If there is any sense to be made. But you're right. We have to get through this together. I'll help you if you'll help me."

Standing, he pulled Kara with him and against him in one move. He wrapped his arms around her shoulders and held her close. "I've wanted to do this since I saw you in Seattle."

She hugged him back, resting her cheek on his chest. He

kissed the top of her head and inhaled her scent. She didn't douse herself in the heavy perfumes his ex-wife had used. Kara smelled like a summer day—sunshine and fresh air. He would have been content to hug her all evening if he hadn't heard Jessica's mile-a-minute chattering coming their direction.

Kara pulled away and turned back to the sink as Phil came in carrying a deck of cards.

"Uno," Jessica said, heading to the table. "We found Uno. Come on, guys, let's play."

And with that, all of Harry's worries about facing the past faded away.

CHAPTER NINE

"Come in," Kara called in response to a knock at her door. She didn't have to turn from her easel to know it was Harry. Two weeks into living in his house, and his presence in her room had become a nightly event. It was odd to Kara how easily they had fallen into a routine. Not just she and Harry but all of them.

Harry's evening routine, however, brought a smile to Kara's face. After dinner, they played a game as a family, usually Uno since it was now Jess's favorite, and then Phil went to work on getting Jessica into bed and did his usual decompressing in front of the television.

Harry sat with him for a while before appearing in Kara's room, usually with wine or a snack. He sat on the bed chatting about things she only half listened to while she worked on whatever project was speaking to her. Jessica used to be her constant companion while she painted, sewed, or created some other artistic vision. She'd grown used to the talking. Otherwise, she probably wouldn't have appreciated his company as much as she did.

He walked in behind her and handed her a mug of steaming tea.

"Decaf?"

"Of course." He took a moment to look at her painting. "Where are the fairytale creatures?"

"No unicorns in this one."

"I think it could use a few."

She lowered her brush and skimmed over the painting. It was darker than her usual work. A reflection of the storm brewing inside her, she suspected. "I told you I have a problem with consistency."

She turned at his lack of response. He was holding up a canvas.

"This one," he finally said.

"What?"

He showed her a piece she'd done for the gallery opening. It was bright swirls and whirls that came together to make up a woman holding a little girl's hand as they stood under umbrellas.

"This is the one I want to buy."

She waved her hand at him. "Take it."

"No, I'll buy it."

Kara dismissed the notion with a laugh. "You are not buying art from me while I am living in your house, Harry."

He lowered the painting. "The first piece you sell here should be to me. How much?"

"Fine. Five dollars."

"I'm serious, Kara."

"So am I. I forgot to get thread for Punky's dress, and I don't have any cash."

"Why do you guys call her Punky?"

Kara shrugged. "I don't know. It just sort of evolved. Pumpkin. Punkin. Punk. Punky. No reason, really."

"Oh. Okay. I thought maybe there was a story I had missed."

"Nope." She sighed as she examined her painting. "This is awful."

"Hardly."

"I can't work on this any more tonight."

He started for the door. "Good. Let's go."

"Where?"

"You said you need thread."

She lifted her brows at him. "Now? It's almost nine o'clock."

"Clean your brushes and come on." He left the room.

By the time she emerged, ready to go, Harry was hanging her painting in the entryway. He'd actually taken down one of the hideous art deco pieces that had been making her cringe every time she entered through the front door.

"Better, huh?" he asked.

"Infinitely."

He chuckled. "I can't believe you haven't painted the walls yet."

"I've been busy."

"Maybe when Jess is in school."

Kara frowned at the thought of Jessica starting a new school while Harry called out to Phil that they'd be back.

"I saw that face you just made. She'll be fine," he said as they left the house.

They climbed into his car, and he was backing out before Kara voiced her fears. "Kids aren't always nice to her."

"Kids aren't always nice to anyone."

"You know what I mean."

He put the car in drive and started down the street. "Does she get teased a lot?"

"Sometimes."

"I hate that."

She focused out the window. "If they'd give her a chance, they'd see she's just like them. She has the same likes and dislikes. It's just getting them to see beyond the Down syndrome."

Reaching over, he put his hand on her knee and gave it a gentle squeeze. "She'll learn how to handle things on her own. She's growing up."

"She probably handles it better than I do."

"What about Phil? How does he handle it?"

"He also handles it better than me." She was quiet for a few minutes before confessing, "These last two weeks, Harry... I don't know what to think sometimes."

"About what?"

She turned her face to him. "Things are going so well. It's scaring me a little."

"Do things usually go badly when you move?"

"Not bad. I guess I'm just used to Phil whining about missing his friends or wanting to do things we couldn't do. He's never been so easygoing with transition before. And he's never gone so long without blaming me for something."

"Maybe he's growing up, too, huh?"

"Yeah. Maybe we all are."

"'Bout time." He squeezed her knee again, and she realized he hadn't removed his hand. She tried to be causal about it, but now that she'd noticed, heat rolled through her.

Nope. Nopity, nope, nope.

They'd fallen into a great little life over the last few weeks. She wasn't going to blow it by letting herself become attracted to Harry. Okay, *more* attracted to Harry. She'd always been attracted to him. She'd decided junior year that she would lose her virginity to him. It had taken her until graduation night to act on it.

She'd been terrified as she'd walked across the room and taken his hand. The loud music had been a great excuse to go upstairs with him. They'd found a vacant room, which thankfully had a bed. She had been expecting to have to kiss him, but she'd looked up at him as the full moon shone through the window and he'd made the first move, pressing his lips to hers. She'd pushed him onto the bed and straddled his hips as he'd stared up at her with wide eyes, looking as terrified as she'd felt inside.

It hadn't been as artfully romantic as she had imagined. It

was uncomfortable. It was awkward. Their kisses had ranged from too dry and quick to too slobbery and drawn out. Her hips hadn't cooperated in the ways she had wanted, and he had finally rolled them over. But then, she couldn't exactly say he'd been graceful either.

Her first sexual encounter had been with the boy of her dreams, but it certainly hadn't lived up to her expectations. She was quite embarrassed about it now. If he had the same memories of that night, she had to wonder why he'd held her in such high regard for so long. Certainly his ex-wife had exceeded Kara in the sex department, at least as far as Harry could attest to. If not, Lord help the poor man.

For some reason the idea of Harry with another woman, even if he had been married to her, didn't sit well with Kara. She certainly had no claim on him, but that didn't seem to stop her from feeling like they were somehow connected in a way that no other woman had business even trying to touch. She hadn't exactly been celibate over the years. Plenty of men had slid into the places that Harry had been the first to touch, but they had always made her think of him.

Was that normal? Did most women think of their first every time after? Or had Harry had the same kind of hold on her all this time that he claimed she'd had on him?

"Kare?"

She blinked until she could focus on him. He was grinning slightly, just his little half grin that was so undeniably adorable. "Hmm?"

"We're here."

Damn it. "Oh."

"You okay?"

She nodded a little too excitedly and then hopped out of the car. He followed her into the craft store as she went straight to the thread section. She dug into her pocket, pulled out the scrap of material for the dress, and started trying to find a matching thread. Once she found what she needed, she turned to head to the counter. Only then did she realize she'd lost her shadow.

She headed to the main aisle and started walking, checking row after row of crafting supplies looking for Harrison. She found him talking to a woman in an aisle filled with canvases. Again, she had a twinge of something—certainly not jealousy—strike her, but she pushed it away and started looking at the paints and brushes in the next aisle.

Her ears perked when she heard him saying, "She had a gallery showing in Seattle. Her agent set it up for her, but he doesn't represent her any longer."

The woman said something in response, but her voice didn't carry as far.

"That's perfect. I'll let her know," he said.

Kara was tempted to poke her head around the rack and find out what he was talking about, but she was too busy mentally kicking herself.

What the hell was that all about? She'd never been the jealous type. One thing she'd learned from what she had perceived to be Harry's rejection was that if someone didn't want her, to hell with them. She'd find someone who did. She'd had relationships before, and never had she been jealous. She wasn't about to start now. And definitely not with someone she wasn't even in a relationship with.

She did her best to look oblivious when Harry's footsteps started down the aisle. He walked by the aisle and then came back when he realized he'd passed her.

"There you are," she said.

He looked at the paint in her hand. "Need that?"

"No. Not really. What is that?" she asked about the canvas he was holding. She guessed the frame was about thirty by forty inches.

"This is for the living room." He held it up. "You didn't have one in your room this size, but this is what we need to replace the print in the living room, don't you think?" He didn't wait for her to reply. "I want you to paint something."

"What?"

He shrugged. "I don't care. I asked this lady what size she thought we'd need to hang over the sofa, and we started talking. She has a little shop where she holds art classes twice a week. She wants to do it more often, but she needs help." He pulled a business card from his pocket and held it out to her.

Kara took it and read the name and then focused on Harry again. "She wants to hire me?"

"Well, she wants to talk to you at least." His smile let her know how excited he was. "I told her you help take care of our granddaughter and need to be able to get her to and from school.

She said if you're right for the position, flexibility won't be a problem at all. She's happy to work with your schedule."

Kara looked at the card again. She wasn't sure how to feel about all this. She hadn't held down a regular job in years, and even then she hadn't been particularly good at it. She'd suffered through while Phil was finishing high school, but it hadn't been easy for her. She wasn't the live-by-a-schedule type.

Then again, this could be the opportunity she needed to find outlets to sell her work.

Harry pulled her from her thoughts by shoving the card into her hand and curling her fingers around it. "Don't look so stressed, Kare. It's just an option."

She put the card in her pocket and pushed past him, not clearly understanding why she was so overwhelmed by the idea of working in a gallery. She wasn't unfamiliar with the job.

They checked out and started for the car, but Harry grabbed Kara's elbow and pulled her toward the ice cream shop instead. She scowled, but he didn't give in.

"Just pretend it's made from organic, all-natural, nonchemically enhanced, free-range chicken milk."

She laughed as they stopped in front of the menu. They stared for a long time, debating before she settled on what Harry informed her was the most boring thing ever—a waffle cone with vanilla ice cream and sprinkles. He, in turn, got a cone with salted caramel ice cream and walnuts, chocolate chips, and chocolate syrup drizzled on top.

"You're going to kill yourself, Harry," she said as they walked back into the warm evening air.

"But my stomach will be happy."

They found a table along the strip center and sat down in wobbly wrought-iron chairs.

She looked out over the parking lot as they ate their treats. "Didn't this used to be a gas station?"

"Gas station and a car sales lot. They had been abandoned a long time when these lots were bought about eight years ago."

"Everything is different, but it's all the same. It's strange."

"Do you still regret coming back?" His eyes betrayed his attempt to sound casual. He was still worried she'd leave and take Phil and Jess with him.

"If we could go on forever not facing our parents, I think I'd be okay. But that isn't realistic, is it?"

"No, it's not."

They sat quietly for some time before Kara said, "I'd forgotten how beautiful it is here. Or maybe I never noticed. Before the weather turns, we should find time to go to one of the lakes and have some downtime. Wouldn't that be nice?"

He smiled warmly. "That would be perfect."

Their conversation turned to plans for a family picnic and swimming day, as well debate over which lake to go to and when. As soon as Kara took the last bite of her cone, Harry pushed himself up and took her hand to help her to her feet. He put his arm over her shoulder, grabbed their purchases, and started for the car, talking about a time his dad took him fishing when he was a kid.

Kara was smiling, listening intently until her wandering gaze landed on a man several stores down. He was standing in a way that made it look like he'd been midstride when he'd frozen in place. His mouth was open slightly, his eyes wide. Her heart tripped when their gazes locked.

Though he was older—his hair was gray, his face thin and pale—she was certain it was the same man who had tossed her into the air as a toddler. Years later, he had used that same strength to drag her out of his house, telling her she would never be welcome there again.

"Hey," Harry said when she stopped walking.

She thought her father recognized her, too, but a split second later, he continued his journey.

Harry stepped into her line of vision, and she blinked several times. He put his hand to her face. "What is it?"

She looked over his shoulder and watched the man climb into his car.

"I...just..." She swallowed hard. "That was my father."

Harry turned just as the car backed out of the parking spot.

"He's gone." She managed to swallow around the tightness in her throat. "He looked at me for a few seconds, but then he...he left."

"If it was him, he probably didn't recognize you. You've been gone thirty years, Kara."

She flitted her gaze to his. "You recognized me, didn't you?"

His frown answered her question. He'd told her over and over how she looked the same, how he had instantly recognized her. She had recognized him, too. And she'd known that was her father. Just like he had known her.

And then he'd left.

Lowering her face, Kara exhaled as pain crushed down on her soul. "Take me home."

Harry thought he'd do just about anything to not have seen the heartache in Kara's eyes when her father had walked away from her. It had kept him awake half the night. He wanted to go to her, comfort her, make things right. But how could he?

She was quiet the next morning, insisting she was just tired when Phil asked if she were feeling all right. She had smiled at Jessica, but it wasn't heartfelt. Harry could see through her, and so could Phil.

"What happened last night?" Phil asked the moment they were in Harry's car and away from Kara.

"We saw a man who she thinks was her father. He looked at her and walked away."

Phil buckled his seat belt and look at Harry. "Was it her father?"

"I don't know. I didn't see him, and even if I had, I've never met the man. But she was certain it was, and she was certain that he recognized her and opted not to acknowledge her."

"What a bastard," Phil whispered.

Harry nodded his agreement as he backed out of the

driveway. He was silent for a few minutes, tapping his fingers on the steering wheel. "After I came home from Seattle, I looked into her parents. They still live in the same house." He drummed his fingers a few more times. "Should I go there?"

"And say what?"

"I don't know. Ask if they want to know about her. If they do, I can push Kara to go see them. If they don't, I can help her let them go."

"I don't know, Harry. Mom wouldn't like us getting involved in her problems."

"Us?"

Phil lifted his brow. "They're my grandparents, aren't they? I have a thing or two I'd like to say to them as well."

"I don't want to confront them. That's for your mother to do."

"She gets to have all the fun."

Harry laughed. "What do you think?"

"I think if left up to Mom, she'd sit on this and let it eat at her for the next thirty years. She's been running all this time. She's not going to stop now unless we make her."

"And the only way to make her is through an intervention." Harry considered it for a few more moments before switching lanes and turning right at the next turn. He rolled through his mind what to say when he got to the Martinsons' house. He knew exactly where it was because, after doing the research, he'd gone to see where Kara had grown up.

Within a few moments, he'd parked along a curb and pointed to a house nearby. "That's it."

"The brick with all the roses in front?"

"Yeah."

Phil laughed softly. "That's where my mom grew up? It's so…normal."

Harry cast a glance at him. "She never fit into this life. She had her own mind from the day I met her. That's what made her stand out. Because she didn't have to try to stand out. All the other girls were so busy primping and flaunting. Your mother didn't need all that. She was smart and beautiful and independent." He glanced at Phil when he sensed his son staring at him. "What?"

"Nothing."

Harry creased his brow. "Nothing, my ass. You're smirking like you know some great secret. Say whatever it is you're thinking."

"The first time I saw you, when you were sitting at the bar with Mom, I saw the way you were looking at her. You still care about her, don't you?"

"Of course I do. She's your mother."

"Harry."

He frowned. "When we were in school, I was beyond the class nerd. People tolerated me because I carried them through group projects or helped them with their homework, but your mom was the only person who ever actually treated me like a person. She'd tell people to back off if they were acting like jerks.

She'd talk to me—sometimes," he added with a laugh. "But she didn't really talk much."

"My mom? She'll talk to anyone."

"Not back then. The one night we were together—"

"Hey, don't go there."

Harry chuckled. "I was just going to say that I wish I had stayed. Things would have been different—in more ways than us being a family. Your mom and I would have been great together. I believe that, even if she doesn't."

"Wait." Phil closed his eyes and shook his head, as if to wrap his mind around the subject. "You guys talked about this?"

"She says she never would have fit the life I would have wanted to her live. I'd like to think I wouldn't have tried to change her, but she's probably right. I would have. I would have wanted her to be what my parents would have wanted her to be. And that wouldn't have been fair to her. She would have been miserable."

"What about now?"

Harry glanced at him. "Now?"

Phil shrugged. "Just...you know. Why not now?"

"Because we have our hands pretty damn full right now." He focused on the house again. "I think you should stay here. I'm just going to tell them that I know how to reach Kara if they are interested."

Phil shook his head. "No. I want to see them."

"Fine, but just...stay calm, okay?"

They climbed from the car and started for the house.

Looking up at the front door as they reached the stairs, he imagined, for what was likely the thousandth time, a teenage Kara standing on the porch, begging to be let back into the only home she'd ever known. The thought cut at his heart and made him ache for her.

Exhaling the anger he felt on her behalf, Harry rang the bell and looked at the porch swing. "She sat right here," he said quietly. "The night they kicked her out. She said she sat there crying, waiting for them to let her in."

Phil sighed. "When I told her I was going to be a father, she smiled and hugged me and promised everything was going to be okay. She said she'd do whatever I needed her to do to help me so I could finish school. I can't imagine a parent acting any other way."

Phil's frustration showed when he reached out and slammed his hand against the doorbell. This time, the door opened and an elderly woman peered out. The resemblance between her and Kara was unmistakable. She had the same heart-shaped jawline and light skin tone.

"Hello?"

"Mrs. Martinson, my name is Harrison Canton. I'm a friend of your daughter."

"Kara?" she whispered as she put her hand to her chest.

He nodded, and the woman's eyes—the same gray as Kara's—filled with tears. Her hand trembled as she reached for Harrison's. He clasped her wrinkled fingers as she met his gaze with pleading eyes.

"Have you seen her?"

"Yes, ma'am."

Her face melted. "How is she?"

"She's okay."

A choked sound left the woman. She stepped back and gestured for them to enter. Harrison walked in first. A quick scan of the room stopped when his gaze fell on a photo of Kara. It was her senior picture. He had seen it in the yearbook and memorized her smile. He'd looked at it many times after their one night together.

He smiled and turned to make sure Phil had seen it. He had. He was grinning, too.

"What's all this?" an elderly man asked, walking into the room.

"They know Kara."

Mr. Martinson looked at Harry, and recognition shone in his eyes. "That was her last night?"

"Yes, sir."

His eyes glazed over, and he shook his head. "I get confused sometimes. I've thought I've seen her so many times over the years, but my mind just plays tricks on me. I didn't want to embarrass myself."

Harry nodded, relieved that it hadn't been what Kara had assumed—that the man just hadn't wanted to see her. He shook Mr. Martinson's hand. "I'm Harrison Canton. This is my son Phil."

"I'm Charles." He gestured to the woman beside him. "My wife, Kay."

"Where is she?" Kay asked, skipping the pleasantries.

Harry gave her a weak smile. "She's been all over the place—she lived all along the West Coast until a few weeks ago."

"What happened a few weeks ago?" Charles asked as he narrowed his eyes suspiciously.

"She came home."

Kay looked from one man to the other as a hint of fear touched her eyes, possibly a bit of doubt. "If she's home, why hasn't she come to see us?"

"To be honest, she doesn't think you want to see her," Harrison said gently. "We've taken it upon ourselves to find out if she's welcome. She doesn't know we're here," he said quickly. "We just thought we'd find out one way or the other and encourage her to either come for a visit or to let things go as they are."

"Oh, my God," Kay choked out as tears fell down her cheeks. "Of course we want to see her."

"We looked for her," Charles said with a sadness in his eyes that Harrison thought was only matched by the grief in Kara's when she thought of her parents. "We didn't know where to go, what to do. The police wouldn't help us because she was eighteen and we had kicked her out. We hired an investigator, but we didn't even know who the boy was..."

He stopped talking, and Harry offered them another smile.

"I'm the boy. And this is your grandson."

They both turned their eyes to Phil, but it was Kay who moved first. She hugged him like she'd known him all his life. Charles embraced them both before putting his hand on Phil's shoulder, as if assessing him.

"You have her smile," Kay said, clutching her blouse collar in her fist.

Phil laughed quietly. "I've been told that all my life."

"You're all grown up," Charles said. "Twenty-seven years if I remember correctly."

"I'll be twenty-seven on March third."

Kay gasped, putting her fingertips to her lips. "Do...Do you have children?"

"A daughter. She's seven."

She looked at Harrison as if she didn't quite understand. "Kara's a grandmother?"

"She's an amazing grandmother," he said.

"How...How can my Kara be a grandmother? She's...She's just a girl in my mind."

Charles put his hand on Kay's shoulder as he focused on Harry again. "Did you marry her?"

"No, sir. I didn't."

Anger flared in Charles's eyes. "Why the hell not?"

Harry lowered his face and sighed as he realized something he hadn't considered when he'd decided to interfere with Kara's life—he was going to have to own up to what his family had done. He gestured toward the sofa. "You might want to sit down for this."

CHAPTER TEN

The first day of school was creeping up on Kara. She'd spent most of the last two days at the sewing machine in her room, using the need to finish Jessica's clothes as an excuse to avoid Harrison and Phil. They should have asked. They should have consulted her instead of going to her parents without her consent. According to the two traitors, her mother had cried. Her father had choked up but managed to restrain himself. She *had* seen him outside the ice cream shop. He had wanted to go to Kara, but he wasn't certain it was her. He'd accepted a long time ago that she was probably dead. That was the only explanation in his mind as to why she'd never gone home—she was dead.

Couldn't have had anything to do with the fact that he had dragged her out onto the porch and told her he never wanted to see her face again.

"Damn it," Kara cursed as the material slipped and she

dragged the outside of her thumb along the sewing machine foot. She pulled her hand back and looked at her wound. The skin was scraped but barely broken.

"That didn't sound good," Phil said from the door.

She exhaled and lowered her hand. "It's fine."

"Coffee?"

The scent emanating from the mug in his hand tempted her to drop enough of her frustration to allow him to enter.

He handed her the drink. "Still mad at me?"

"Yes."

He lifted up a dress that was nearly finished. "Is this the pink dress the principal was wearing?"

"Yes."

She sipped her coffee as he carefully put the material back down.

He grinned at her. "Jessica is pretty lucky to have such a wonderful grandmother."

"Don't try to butter me up, Phil. You and your father crossed a pretty serious line."

"Do you know me at all, Mother? I'm not buttering you up. I'm laying out a guilt trip."

She smiled sarcastically. "Oh, goody. It's been a few days since we've gone on one of those."

"Harry and I may have crossed the line, but we did so because we love you. You were torturing yourself over whether or not your parents wanted to see you. We simply stepped in and asked them what you were too afraid to. They're truly sorry for what they did, Mom."

"That doesn't mean I'm ready to face them."

"I know. And that's okay. But it's really unfair that you're angry with me for doing the exact same thing you would have done." He nodded when she looked at him curiously. "Remember when I didn't get invited to Joey Cambridge's tenth birthday party? I was devastated, but I refused to ask why. He was my best friend. How could he not ask me to a party? So you went to see his mom, and it turned out she just didn't have enough invitations and thought that my being there was a given. She didn't realize not getting a paper invitation had hurt my feelings."

She scoffed. "This was a little bit bigger than a party invitation, Phil."

"I know. But it's the same principle. I was hurting. You knew the only way to fix it was to face it, and when I couldn't, you did it for me. You were too scared to face your parents, so Harry and I did it for you. If they had decided they didn't want to see you, we knew you would take it better from us than from them. Maybe we should have talked to you first, but you would have told us not to go, and you'd still be sitting here wondering if your parents love you. They do, Mom."

Her lip trembled, and she shook her head. "I'm not ready."

"Okay." Leaning down, he put his arm around her shoulders and kissed her head. "But will you at least try to understand why we did what we did and stop hiding in your room?"

"I'm not hiding. I'm—"

"You're hiding. Which is better than running, but it's still childish."

She gawked at him as he started for the door.

"I'm going to tell Harry it's safe to come in," he said. "He's been pacing outside your door all morning."

Before she could argue, he was gone, her bedroom door left wide open. She frowned as she looked at the shirt she'd been working on. She rotated the needle up, released the foot, and started gently working the material free. By the time she was cutting the threads, Harry was closing her door behind him.

"Phil said you wanted to see me?"

She rolled her eyes and shook her head. "Your son is frighteningly misguided."

"So…you don't want to see me?"

She set the shirt aside and focused on him. "I don't want to be pushed, Harry. I don't want to be made to feel like I have to forgive when I'm not ready. Or forget when I can't." She looked at him. "Have you called your mother yet?"

He lowered his face. "No."

"Why not?"

"Because I'm still angry."

"Well, I'm angry, too. Maybe they did go look for me. Maybe they were sorry. But if they hadn't done what they had, I never would have turned to your mother for help. I never would have been sent away. You would have known about Phil from the start."

He gave her a pathetic look, much like the one Phil used to give her on the rare occasion he'd upset her enough to ground him. "I just saw how much you were hurting, and I wanted to fix it."

She leaned back in her chair and crossed her arms. "I know you did. You've always been a passive-aggressive hero—saving me from paint spatters and emotional turmoil."

"And you've never needed my heroism."

"That's debatable, I suppose. I probably would have been suspended for giving the school Ken doll a black eye if he'd squirted paint on me, even though I started it." After pushing herself up, she took his hand and pulled him to her bed. After sitting back against the pillows, she curled her knees to her chest while he settled next to her. She'd sent him away the last few evenings, not wanting his company as she worked, but she had missed him. She hated how much she had missed him.

Seeing him leaning against the window ledge, looking at her through sad eyes, made her realize just how much. She turned her attention outside. Jessica ran to the swing set Harry had bought for her. He and Phil had assembled the two swings, teeter-totter, and a slide coming from a little wooden clubhouse. Jessica had been in heaven since.

Phil wasn't far behind, following his daughter as she yelled for him to push her.

"You spoil her," Kara said.

"That's what grandpas are for."

She returned her attention to him. He was pouting ever so

slightly as he fiddled with a string on her blanket. "I'm not mad at you for trying to help. Hell, I'm not even mad at you, really. I'm just mad."

"I know."

"What am I going to say to them, Harry?" She creased her brow as she fought the emotions bubbling inside her. "'Hey, don't worry about that time you disowned me. It's cool. Let's just act like that never happened.'"

"I don't know." He broke the string free and rolled it around until he had created a tight ball between his fingers. "I'll go with you, if you want, though. So when you say whatever you need to say, you aren't alone. But you have to face them, Kare. So you can embrace this new life we're building. We both have to."

She watched him playing with the string as she pondered his words. "What is this new life we're building, Harry? What are we doing?"

He shrugged. "I don't know. Taking a day at a time, I suppose. That's all we can do. I just want Phil and Jessica here. With me."

"And I'm part of the package."

A smile tugged at the corner of his mouth. "I didn't mean it to sound like that."

"You don't have to apologize."

"I'm not apologizing, because I didn't mean it like that. I'm happy you're here. I'm not happy about the circumstances, but I'm glad you're back in my life."

She ran her hand over her hair. "The circumstances suck."

He scoffed. "Yes, they do. Next weekend is my parents' wedding anniversary. I've taken Mom out to dinner every year since Dad died. What am I supposed to do now? Take her out and act like everything is fine? Like you said. 'Hey, let's just forget about that time you lied to me about being a father for twenty-seven years.' I can't do that."

"Has she called again?"

He shook his head, and Kara frowned, hating how much pain they were both in. She'd been so miserable. She couldn't remember the last time she'd just taken a breath and relaxed. The sound of Jessica and Phil laughing wafted through her window, and she hopped off the bed.

"Let's go."

"Where?"

"We're getting out of here." She grabbed his hand and pulled him to his feet. "No more stress today. I can't handle it. I need some fun, and you, Mr. Passive-Aggressive Hero, are going to give it to me."

Kara's idea of fun had been finding a lake and spending the day exploring and swimming. But she had told Harry he was going to give her fun, and his idea of fun was completely different. He wondered now, as the roller coaster crested its highest peak, if he had made the wisest choice.

Kara screamed beside him as they plunged downward and

then were jerked right and left. She didn't seem to stop screaming the entire time they were rolled, twisted, and tossed by the ride. When they finally came to a stop, she laughed.

The safety bars holding them in released.

Kara shoved hers up and struggled to climb out. "We are not doing that again."

Instead of admitting he agreed with her, he said, "One more time. Come on."

"I'll get sick. I swear I will."

They walked down the ramp and met Phil and Jessica finishing a funnel cake.

Jess bounced toward them. "I heard you screaming, Grandma."

"Seriously, Mom." Phil tossed their trash in a can and brushed his hands on his shorts. "That was hilarious."

"I'm glad you appreciated it."

Jess grabbed Phil's hand. "Let's do the tea cups again, Daddy."

"That's all the way on the other side of the park, Punk."

She put her hands together and pressed them to her chin. "Please."

Harry waved them off. "Go on. We'll catch up to you." Exhaling loudly, he eased onto a bench.

Kara smirked as she sat next to him. "So I'm not the only one who thinks that roller coaster was not a good idea."

He chuckled and put his arm around her shoulder. He was surprised when she leaned closer to him and her hand fell to his knee. "You're having fun."

"I'm having fun. Jessica is going to sleep like a rock tonight."

"So am I," Harry said. "I'm getting too old for this amusement park thing."

"Oh, no. No. Not too old. Too distinguished. Too mature. Too sophisticated. Never, ever say you are too old."

"Hmm. I'm too distinguished for this amusement park thing."

She laughed and her head fell to his shoulder. Harry thought his heart might burst from the excitement. For the millionth time in his life, he wished he hadn't been such a chicken shit back then. He wished he'd taken the chance and told her how he felt. How their lives would have been different. They would have had years filled with days like this. Years of laughter and days of getting away to forget the stresses of their lives. Instead of something new, this would have been normal for them. This would have been their life.

He couldn't resist the urge to turn his face and bury his nose in her hair. Then he kissed her head and froze as realization struck him. "This is it," he said.

She leaned back and gave him that look that he had already become re-accustomed to. The what-the-hell-are-you-talking-about-Harry look she had. It cemented what he suddenly knew.

He smiled. "This is it."

"What?"

Turning on the bench, he put his hands to her face and brushed his thumbs over her cheeks. "This is the happiest day of my life."

The crease between her brows softened, and she smiled. "I think it could be mine, too."

Leaning down, he kissed her cheek and pulled her into a hug. He held her for a long time before pulling back. He put his forehead to hers and exhaled heavily before pressing his lips to the corner of her mouth. An audible gasp caused Harry to lean back.

Phil and Jessica had emerged from the crowd and were standing next to them. Jessica had both her hands over her wide-open mouth, and her eyes looked nearly ready to pop out of her head.

Phil's gaze danced between his parents. "She, uh, she changed her mind. She wants to go to the carnival games. We can, um, go without you."

Harry grabbed Jessica's hand as he stood and started toward the games. "Absolutely not. It's not a day at the amusement park until I win an oversized bear."

"You kissed Grandma."

Harry glanced at Kara and winked. "Yes, I did."

"Don't say a word," Kara said to their son.

Phil laughed in response but heeded his mother's warning as Harry led them toward the ring toss.

Kara slipped into a pair of house pants she'd sewn together out of scrap material and tugged on a T-shirt before pulling her hair back in a loose bun. She scrubbed her teeth clean and washed her face in the half bath before trekking back into her room. She wasn't expecting to see Harry sitting on her bed. They were all exhausted from the day at the amusement park, and she figured he would be asleep by now.

"Aren't you tired?" She closed the door behind her.

He stopped looking at his phone and grinned. "I'm digging those pants, Kare."

She looked down at the patchwork she was wearing. "Yeah? I'll make you a pair."

"I'm holding you to that."

She sat on the bed next to him, tugging the covers up and dropping them over her legs as she sagged back against her pillows.

Once she was settled, he asked, "Do you want me to leave so you can get some sleep?"

"Nope. I can sleep with you here." She smirked at him. "What's on your mind, Harry?"

"Why do you think I have something on my mind?"

"Because you're tired, and instead of going to bed, you are sitting here with me."

"I had an amazing day."

"The happiest day," she reminded him.

He nodded. "It was the happiest day." He found another string on her blanket to tug on. "I'm sorry if I embarrassed you with that kiss. I didn't...you know...mean anything by it."

"I know. And you didn't embarrass me. This one time, the

day after high school graduation, I tried to sneak out of this girl's house without everyone realizing I'd been dumped by this guy I'd just had sex with. *That* was embarrassing."

Harry chuckled. "What kind of jerk dumps a girl he just had sex with?"

She lifted her brows in response, and he sighed.

"I need to tell you something," he said.

The seriousness of his tone caused her to take pause. "What?"

He looked at her for a long moment. "I really hated that roller coaster."

"Me, too. Maybe next time we just go to the lake like I suggested?"

"Yeah. That's probably a good idea."

"But that's not what you wanted to tell me."

He shook his head.

"What is it?"

"I was really scared."

"On the coaster?"

"When you were mad at me. I just kept thinking, what if she leaves? What if she runs away? I know that we aren't… whatever…and I'm not expecting that," he amended, "but this family, this home…we wouldn't be complete without you." He put his hand on her knee. "Promise me that you won't ever just leave. That you'll always try to work things out before giving up on me."

Kara wondered if this was the result of his divorce. Had his wife just left without warning? Or was he so convinced by his own theory of why she'd drifted so much that he really thought she would just disappear without so much as a goodbye? She decided now wasn't the time to psychoanalyze his request.

"Promise," she whispered. "And you promise me that you won't go around trying to fix my problems all the time."

"Promise."

"Come here," she said, patting the bed next to her.

He hesitated before stretching out on top of the covers and putting his head on the edge of her pillow. They looked out the window up at the stars.

Reaching down, she curled her fingers in his. "This is the perfect end to the happiest day."

CHAPTER ELEVEN

Harry couldn't remember ever having such a hard time picking out flowers, but none of the bouquets in the floral department at the grocery store were "speaking" to him, as Kara would have said. He'd awakened in the morning with her curled next to him. Her mass of hair had worked loose from the bun she'd put it into the night before, and his face was buried in the tangled strands. His arm was asleep and he was cramped in the tiny space on her bed, but he hadn't moved. Hadn't dared.

Thirty years before, he'd missed his one and only chance of waking up with her in his arms. He wasn't blowing it this time. He lay there listening to her breathe, feeling each rise and fall of her chest and the heat of her body against his for what seemed an eternity. When he couldn't take the discomfort any longer, he eased his arm into a different position, careful not to wake her, and pulled her just a bit closer. He closed his eyes and stayed that way until she shifted and eventually awoke. She'd blushed and crawled from bed to start the coffee while he used the bathroom.

After he went back to her room, they sat on her bed sipping coffee, nibbling fruit, and telling stories. He loved listening to all the things she'd seen. He envied her life more than just the time spent with Phil. She'd seen and done things he never would.

Jessica had come in as they drank their second cups of coffee and snuggled under the covers with Kara, enhancing the stories with her seven-year-old point of view. It had been a perfect morning. He couldn't stop thinking that was how every morning of the last thirty years should have been.

After breakfast, Kara worked on finishing up Jessica's new school clothes while he and Phil ran errands. As soon as they walked into the store and Harry saw the flowers, he decided Kara needed a bouquet in her room. He just couldn't decide which ones.

Finally, out of sheer frustration, he grabbed a dozen red roses and a box of chocolates from a nearby display and silently chastised himself for putting too much thought into it. He just wanted her to feel special. And appreciated. He had a suspicion she'd spent much of her life feeling neither. He was going to change that. She did so much for them. He was going to do something for her. Women liked roses and candy. Those kinds of things made them smile. At least from what he could remember. It had been an embarrassingly long time since he'd tried to woo a woman. Not that he was trying to woo her. Not exactly.

He looked at the gifts in his hand and doubt found him. This was a stupid idea. Stupid. What if he *was* trying to woo her? What if she didn't want to be wooed? What if, instead of making her feel appreciated, he made her feel awkward? Or obligated? The last thing he wanted was to put her in a position of feeling like she owed him something.

"Shit."

"Harry?"

He figured he looked as confused as he felt by the way Phil eyed him.

He grinned slowly and pointed at Harry. "Date night?"

"What?" He looked at the roses. "No. No, I-I…" He lowered the flowers and sighed. "I wanted to do something nice for Kara, but I don't think…I mean…"

Phil's smile widened. "Harry, do you want to date my mom?"

"No. Maybe. I mean…would that be okay? Would it be strange?"

"My entire life has been strange. Mom won't eat those."

Harry looked at the chocolates for a moment before the light bulb in his mind lit. "Oh, right. Processed sugars. Chemicals. All that."

"Roses don't really scream Kara either."

A feeling of defeat washed over him. "This was a bad idea."

"No. You're just treating Mom like the traditional female, and trust me, she's not. She likes flowers, but she prefers them live." He walked them back to the floral area and looked at the selection of potted plants ranging from ferns to bonsai. "She'd like any of those."

He took the roses and returned them to the pail of water with the other bouquets. Harry picked up a dark purple orchid and waited for Phil to approve. With a nod, Phil took the candies and gestured for Harry to follow him to the health section. Phil swept his hand like a game show host at the bins of bulk nuts, dried fruit, and granola. "This. Any of this."

Harry had never felt so overwhelmed by food before. He picked up a small brown paper bag, clearly marked to show it was made of recycled materials—a far cry from the fancy candy box he'd initially picked out—and settled on a mix of unsalted nuts. He filled the bag halfway and glanced at Phil, who again nodded his approval.

The bag was just about the most unromantic package he'd ever seen. The plain wrapping made the gift seem more friendly than whatever he might have been going for. Maybe that was a good thing. He was jumping the gun. Kara hadn't been back in his life nearly long enough to start dating.

"Dating is kind of a strong word," Harry said as he followed Phil to the front of the store. "I mean, I-I don't think it's the right word."

"Why not?" Phil pulled the cart to a stop in front of a display of toilet paper. "I, for one, would like to have at least a brief time in my life when my parents are a normal couple."

"Yeah, but..."

"But?"

Harry looked at his gifts again. "This probably isn't the best time. I mean we just… We're just getting to know each other again, and we have so much going on. She's probably not interested in me anyway. I'm not exactly the poster child for the hippie lifestyle."

Phil took the orchid and the nuts and put them in the cart. "First thing, Mom has the least defined standards for men I've ever known. You fall well within the range of what is and isn't acceptable in a boyfriend. She's dated artists, businessmen, and academics. You treat her well, and you have a pulse. Those are about the only two things that have been consistent in the men she's introduced me to. Second, I saw you together yesterday when you thought Jess and I had left. She likes you."

Harry frowned. "I just want her to know I appreciate her. It's not like…"

"It's not like high school, when you wasted all that time that you could have been together because were too scared to tell her you liked her?"

Harry's scowl deepened when Phil walked away. "You're a smartass. You get that from her, by the way."

"Yeah, I know."

Harry paid for their groceries and fretted all the way home. He was on the verge of hiding the orchid and just putting the nuts on the counter like he hadn't agonized over their purchase when Phil shoved the gifts in his hands and nodded toward Kara's room.

"Just be cool," he whispered, but then he yelled over Harry's shoulder. "Hey, Jessica, come see what Daddy got!"

The girl darted from Kara's room. Harry froze, but Phil urged him toward the door as he distracted Jessica with a box of all-natural popsicles. Harry exhaled and gripped the plant and bag of nuts.

Kara sat at the sewing machine squinting at the tiny needle, her reading glasses perched on the top of her head. A long, messy braid hung over her shoulder. She was wearing an ankle-length sundress in shades that reminded Harry of a peacock. He couldn't stop the smile that spread across his face as she focused on threading the machine.

"Tell me he didn't get her candy," she muttered, not lifting her attention from the eye of the needle. "She's wound up enough without all that sugar."

"No. No, we didn't buy any candy." Before he could chicken out, he thrust the orchid toward her. "I got this for you."

She looked up, and he could swear her cheeks blushed just a touch. "Oh, Harry, it's beautiful."

"I thought...you know, you needed...a plant." *What?*

"It's lovely." She stood and took the orchid. "I gave all my plants away when we moved." She touched the petals of one of the flowers, admiring it with a smile. "Thank you."

"And some nuts. Unsalted. I hope that's okay."

She looked at the bag for a moment, and his heart tripped a bit. She suddenly appeared tentative. She lifted her gaze to his, and he could read the questions in her eyes.

"Thanks," she said with far less enthusiasm than she had just moments before.

His hopes sank. "I just thought…"

"Phil picked these out."

He opened his mouth and closed it, trying to process if her words were merely an observation or an accusation. "Well, not exactly. He pointed me in the right direction, but I picked them out."

She took the bag from him. "Why?"

"What do you mean?"

Putting the gifts on the table, she turned and faced Harry, crossing her arms over her chest. "Why are you buttering me up, Harry?"

"I'm not."

She tilted her face, silently letting him know she didn't believe him. He exhaled all the breath and excitement he'd been holding.

He shrugged. "I wanted to do something nice for you."

Her brow knitted. "Why?"

He stared at her for a few heartbeats. "Because."

"Because?"

"Just because."

She gave him that look again, like she couldn't quite decide if she should buy into his story.

"When I woke up this morning, I was so happy. Hanging out with you and Jess put me in a great mood. I just wanted to do something nice for you."

Finally, the suspicion faded from her face and she smiled. "Oh. Thank you."

"You're welcome."

She put the pot on her dresser and carried the bag of nuts with her to the bed. She looked out the window. Phil and Jessica sat at the newly added picnic table. Harry's backyard had transformed from barren to a family gathering spot in just a few weeks. He had already promised next summer there would be a pool. Jessica hadn't stopped talking about how awesome it was going to be.

He crossed the room and sat on her bed, taking up his usual spot leaning against the window ledge. She opened the bag and dumped out a handful of nuts for him. He picked a few and popped them into his mouth. She stretched her legs out, not seeming to mind that her toes slid under his thigh. He, on the other hand, felt the contact buzz throughout his body.

"I finally got started on my curtains this morning." She pushed the nuts around, as if looking for something particular. She plucked a cashew up and put it in her mouth. "Do you have anything I can use as rods?"

"We can go to the hardware store this afternoon."

"I need to go the thrift store. I'm sure they have some."

"What do you need from the thrift store?"

"Well, as soon as I get done sewing all these new dresses that Miss Jessica has requested, I'm going to have start working on making some sweaters. Fall isn't that far away. I need some yarn. There's usually some at the thrift stores."

"You knit, too?"

"When I was so pregnant with Phil that I could no longer move, one of the ladies gave me a basket of yarn and about ten minutes of lessons. By the time he was born, I had managed to make him a pair of booties, one about twice as large as the other." She laughed. "I think I still have those somewhere. Luckily, I got better with time."

"I think it's amazing how self-sufficient you are. If the zombie apocalypse happened tomorrow, you would be one of the few survivors. You can garden, sew, knit, live on nonchemically altered foods. That's very impressive."

"Well, you could negotiate your way out of having your brains eaten. You should have been a lawyer."

He smiled and lifted his gaze to her. "Still regret coming home?"

She looked out the window as Phil chased Jess around the yard, his arms up like he was a monster. "No. Today I'm very happy that I came home."

He dropped his hand onto her ankle and brushed his thumb over her soft skin. "So am I."

Kara pressed her heel into the ground, and the swing swayed back and then forward. She looked at the setting sun painting the sky brilliant pinks, purples, and oranges. She committed the scheme to her mind, planning to use the colors in a work of something she hadn't quite determined yet.

It had been hours since she and Harrison had left her bed after sharing half the bag of nuts and chatting about nothing. His hand had fallen to her ankle, and his thumb had rolled over her skin. She'd swear she could still feel his heat boring into her.

She'd looked at the orchid on her dresser a hundred times, and each time the flower sent a thrill through her, which was almost immediately followed by a silent warning that she shouldn't even consider getting caught up in Harrison Canton again. Sure, things were a lot different now than they had been when he'd just been a crush she fantasized about, but they had so much baggage.

Yet, when he was sitting with her, talking about nothing or something as serious as their parents' actions, she didn't want the moments to end. He'd fallen asleep in her bed the night before, and when she'd awakened in his arms, she couldn't have been happier. She was embarrassed because, even though she was far from vain, she knew she must have looked awful. He hadn't cared in the least. He'd crawled back onto her bed in his same wrinkled clothes, his hair sticking up as he sipped coffee and had another of their pointless conversations.

This evening, instead of going into her room to paint or sew, she'd slipped outside while he and Phil watched their customary hour or so of television. She needed to clear her head, and being in her room just reminded her how much she enjoyed being with Harrison. She was as drawn to him now as she'd been thirty years ago, only now she had a much clearer understanding of what that meant. This life, as conflicted and confusing as it was, was filling a hole inside her she had ignored for far too long.

Recognizing and accepting that brought a strange mix of emotions—contentment wrapped in terror. She hadn't expected to feel such a sense of belonging when she came back to Stonehill. She hadn't expected to have the same stirring of emotions every time she looked at Harry. And she certainly hadn't expected to have this longing to see her parents.

She felt as if she were on the cusp of having everything she was supposed to have had back then. Her son, his father, her parents, even Elaine, if Kara were being honest. They should have been a family. This should have been her home. Her life. And now everything was right there. All she had to do was take it.

But that was the hardest part. What if she reached out and everything was pulled away from her? What if her parents changed their minds about wanting to see her? What if Harry changed his mind about wanting her as part of his family? What if… What if she let herself count on them and they all just walked away again?

Kara closed her eyes and tried to push the doubts away, but they always won. She could daydream about this wonderful life all she wanted, but her dreams always ended the same. With the realization that she was opening herself up to being emotionally obliterated all over again. She just didn't know if she could do that.

She looked to the house when the screen door opened. So much for alone time. Harry was walking across the yard, a glass in each hand, ice clinking the sides with each step he took. He held one out to her as she skidded her slow-moving swing to a stop.

"Want some company?" he asked.

She thought she should tell him no, given the tangle of emotions she'd been trying to process, but instead she nodded toward the darkening sky. "You missed a hell of a sunset."

He shifted his gaze upward. "I'm sure you saw them all the time on the coast."

"There is something to be said for the sun sinking into the ocean."

He sat awkwardly, trying to fit in a seat made for children. "Do you miss it?"

"The coast? Only every second of the day." She smiled at him. "The sacrifice is worth being here with you guys, though."

"Thanks for including me in that," he said with one of his sexy half grins.

"Jess in bed?" she asked instead of acknowledging something she hadn't realized she'd done.

"Yes. And Phil is watching some crime show."

"He likes those."

They both took drinks from the lemonade she'd made earlier.

"I missed a call from my mom," Harry said after a few moments of silence.

"Are you going to call her back?"

He focused on the sky. "Yeah. I guess I have to. I'm sure she's wondering about dinner next week." He laughed, but it wasn't genuine. In fact, the forced chuckle sounded pretty damned miserable. "She must have some kind of radar. Whenever I start getting too content, she calls and shakes me up again."

She ran a hand over his back, not sure what else she could do to offer him support. "We've had a good weekend, huh?"

"We've had a great weekend. I really don't want it to be over."

She pressed her lips together and stilled her hand as another reality she'd been ignoring sank in. "Jess starts school tomorrow."

"You nervous about that?"

"I'm very nervous about that."

"She's going to be okay."

"I'm sure. I just worry about her."

"I get that." He sipped his drink and shifted on the tiny seat. "Have you decided what to do about your parents?"

She sighed. "I have to go see them. I just haven't figured out when."

"Is it a matter of finding the time or finding the courage?"

"Courage. Definitely the courage."

"They want to see you. They want to tell you they're sorry."

"And your mother wants to tell you that she's sorry. Does that make facing her any easier for you?"

He sighed. "Not in the least. But I do have to face this eventually, Kara. So do you."

A breeze flitted through the backyard, and she shivered. The wind hadn't made her body shudder, however. His words had set her nerves on edge and made her quiver. Even so, she said, "Sun's barely down, and I swear the temperature has dropped by ten degrees already."

He pushed his swing closer to hers and put his arm around her shoulder. His heat radiated into her, sending a flush throughout her body.

"Better?"

"Mm-hmm."

"You looked pretty deep in thought when I came out. Are you okay?"

"Just trying to figure some things out."

"What things?" he asked quietly.

Kara drew a slow breath and held it for a moment before sighing. "Everything."

"What to talk about it?"

She looked up at the sky again. "This could be our life, couldn't it? You and me. Phil and Jess. We could...we could be happy, couldn't we?"

"I think so."

"We could be a family. A real family, not just... Not just strangers in a community who agree to take care of each other and call it family. But a real family. The four of us."

"I want that, Kara. More than anything."

She blinked, surprised at the tears in her eyes. "Me, too. But..."

"But?"

"Family leaves," she whispered.

"Oh, honey." He tightened his hold on her. "People make mistakes. People hurt other people, even when they care about them. And, yes, sometimes family leaves. But they're still your family. Your parents, even after all they did, still love you. My mother, bat-shit crazy as she is, still loves me."

Kara laughed softly, but her amusement didn't last. "I want this life. So much. But I am absolutely terrified."

"I know. But, Kara, this scares me, too. Opening yourself up to someone else means trusting they won't hurt you. When you've been hurt and betrayed before, trust comes a little slower. And that's okay. What isn't okay is running away before you let people get close enough to care."

She smirked. "I hate when you slip in your little bits of psychoanalysis."

"Do you deny doing that?"

She took a moment to think back on her life and how she would barely get settled before she started thinking of where to go next. There were few people in her life, other than Phil and Jessica, who she had allowed into her heart. Most of those were the women who took her in when she had nowhere else to go.

"No," she finally whispered. "I don't deny doing that. I keep people at arm's length and run before they have a chance to get closer. And I do that because I never dealt with what our parents did. I just shoved it down and buried it, and now I can't do that and it is burning me alive. I'm an adult. A grandmother. And I still treat my problems like I did when I was kid. I just ignore them until they consume me, and then I leave. I'm sorry, Harry. I just don't know how to be any other way."

"Yes, you do, Kara. It's just not as easy."

She swiped at her cheek. "So I face them. Then what?"

"Then you take a step at a time until you wake up one day and realize the anger is no longer controlling you. I need you to hear me, Kara, really hear me when I say I will always, until my dying day, be here for you. No matter what happens between us, no matter where life takes us, and no matter how much you push me away, you're never going to be alone again."

He pulled her closer and leaned over to kiss her head. She should have pulled away, but she didn't. She lifted her hand to where his rested on her arm and soaked in the feel of his embrace. Being close like this was a mistake when she was feeling so mixed up inside. She shouldn't even consider what she was thinking, but she lifted her head, their gazes locked, and electrical heat pulsated through her. All the logic left her mind, all her reasons for not being there were forgotten, and all she wanted was Harry. He had a way of making all her problems fade away. He always had. One look, one touch, and she was lost in him. And, damn it, she needed to get lost right now.

She smiled slightly at the questions in his eyes. Seeing his uncertainty reminded her of their one night so long ago. Just like that night, there was something alive between them. And just like that night, Harrison made the first real move, closing the gap between them and putting his mouth on hers.

Unlike that night, however, his kiss wasn't awkward and unsure. His lips pressed against hers with confidence. His hand pulled her closer, and his mouth worked over hers.

Everything disappeared except his heat, his scent—hints of ginger from his fading cologne—and his tongue brushing her lips. Her lemonade wasn't exactly forgotten. She simply stopped caring about it. She lowered her hand and slowly released her hold. The glass thudded to the ground, and she used her free hand to cup Harry's face. She opened her mouth and moaned when he deepened the kiss. He must have dropped his lemonade as well, because his fingers threaded into her hair, holding her as he slid his tongue over hers.

Their position—on separate tiny swings—was uncomfortable and prevented them from increasing contact. As Harry pulled back, Kara wasn't sure if the distance was a good or bad thing. He put his forehead to hers, panting quietly, and she immediately missed his mouth on hers. She stroked his cheek, brushing over the prick of his stubble, and sighed.

"I've wanted to do that for so many years," he whispered. "You were always on my mind. All this time."

She smiled, and he slid his thumb over her bottom lip. "I've thought of you, too."

Harry grinned. "Probably not as favorably, though."

"Depended on the thought." She tilted her head and caught his mouth again. The kiss lingered, making her heart race and her fingers tremble.

Harry tried to pull her closer, but the chains prevented her swing from moving any further. She was still undecided on the distance between them, but clearly he wasn't. He untangled his arm from around her and pulled her up as he stood. His palms pressed to her face, his fingers digging into her hair, as he held her for another kiss. She wrapped her arms around him, pulling his body into hers.

Had they fit so perfectly together when they were teenagers? She couldn't remember, but the kisses they'd shared hadn't been anywhere near this electric. The touch of his mouth on hers made every cell in her body feel alive. She wanted to cling to him and crawl inside him at the same time. He was definitely much better at kissing than he had been thirty years ago. She questioned what else he was much better at doing. She broke the kiss as that thought rolled through her mind.

He seemed in tune with what she was thinking. He touched her lips with his thumb again as he took a moment to catch his breath.

"I'd really like to do things right this time." He ran his hand over her hair before meeting her gaze. "No more running scared every time you look at me."

"You never ran, Harry. You tripped and stumbled a few times, but you never ran."

He chuckled, but as he stroked her face again, seriousness filled his eyes. "I know trusting doesn't come easy to you. I know you've had a lifetime of feeling betrayed, but please, please trust in me. Believe in me. Let us have our life, Kara. The life we should have had."

She leaned forward, putting her cheek to his chest. His heart pounded in her ear as he wrapped his arms around her and she nodded. "I'm ready to let go of the past and embrace the future. We have to face them to do that, don't we?"

"Yes, we do."

"That's not going to be easy."

"No."

She closed her eyes and soaked up the feel of his arms around her. Though his body was warm, the air was getting cooler, and she could no longer ignore how chilled her feet and arms were getting.

"Let's go in," he said when she trembled. He pulled away from her and gathered their glasses. With his arm around her shoulder, he led her inside, entering the kitchen through the back door. "Go get ready for bed." He put the dishes in the sink and looked at her. "I'll be there in a few."

She cocked a brow, and he smirked.

"To say good night." He kissed her forehead and disappeared out of the kitchen.

She took a clean glass from the cupboard and shook her head as she considered how things had changed between them over the weekend. Friday night she was still pissed at him for sticking his nose into her relationship with her parents. Saturday night she'd pulled him onto her bed and they'd fallen asleep.

Tonight? Who the hell knew what tonight would bring.

She was distracted from filling her glass with water when Phil stepped next to her and reached for a glass himself.

"Going to bed?" he asked.

"Headed that way soon." She glanced at him and frowned at the way he was starting at her, his mouth in that thin line of disapproval. "What?"

"I know Harry didn't come upstairs last night."

"He slept in my bed, but that's all he did. And in case you missed it, your dad is all grown up now, Phil. He can make his own decisions."

"I just... I think it would be great if you guys...you know... were like normal parents, but do me one favor."

"Use protection this time?"

He closed his eyes and sighed. "Come on, Mom. I don't need these visions in my head."

She chuckled. "What can I do for you, Phil?"

"Be careful. For both your sakes. I think Harry has this grand idea of us all being a family and all that entails. You tend to grow skittish when relationships get too deep. I don't want to see either of you get hurt. If you aren't interested in his idea of happily ever after, you should tell him."

She exhaled slowly. It had been a few days since Phil had reminded her of her ability to do everything wrong. She guessed it was probably time he brought up something of which he didn't approve. Why not point out how terrible she was at long-term relationships? Hadn't she and Harry just discussed her life's motto of run before falling? Hearing it from Phil stung, though. Taking a breath, she cocked her head and scoffed. "I promise to go easy on him, okay?" She took her glass and started out of the kitchen. "Good night."

"Lock your door if there's anything going on that Jess doesn't need to see," he called. "You know how she likes to sneak into your room."

"Sure thing, *Dad*."

She left him standing there as she went to the half-bath that had been designated as hers when she'd moved into Harry's old office. Closing the door behind her, she frowned at her reflection and the distinct red ring around her mouth. Whisker burn. Ah. That explained a bit of her conversation with Phil. She got ready for bed and walked into her room, closing the door behind her. She pulled a pair of pajamas out of her drawer, and for the first time in recent history, she wished she had something sexy to wear—or at least something that wasn't so casual. She imagined Harry liked satin and lace. She didn't own either.

She bit her lips as she debated whether or not she should correct that.

Harry started to knock on Kara's door and then stopped. He wasn't expecting sex. He wasn't opposed to it, but he'd meant what he said when he told her that he planned to do things right. Even so, he had to question if going to her room after the kisses they'd shared was a good idea. She had him tied up in knots. They were the best kind of knots but knots all the same. His mind was spinning at the possibility that everything he wanted was at his fingertips. But he wasn't foolish enough to believe that things could be so simple. Being with Kara was easy. Things felt right. But he'd thought things had been right with his ex-wife, too. Just because things were going smoothly now didn't mean they always would. Kara wasn't the only one who had fears and reservations.

He had his hand up, still debating if he should visit with her this evening, when her door opened and she jolted with surprise to find him standing there, prepared to knock.

"Shit," she breathed.

A chuckle bubbled up in him, but he swallowed it down. "Sorry."

"I can tell by that smirk on your face."

Harry closed the door behind him as he came in. Instead of taking his usual seat against the window ledge, he stretched on the bed, putting his head on a pillow. He'd fallen asleep like that the night before and wouldn't mind doing it again, but she had other ideas. She grabbed a photo album and leaned against her headboard. He put his arm around her legs as she opened it. He grinned at a photo of a tiny bundle wrapped in Phil's arms. Kara flipped through the pages, taking time to tell him the story of each day captured in the glossy prints.

This was part of their time together that he cherished. Not just being with Kara but hearing about the life he had missed. She and Phil may have had their issues with his childhood, but they hadn't been as bad as Phil had said or he wouldn't have integrated Kara so deeply into his life with Jessica. From the start Kara was there, taking photos, painting rooms, making clothes and blankets. Offering Jessica the same tokens of love she had given to Phil.

"His wife left when Jess was about six months old," Kara said, drawing Harry back to the conversation. "When they were told Jess had to have surgery on her heart. I can't imagine leaving my baby, especially when she was so sick."

"I'd guess that is why she left," Harry said. "She couldn't handle the stress of it."

"She didn't want her." Kara traced her fingers over Jessica's image. "She wanted to abort her. Phil wouldn't allow it."

"Thank God, huh?"

Kara nodded. "This little girl brought us back together. Phil and me. I don't think he ever would have invited me to be an integral part of his life if she hadn't come along."

"I don't believe that."

She cast him a sideways glace, and Harry massaged her thigh reassuringly.

"He adores you, Kara. He watches you when you are with Jessica. You may not have noticed, but I have. He is reminded of how you were with him when he was a kid."

"Did he say that?"

"No. But I can tell by the way he looks at you." Harry paused and then wondered out loud, "I thought you two were doing better."

"We are. He's not voicing his resentment at not growing up in Mayberry, and I'm not constantly feeling defensive. It's nice."

"So why are you back to feeling like the world's worst mother?"

She chuckled. "I wasn't. I was just pointing out that he had gone his own way when he found out Katrina was pregnant. I don't think any of us were really surprised when she left, but I was stunned Phil wanted me to help him take care of Jess. Honored but stunned."

"You couldn't be better suited for the role of mother and grandmother."

She gnawed at her lip for a moment. "He's afraid I'm going to hurt you."

Harry focused on her face. "Why?"

She closed the photo album and set it on the floor. "You said it yourself, Harry. I'm a runner, not a lover. I'm not so great at relationships. I have a way of messing things up."

"Hmm. How many times have you had sex with the girl of your dreams and then disappeared without a word?"

She smiled. "None, that I can remember."

He sobered a bit. "And how many times have you married the wrong woman just because you felt like it was expected of you?"

She rolled her eyes as if considering. "Never."

"And how many times have you been divorced?"

She looked at him, and the amusement left her eyes. "None."

"So I'm thinking I'm far less successful at relationships than you are."

"At least you got married. I never even gave myself the chance. I just run away from…everything." She frowned.

He ran his hand over her thigh. "I hate how hard you are on yourself."

"I wasn't like this until I came back to Stonehill. Being here…" She exhaled heavily and pulled her knees up to her chest. "Being here is like having every mistake I've ever made piled on top of me all at once. I'm suffocating under the weight of it."

"What mistakes?"

She looked down at him and offered him a weak smile. "Sometimes it seems like every decision I've ever made has been wrong."

His hand fell to her foot. He rubbed his fingers over her skin. "Everyone feels like that sometimes, Kare."

"But it's more true in my case than in others."

"No, it's not." He pushed himself up onto his elbow so he had a better view of her face. "I've made mistakes, too. But we're here now. We're trying to make things right. That's all anyone can do."

She slid down the bed and rested her head on the pillow next to his as she looked out the window at the stars. "I don't have a lot of faith in gods or karma," she whispered, "but it seems like the universe is putting us here now because we never would have made it back then."

His arm settled across her, and he pulled her a bit closer as he kissed her temple. "Maybe. But she sure is a bitch for making us wait twenty-seven years."

Kara laughed quietly. "Yes, she is."

She traced her fingertips over his arm, and he hugged her closer. When they were together like this, when it was quiet and all he had to do was be close to her, Harry could swear time had faded and three decades hadn't slipped away from them. Closing his eyes, he put his nose to her hair and inhaled the scent he'd already come to love.

"I like to think we would have been strong enough to last," he whispered. "That's wishful thinking, I know. We were too young, too insecure in ourselves, but that doesn't mean I wouldn't have tried my damnedest."

He moved his hand over her hair, lightly stroking the soft strands. He wanted to feel all of her now that he was allowed to be this close. He'd been starved of her for far too long, and now he couldn't get enough.

"When Laura left—hell, before she left—I used to think about us. About what we could have been. I felt like a piece of me was missing without you. I would wonder if you were happy. If you were married with kids. I wondered if you ever thought about me like that. If you ever wondered what happened to me."

She put her hand over his and held it as she pressed her cheek into his palm. He sensed she was struggling with how to respond to his confession. He was about to tell her she didn't have to say anything at all, but then she exhaled a quivering breath.

"When I first got to Oregon," she said quietly, "I kept telling myself to be strong and to be patient. That you had to finish school, like Elaine said. You had to be able to provide for our baby. I had to stay there and learn to be a wife and a mother. I had to do what I could to take care of you because you were going to be working so hard to take care of us. So I'd get up every day and learn everything I could about making a home, and at night, when I felt all alone, I'd write those stupid letters—"

"They weren't stupid."

"They were." She sniffed and wiped a tear from the side of her nose. "I kept imagining us living in a house with a garden, and you'd come home after a hard day and we'd have dinner and…and just…be happy. I kept telling myself if I held on long enough, you would come. I lied to myself for so many years. 'He's just busy. He's just working so we can have a good home.' But deep down I knew. When I hadn't heard from you by the time Phil was born, I knew you weren't coming, but it took me another five years to finally let you go. I couldn't keep putting my life on hold for something that was never going to happen. So I pushed all the hurt and the anger as deep down as I could. I left the community to start over, and I told myself I'd never look back. But you were always there. I don't know if it was because of Phil or something deeper. I missed you, Harry. I missed the life I wanted us to have. But I hated you at the same time. Does that even make sense?"

"It makes perfect sense." He wiped away another droplet that had fallen from the corner of her eye and slid down her nose.

Over the last few months, he'd had his fair share of time feeling like shit over what Kara had been through, but in that moment, he felt like the worst kind of asshole. "I wish I'd known."

"I know. And I wish I'd had the courage to face you and our parents. Even if we hadn't gotten married and settled down, I think I could have let someone love me if I'd just been stronger. Maybe I wouldn't be so scared right now."

He caressed her cheek. "I'm scared, too, Kara."

"You are?"

He nodded. "It would tear me apart if I lost you again."

"Me, too," she whispered. Closing her eyes, she sighed contentedly and snuggled deeper into his hold. "Will you stay with me again tonight?"

His heart skipped a beat at her request. He kissed her head and pulled her even closer. "I'll stay with you every night if you want me to."

CHAPTER TWELVE

Kara's heart raced as she prepared to drop Jessica off for her first day of school. While her granddaughter leaned from one side to the other in the back seat, desperate to find out what was taking so long, Kara inched forward with every student dropped off by the door. When she got to the spot where she was supposed to let Jessica out, she unbuckled her seat belt and reached for the ignition. Before she could cut the engine, Jessica opened the back door and slid out.

"Bye, Grandma! See you after school."

"Jess—" Kara's voice cut off with the slamming of the door.

Jessica bounded up the sidewalk to where the principal had told her second graders waited to go inside the building. Each grade had a designated location. At the school's open house, Phil had asked Ms. Fisk, Jessica's teacher, to walk Jess through the routine several times. She had, and apparently that was all Jessica needed to feel like she didn't need Kara to help her find her place.

Even so, Kara sat, hand on the key, watching as Jessica confidently headed toward the other second graders. Several kids glanced at her and then turned away, causing Kara's heart to ache with each step Jessica took. Finally, the girl, in her bright pink dress, stopped and looked around at the other kids.

"Notice her," Kara whispered. "Somebody notice her."

She was ready to get out of the car and go stand with her granddaughter when Jessica smiled and waved at one of her peers. One of the girls from the playground waved back and moved to Jessica's side. Kara ignored the car behind her when the driver honked the horn. She had more important things to worry about than whether or not she was holding up the line. She waited, silently pleading, holding her breath until the girl said something and Jessica smiled again. The girl took Jess's hand and led her to a group of kids all decked out in shades of pink and purple. In her new dress with her hair curled to perfection, Jessica fit right in with the rest of the seven-year-old princesses.

Tugging her seat belt around her again, Kara waited a few more seconds, just to be sure, before leaving Jessica on her own. As much as she wanted to make sure nothing and no one ever hurt her granddaughter, it wasn't logical. It wasn't easy to know that sometimes people were going to reject Jessica because she looked different, because she was slower, because her voice was hard to understand, or just because it was easy.

Phil had talked to Ms. Fisk and a few other parents, staying much longer than most had during the open house, giving Jessica the best possible chance at being accepted. Kara had no choice but to stand back and see what happened, but damned if it didn't make her stomach roll and bile rise in her throat.

Kara's plan was to go home and start the painting Harry had requested for the living room. She'd decided on the same swirl-patterned style that he had hung in the entryway, but the painting for the living room was going to be the skyline of an amusement park.

It had been three days since their time on the rides, but the fun they'd shared had stayed with Kara.

However, after last night, she was tempted to paint a romantic scene on a swing set.

She'd awakened this morning with Harry wrapped around her. Turning off the alarm, she had wished to go back to sleep in his arms. He'd stretched, sighed, hugged her to him for a few minutes, and then he'd kissed her and slipped from her bed. She'd brushed her teeth and dressed before getting Jessica ready for her big day, but there had been a shadow hanging over her.

Every time Kara stopped moving long enough, thoughts of her parents crept into her mind. They wanted to see her. They wanted her forgiveness. She wanted to give it and move on. Just like she and Harry had discussed last night.

She was driving on autopilot, not really thinking about where she was going until she stopped at an intersection and realized she was less than a block from her parents' house. She hadn't intended to go there. She had a million excuses not to be there. She was still angry. She had a busy day planned. She hadn't even showered this morning—she'd just pulled on a long skirt and T-shirt and tugged her hair back in a bun. She wasn't dressed for a family reunion.

Even so, she felt compelled to make the right-hand turn that would take her to the place she had grown up. Biting her lip, Kara parked across the street before taking a deep breath and finally looking at the house she hadn't seen in almost thirty years.

It looked the same. Exactly the same. A swing still hung on the far end of the porch. It was where she'd sat holding out hope the night she'd been kicked out. She'd waited for what seemed like hours before finally walking three blocks to the convenience store and looking up Harry's parents' address in the phone book dangling in the booth. She'd then walked to the other side of town with nothing but a backpack of mismatched clothes and a toothbrush. Somehow she had worked up the courage to knock on the door. She didn't remember much after that.

Harry's mother had been the only one home, and when Kara had broken down crying, she had ushered Kara in and Kara had told her everything.

She was pregnant. Harry was the father. Her parents kicked her out. She didn't know what to do. She'd begged Elaine to help her. Help her, she had. Helped her onto a bus that took her straight to Oregon and into the arms of a stranger who became the only family she'd have while she learned to be a mother.

Kara never thought she would come back here again. This

place was too painful to even think about. Glancing toward the house once more, she could have sworn she could still hear her mother sitting at the kitchen table crying and her father screaming ugly words at her as she pleaded for him to stop.

"I mean it, Kara. Don't come back," he had yelled before slamming the door.

Kara was looking at the house when movement caught her eye. The man she had seen while out with Harry walked onto the porch and stood at the banister. He was staring at Kara. Her father was stooped a bit now, and his steps were slower as he moved across the porch.

The urge to put the car in gear and drive away was nearly uncontrollable. Putting her hand on the gearshift, she debated, wanting to leave before she had to come any closer to facing her parents than she was already, but her father took the first stair and then the second.

Kara exhaled and turned off the ignition. She closed her eyes and wished Harry was there. Somehow things were always easier with him at her side. Swallowing as much of her fear as she could, Kara unbuckled her seat belt and let it retract. When she looked again, her mother was there, too, standing on the porch staring at her. Waiting.

One more breath and Kara opened the car door. Her hands trembled as she grabbed her handmade bag and put the strap over her shoulder. She stepped out and closed the car door, focusing far more than necessary on pressing the lock button on the remote. Another deep breath and she crossed the street.

Much like when she was driving, autopilot took her up the sidewalk. She was standing directly in front of them before she finally lifted her face and looked up.

Tears were falling down her mother's cheeks. Her father's lip was quivering. All the anger that Kara had been holding on to somehow faded. Instead of lashing out and demanding the apology she had wanted for so long, she crumbled. Leaning forward, she fell into her father's arms and started crying as he hugged her.

She buried her face in his chest like she used to do when she was young and everything was wrong in her world. He'd hugged her when she didn't place in the junior high art contest and when her cat had died. It had been his hugs that had made everything better, which was why it cut so deep when he was the one who had turned her out.

His hand, not nearly as strong as it used to be, stroked her hair as he breathed out her name. She clung tighter until she felt a smaller hand on her back.

She untangled from one hug and lurched into another. "Mama."

sh

Jessica hadn't stopped talking since she got home from school. Kara could barely keep up. All she knew was that her granddaughter had had a fantastic first day of school. She shared in the girl's excitement. She'd had a wonderful day as well.

As soon as Phil and Harry got home, they were very nearly assaulted at the door. Jess was on Phil, telling him all about her teacher and classmates, and Kara grinned at Harry, waiting for the right time to let him know she'd spent the day with her parents.

Phil led Jess into the kitchen as she started in on recess and how the swings at school are even better than the swings on her set. Kara tuned her out, as she'd heard that assessment several times. Taking Harry's hands in hers, she backed into the living room, pulling him toward the couch.

He leaned forward, kissed her cheek, and then leaned back just enough to eye her suspiciously—narrowing his eyes and tilting his head slightly. "You look awfully pleased with yourself."

"I am." She sank down and smiled. "I did it."

"Did what?"

"I saw them."

His brows shot up. "Your parents?"

She nodded, and he brushed his hand over her hair.

"How'd it go?"

"All these years, I thought I would be so angry when I saw them. I imagined all these horrible things I wanted to say to them, but when I got there, I just broke down. I cried, and they cried. It was a very snotty reunion."

He laughed. "I bet."

Her smile fell a bit. "My dad isn't doing so great. He forgot who I was twice. I missed so much of their lives, and now he's fading."

"You're here now. That's what matters."

"I stayed there all day, talking to them, telling them everything. I'm going to go tomorrow with photo albums."

"That's great."

She put her hand to his face. "I wouldn't have done it if you hadn't pushed me. Thank you."

"You did the hard part."

"The thing is, it wasn't that hard. Well, not after I worked up the nerve to get out of the car." Her shoulders sagged. "My grandparents are dead. I knew that, but…"

"But they confirmed it." He rubbed his hand over her back as she nodded. "We should take flowers to their graves."

She leaned into him, loving the security she felt when his arms slid around her. "That would be lovely."

"Now? Phil is planning on taking Jessica out to dinner to celebrate her first day."

Kara's breath caught as emotion surged through her at the thought of seeing her grandparents' names spelled out in stone, but she forced the air out and nodded. No more running. "Okay. Now."

Leaning forward, he kissed her head. "Let me change first."

He pushed himself up and disappeared, and Kara sank back on the sofa. Her head spun whenever she spent too much time considering how quickly things were changing. She and Harry were…not exactly a couple but close. She and Phil were, for the first time in years, in a place where they weren't bickering constantly. Jessica was incredibly happy with her new school and their new life. And Kara had made peace with her parents. Things couldn't be better.

For her, at least. Harry was still struggling with his mother. Kara wasn't sure what, if anything, she could do about that. She didn't want him to resent her involvement the way she had resented his. And even if she did want to get involved, she wasn't sure what she could do. She wasn't any more ready to forgive Elaine than Harry was. But one thing Kara had realized today was that their parents were frail. If Harry ever planned to recover his relationship with his mother, he needed to start working on that. The woman was aging every day. He wasn't going to have an infinite amount of time to settle things.

"Hey," Phil said, coming into the living room. He smiled brightly. "She had a good day, huh?"

"She had a wonderful day. Some of the girls in her class seem to have taken her in."

"That's great."

"Yes, it is."

His smile faded a bit. "You okay, Mom?"

She exhaled. "I visited your grandparents today."

His face lit. "How'd it go?"

"It went well. I'm going to take them some photos tomorrow. They are very impressed with you."

He sat beside her. "They seemed like nice people."

"They want us over for Sunday dinner. All of us."

"Including Harry?"

"Yeah. They were impressed with him as well." Kara changed

the direction of the conversation. "He said you're taking Punk out for dinner?"

"Yeah. She's earned it. What are you and Harry doing?" He scrunched up his face. "Or do I want to know?"

She laughed slightly. "We're going to the cemetery to put flowers on my grandparents' graves." She didn't mean for the tears to spring to her eyes, but they did and she couldn't hide them.

"I'm sorry," Phil said sincerely.

She sighed. "It's not like I thought they'd still be alive. It's just a reminder that I've spent the last thirty years with my head selfishly stuck in the sand. I spent so much time being angry and blaming my parents. I should have used that time working up the nerve to come home. I could have told Harry about you, fixed things with my parents. Seen my grandparents. And, who knows, maybe you would have had a better life."

"I had a great life, Mom."

"No, you didn't."

"I did. I'm sorry I always gave you such a hard time. I was angry, too, but Harry is right when he says I probably would have hated growing up in suburbia. There isn't a single ocean in Iowa."

Kara smiled, but her amusement didn't linger. "I was just scared. I was too scared to come home. And we all suffered for it."

"You thought Harry didn't want us. You thought your parents didn't want us. Why would you come back when you thought we weren't welcome?" He put his arm around her shoulder. "Do you remember my tenth birthday? I kept asking for a brand-new mountain bike. It was all I wanted, but you didn't have the money for it, so you did some artwork for that guy named after an animal—"

"Bear."

"And he made me a bike. Remember? It was the coolest thing I'd ever seen because he welded my name on it. Nobody else had a bike with their name on it. I rode that bike even after I'd outgrown it. It was better than anything you could have bought, Mom. You did the best you could, and I know I've always been the first to knock your parenting, but I just didn't know back then what I know now. You didn't bring us home because you didn't think it was the right thing for us. You did what you could, and that's all anyone could ask."

"Do you have any idea what it means to me to hear you say that?"

"I'm sorry I didn't say it sooner. I know it wasn't easy for you to come back here, and I know you did it for Jessica and me. Everything you ever did was for Jess and me. I know that. And I want you to know that I do appreciate it, and I do love you."

Leaning over, she gave him a hug. "Thank you."

"I'm ready, Daddy," Jess yelled, running into the room.

She hesitated as she looked at Kara, who forced a smile to her face. Seemingly appeased, Jess returned her focus on getting Phil up and out the door.

Once they were gone, Kara took several deep breaths, trying to prepare herself for saying goodbye to her grandparents.

"Would you mind…" Kara started but didn't finish. She looked out over the headstones, four peace lilies in her hand. "I think I'd like…"

Harry put a kiss on her head and then gestured toward another section of plots. "I'll be over there if you need me."

She offered him a sad smile that tugged at his heart. "Thanks."

He watched her walk away before shoving his hands into his pockets and scanning the memorials he'd pointed to a few moments before. Walking down the path, he veered to the right, going to a headstone he hadn't visited in a long time. Stopping, he stared down at his father's marker.

Beloved Husband and Father.

Nothing about being a grandfather.

He looked up and noticed Kara had stopped moving. She'd found at least one set of grandparents. He suspected when they curled up in bed later that night, she'd tell him about them. He wondered if they would have turned her out as well. If she had gone to them instead of his mother, would things have been different? Would they have taken her in and given her the love and support she'd needed? Or would they have turned their backs on her as well?

He returned his attention to the grave at his feet. "What the hell were you thinking, Dad?"

"Your father wasn't much for talking when he was alive," his mother's frail voice said behind him. "I doubt he'll answer your questions now."

Harry's heart did a barrel roll in his chest. He took a breath to steady himself before facing his mother. She gave him a timid smile when he turned around.

He sighed at the hopeful yet reserved look on her face. "I should have known you'd be here sometime, Mother."

"We would have been married fifty-six years tomorrow."

"I've been trying to decide what I should do about that."

She looked down at the flowers in her hands. "We didn't want you to throw your life away because of one mistake—"

"It wasn't a mistake," he said, cutting her off. "Kara was never a mistake. I loved her, Mom. I know I was a kid, but she was like… She was the only ray of sunshine in my life. She was the only person in the world I felt connected to. Being with her wasn't a mistake. No, I didn't mean to get her pregnant, but I don't regret it. I don't regret being with her, and I don't regret having a child with her. She was not a mistake."

Elaine hesitated. "We thought we were protecting your future. We were going to tell you after you were done with school. If you had wanted her in your life after you had a way to support her, we would have brought her and the baby home. You couldn't have taken care of her if you'd dropped out of school, Harrison, and we didn't want you to give up having an education."

"You never told me, Mom."

"Your father died, and I thought... What if you didn't forgive me? He was the peacekeeper, the one who could smooth things over. What if you hated me? I couldn't take it if I lost both of you, Harry."

"So I lost my son instead. How is that right?"

"It isn't. It isn't right, but I could never find the courage. I didn't want to be alone."

He nodded. "But you wouldn't have been alone. You would have had me, and Kara, and our baby. We could have been a family. For twenty-seven years, she thought I didn't want my son. She thought her parents didn't want her. That we'd all just washed our hands of her like she meant nothing to us. She's been hurting so much all these years. You did that to her."

Elaine lowered her face. "I know."

"How did you feel, reading her letters, looking at pictures of my boy, and all the while knowing that I didn't even know he existed?"

She was silent for a few moments. "He looked so much like you. I couldn't believe how much he looked like you. Whenever her letters would come, I'd get so excited. I couldn't wait to see him."

"You mean see pictures of him. How was that enough? Didn't you want to see him? Hold him? Instead of just some piece of paper?"

She sobbed. "Of course."

"You didn't have to send her away. We could have figured out a solution. Maybe I would have dropped out of school. Maybe I would have given it all up. But it would have been worth it, Mom. They would have been worth it, but you didn't even give me a chance to be a...a beloved husband and father." He gestured to his father's grave. "You had all these years to come clean. Why didn't you?"

"It just got harder and harder, Harry. When the pictures stopped coming, it broke my heart. I wanted to know what he looked like, what he was doing, but how could I ask?"

"She said she sent you her address."

"I sent money."

"Until he was eighteen. What about college? Didn't you think maybe she needed help putting him through college? I mean, we wouldn't want him to give up having his education, would we?"

She lowered her face again. "Saying I'm sorry isn't enough—"

"Damn straight."

"What do you want me to do?" she demanded as she lifted her face to him again.

He'd never seen his mother cry. Even when his father had died, other than a few sniffles, she'd kept herself together. He had wondered then if she were even capable of it. Now, standing before him with tears on her face and her voice cracking, he wondered not if she were capable of crying but if she were being sincere. He swallowed and looked to where he'd left Kara. She was watching from a distance. She had no more flowers in her hands. Apparently she'd finished what she had come to do.

"Kara doesn't want anything to do with you," Harry said. "She says she doesn't want someone in her life who is capable of doing what you did to her. And I don't blame her, because I'm struggling with that myself."

"Harry," she called when he started past her. "I made a mistake. I was too scared to try to fix it. Being a parent means making mistakes, being scared that you're going to lose the one thing that means the world to you. But those mistakes are made in the name of protecting your son."

He sighed as he looked at her. "I have the most incredible granddaughter. She hugs me, and I forget all my problems. She is the single most amazing gift I've ever gotten. You didn't just rob me of my child. You robbed yourself of your grandson. Do you think he wants to run up and hug you? Do you think he is ever going to look at you like you hung the moon? I'll never have more children, Mom. You'll never have another grandchild. You threw away the only chance you ever had at knowing how amazing it is to be a grandparent."

"I didn't mean for things to turn out like this, Harry."

"Well, they did turn out like this. And it is your fault. You may have lost out on your chance, but I have my son back now. I have his mother back. And we're doing everything we can to set things right. I don't know if there's room for you in that."

"You have to forgive me."

"No, I don't." He left her standing with her mouth hanging

open as he walked to where Kara was waiting. Her eyes were still red from crying, and it made his sorrow run that much deeper.

"Are you okay?" she whispered as he neared her.

He pulled her into his arms, digging the fingers of one hand into her hair as he held her to him. He choked back his tears and hugged her for a long time. Finally, without a word, he eased up enough to guide her back to the car.

"Harry?" she asked when they were inside the car.

"They planned to tell me after I finished school, but Dad died and she chickened out."

The weight of Kara's sympathetic gaze on him was suffocating. He shook his head, hoping she understood he didn't want to talk about it. She looked out the window as he left the cemetery. They drove home in silence. Phil and Jess hadn't returned yet, making the house so quiet it set Harry on edge. He'd never liked the silence of an empty house, but now that he was used to hearing Jessica talking and Phil watching television and Kara telling him stories, the silence seemed so sad.

He dropped his keys on the table and looked at Kara's painting hanging on the wall.

Kara put her hand on the small of his back and looked up at him. "You must be starving. I'll make some dinner."

He caught her hand as she started to walk away. "It wasn't a mistake."

She creased her brow. "What?"

"Graduation night. Us. It wasn't a mistake."

She smiled slightly. "No. It wasn't a mistake."

Pulling her back to him, he captured her mouth with his. She parted her lips, deepening the kiss as he'd done the night before. Harry was very nearly about to give up on his notion that he romance this woman before taking her to bed, but the slamming of car doors saved him from his lust. He gave her one more quick kiss and wiped her lips dry.

He turned and opened his arms as Jessica darted in. She wrapped herself around his waist and hugged him, and just like he'd told his mother, all his problems disappeared. At least for the moment.

CHAPTER THIRTEEN

Kara knocked on Harry's door. When he didn't respond, she eased the door open and frowned. Exactly as she'd feared. Self-inflicted pity party. Not that she blamed him. She'd been there and had most definitely done that. "May I come in?"

He finished taking a drink from the beer in his hand and nodded. Tossing a photo next to him on the bed, he leaned his head back on the pillows and watched her close the door and cross the room to him. She sat on the edge next to him and picked up the picture he'd discarded. She smiled at the image of a tiny Harry standing next to who was obviously his father. They were fishing on a pier somewhere.

"The resemblance between you Canton men is remarkable."

He started to smile, but it faded. "Phil's a Martinson, remember?"

She caught his gaze. "He's a Canton, Harry. He's your son."

She picked up the pictures, scanning them, pausing every now and then when one would catch her eye. Finally, she set the photos on the dresser. Rubbing his thigh as he finished his drink, she said, "Talk to me."

"About what?"

She was torn between the urge to leave him alone and chastise him for being difficult. Instead, she grabbed one of the photos—a ten- or eleven-year-old Harry with a black dog—and showed it to him. "This day. Tell me about this day."

"That's Buster. He was my best friend. My only friend. I would take him for walks. Feed him. The only thing I didn't do was clean up his shit, which infuriated my mother. One day he disappeared. She told me he ran away. I overheard her a few weeks later talking about how she'd taken him to the pound. I was furious. I smashed open my piggy bank and rode my bike to the shelter to save him, but he'd already been euthanized."

"Oh," she gasped. "Harry."

"She wasn't even remorseful. She just said if I'd cleaned up his messes, she would have let me keep him. My entire life she's been taking things from me. She's such a selfish bitch. You're right. You're so right. There is no room for her in our family. Not after everything she's done."

Kara put her hand on his face, but he turned away.

"Don't. Please. I just need to be alone right now."

"Harry."

"Please, Kara," he pleaded on a whisper. "Just let me go through this."

She hesitated, debating if she should push him harder. After a moment, she conceded with a nod. She went downstairs to her room, closed the door, and collapsed on her bed. She hated seeing Harry so torn up. He was the strong one, the one who talked reason into her, the one who reminded her that forgiving her parents was the equivalent of freeing herself from the pain. And he'd been right. The years of stress pulling at her had already started to fade. She had a long way to go with her parents, but the first step on the road back to being family had been taken, and with it, so much of her anger had left her.

She wanted that for Harry. She wanted him to find the peace that only forgiving his mother could bring. The problem was Kara hadn't quite figured out how to forgive the woman herself. She could remember it like yesterday, how Elaine had put her on a bus and promised her she'd be well taken care of until Harry could come for her.

Had Elaine genuinely intended for Harrison to go to Oregon to collect Kara and Phil? Or had she just written them off like they were nothing? Had she gotten scared, like she said, that Harry would reject her and she couldn't stand the thought of losing her husband *and* her son?

It was unfathomable to Kara, but who the hell knew what one person would do for the sake of keeping another. If she'd learned anything in her life, it was that everything could be justified if emotions were high enough. She'd justified not coming home for thirty years out of fear of rejection. Elaine had lied for thirty years.

And now Harry was feeling the same pain Kara had so long ago. So much anger and such a sense of betrayal.

He had pushed her to do what she needed to forgive her parents or at least move forward. She owed the same courtesy to him. Grabbing her cell phone off the nightstand, Kara connected to a search engine and looked up Elaine's address. She knew she was in the same house, but it had been far too long for her to remember where that was. She jotted the house number and street name down on a piece of paper and headed for the front door before she could change her mind.

"I have to run out for a few minutes," she called, passing the living room. "I'll be back soon."

"Okay," Phil responded over the sound of sirens blaring from the television.

She climbed into Phil's car and drove several blocks. She slowed as she neared Elaine's address. Her heart was in her throat as she pulled into the driveway. Looking up at the two-story brick, she easily recognized it. Years ago, she'd stood on the sidewalk, staring up the house and working up the courage to knock on the door. She didn't let the fear stop her now. If she was going to do this, she need to just get it over with. Just like she'd done with her parents.

Face it. Deal with it. Move on.

She rang the doorbell and held her breath. In those few moments, fear sneaked up on her, but she forced it down. She didn't need anything from Elaine this time. She just needed to say her piece and leave.

The door opened, and the woman who answered poked her head out. Her curious eyes instantly saddened. "Hello, Kara."

She swallowed hard. "Elaine."

They stood in an emotional stalemate for a moment before Elaine stepped aside and allowed Kara to enter. The house looked familiar, but so much had changed since the last time she was there. Even so, when Elaine turned and started to walk away, Kara knew she was leading the way to the kitchen.

"I think we need some tea for this, don't you?" Elaine asked without waiting for an answer.

Kara stopped in the kitchen doorway. The table, though different from the one that had been there before, was in the same place. She'd sat there and told this woman that she was pregnant with Harry's child. She'd told her she'd been kicked out by her parents and she had no place to go. She'd begged Elaine to call Harry because he would know what to do.

She'd been sitting there when Elaine served her eggs and toast the next morning and explained how important it was that Harry finish school so he could support Kara and the baby. Elaine knew where Kara could go for the help she needed until Harry could come for her.

"How did you find the place where you sent me?" Kara asked without thinking.

Elaine finished filling the teapot with water. "My husband's cousin told us about it while visiting over the summer. She lives in Oregon. She'd bought produce from the farm. She was very impressed by their mission—helping young, unwed mothers."

"I imagine you were horrified."

Elaine turned on the burner and faced Kara. "I wasn't raised to have sex out of wedlock. Neither was my son."

Kara lifted her brows. "And then I came along and ruined him, right?"

"As soon as you told me your name, I knew you were the girl he had been babbling about for years. He adored you. I had no doubt your baby was his."

"And yet you still sent me away."

Elaine returned her attention to her task, reaching for two teacups. "We thought we were doing what was best for our son."

She scoffed. "What about *his* son?"

The cups clanked on the tile countertop as Elaine faced Kara again. "Your parents had kicked you out. Harry had no means to support a family. What did you want me to do? Adopt you?"

"A little fucking sympathy would have been nice."

"Don't you cuss at me."

"Don't you pretend you had no other choice. You didn't want your precious little boy's life to take a turn you hadn't predetermined to suit your plans for him, but you never once, not for one minute, considered his little boy. My son, Harry's son, grew up without a father, Elaine. He grew up thinking his dad didn't want him. You were so scared that you'd lose your family that you robbed Harry of his."

Her lip trembled almost as much as her hands. "What did you want me to do?" she repeated.

"You should have told him. You should have given him my

letters. You should have let him decide what his life was going to be."

"How could he have supported a family with a high school diploma? He deserved more than that."

"But I didn't? I was going to go to college, too, Elaine. I wanted to work in a museum preserving art. But instead of learning the proper technique for restoring paintings, I learned how to barter for diapers and food for my child." Her vision blurred with tears that fell before she could stop them. "You tossed me out without a thought for the child I was carrying. I didn't deserve what you did to me. None of us deserved what you did."

The teapot whistled. Elaine stared at Kara for several long moments before she moved the kettle from the heat and turned off the burner. "Chamomile?"

Kara sighed and wiped her face. "Why not?"

"Sugar or honey?"

"Honey."

"Sit at the table. I can't stand you hovering with that disapproving look on your face."

Kara cocked a brow and crossed her arms over her chest instead of sitting.

Elaine laughed quietly in response. "He was enamored by you. Still is, if I read him correctly at the cemetery. It took him a long time to get over you. I was so proud of him when he married Laura. She was so…"

"Boring?"

"Stable. I'd heard Harry's stories about you. Free-spirited, sarcastic, rebellious."

"The first two maybe, but I was far too intimidated by authority to be rebellious."

"You're the one who covered that boy in paint, aren't you?"

She smirked. "That was me."

"Harry very nearly got himself in trouble saving you."

"I didn't ask him to."

"Every now and then, even after he was married, he'd tell stories about you. It was like twisting a knife in my stomach. As if he knew on some level and couldn't quite let you go. Out of the blue, he'd talk about how you defended his Mount Rushmore project or how you were a great artist. He'd see a painting and say something like, 'Remember Kara Martinson—the girl I went to school with? I sure hope she's still painting.'"

"Yeah, well, sometimes I'd see a man with his kid and think something like, 'Remember Harry Canton—the boy who knocked me up and disappeared without a word? I sure hope he contracted an STD and his balls rotted off.'"

Elaine frowned as she held out a cup. "Sit. If we're going to hash this out, we're going to do it civilly." She lifted her brows. "I assume you came to hash this out."

Kara accepted the cup and sat at the table. "Harry is hurting because of this. I'd like to fix that if possible."

Elaine stirred her drink. "I told Harry what happened. His father had died. I was alone." She shrugged her frail shoulders. "I thought if I told him, he'd leave me here without anyone." She lifted her gaze. Her eyes were watery. "He was all I had, and I didn't know what I would do without him."

Kara laughed at the irony.

"I read your letters," Elaine defended. "You were raising Phil well. You'd made a life for him."

"A life? Is that what you call it?"

"He was happy. I could see it in the pictures."

"He was miserable not having a father, and he blamed me for that."

Elaine waved her hand dismissively. "All teenagers are miserable and blame their parents."

"He just wanted a normal life, a house, a dad." Kara rotated her jaw angrily. "I couldn't give him that."

She looked into her mug. "Every time I got one of your letters, I tried to make myself give it to him. To tell him the truth and beg him to understand. Then the letter came that said you wouldn't be writing again. I didn't know what to do. I cried and cried. I wanted to write to you then, confess everything. I even considered asking you to help me tell Harry the truth. I thought he would be more forgiving if it came from you."

Kara laughed bitterly. "Wow. What did you think I was going to do, Elaine? Pretend I hadn't spent years trying to get him to accept his son via the postal service?"

"After the letters stopped," Elaine continued as if Kara hadn't spoken, "it started to seem like maybe it had never happened. Maybe it hadn't been real. I could bury it. Forget. But every now and then, I'd pull out the pictures and look at Phil's little face, and I'd wonder what he was doing."

"You had our addresses. I always sent you our addresses."

"I know. But I wasn't brave enough to use them."

"You sent money."

"That was easy. That was impersonal."

Kara lifted her brows. "He was your grandson."

She nodded. "He must think I'm a monster."

"I can't say any of us have a very high opinion of you right now."

Tears fell down Elaine's cheeks.

Kara shook her head. "I can't, for the life of me, begin to understand why you did what you did. I don't know that I can forgive you, but I do know that the anger Harry is feeling right now is tearing him up, and I can't stand to see that. I'm going to do what I can to help him come to terms with things and make peace with them. That means I have to make peace with you. But I want to make one thing very clear: I am doing this for Harry's sake. Not for one moment am I taking you or your feelings into consideration. I am doing this for him. Not for you. Never for you."

"I'll never forgive myself. If that counts for anything."

"It doesn't." Kara looked in her mug and sighed. "You're going to let Harry set the pace for what happens next. Don't call him or push him. I'll help him take the next step, but it's up to him if and when that happens. He's got a lot of things to figure out, and you aren't going to compound it with this I-was-doing-it-for-you bullshit."

"You're cussing again."

"I don't have to respect you," Kara stated. "I'll try, for Harry, but I don't have to. When you play the protective mother card, all you are doing is projecting your guilt onto him, like it is somehow his fault that you lied to all of us. It isn't. That was your choice. Stop making it about his education and own that it was your fear. As for my son, it is up to him whether or not he invites you to be a part of his life. That isn't my choice, and that isn't a relationship that I will push on him. If he asks for my help, I'll give it, but I will not help you. Do you understand me?"

"Yes," she said on a breath.

Kara pushed herself up, but Elaine grabbed her wrist. Her eyes were sad, pleading.

"I'd at least like to see what my grandson looks like now. I'd like to see his daughter. Do you have photos?"

Kara considered the request for a moment. "I think that's for Harry to decide."

"Wait," Elaine called as Kara pulled free. "I know it doesn't mean much, but I am sorry that I hurt you."

She nodded just enough to acknowledge the apology before heading for the door.

Kara walking into the kitchen was like taking a breath after nearly drowning. Harry pulled her to him, wrapped his arms around her, and buried his face in her hair as relief washed through him.

"I'm sorry," he whispered.

"For what?"

"For sending you away."

She leaned back and met his gaze. "You said you needed to be alone."

"I didn't mean it." He stroked his fingers over the braid that started at her temple and disappeared behind her head. "I didn't want you to leave."

"I'm not going anywhere, Harrison."

He lowered his face, embarrassed that she'd read his fear. She'd spent her life running. He was terrified she was going to run again. He didn't want to lose her. "It's been a hell of a few days. I'm so worked up about my parents' anniversary. Running into Mom today didn't help."

"I know." Kara took a breath. "That's why I went to see her."

Harry's stomach flipped. "You what?"

"I told her I am going to put it all behind me and focus on the future. I want a life here, Harry. With you and my parents and our son and granddaughter. And, I suppose, with your mother. The holidays may be uneasy, but a lot of people don't get along with their in-laws."

Harry lifted a brow and smiled. He didn't think she'd even realized what she'd said. "In-laws?" he asked before she could continue her rambling.

Kara flattened her mouth and cocked a brow—the same disapproving look she would get so mad at Phil for giving her. "You know what I mean."

She started to walk away, but he wrapped his arm around her stomach and reeled her back to him.

"Are you asking me to marry you?" he teased.

Her eyes widened and her mouth dropped, causing him to laugh. "Hardly."

He grinned at her, amazed that all it took was a few minutes of being with her to make him feel so much better. Five minutes ago he'd been about to lose his mind. Now, he leaned against the counter and used her hips to nestle her between his legs. "I'd have to consider all my options, but I could probably be swayed with a little romance."

"Harry," she said, but her chastisement was light.

He dipped his head down and kissed her. "A few candlelit dinners and walks along the beach would probably convince me of your sincerity."

She dragged her hands up his arms and around his shoulders. "Harrison."

He kissed the corner of her mouth. "I think I'll keep my last name, though." He pressed his lips to her jaw line. "I'm a man of independence. I'd like to have my own identity."

She sighed heavily and rolled her head back as he put his mouth to her neck. "You're impossible."

"You love it." He moved his lips higher.

She gasped. "Maybe on some deep, dark, masochistic level that I never realized existed."

He moaned as he nipped her ear lobe. "I think I'd like to get to know this deep, dark, masochistic level of yours."

"It must be the same side that drove me to visit your mother."

He exhaled. "And my good feelings are gone." Leaning back, he frowned at her. "I know you aren't much for abiding by rules, sweetheart, but let's agree on one: no mentioning my mother when we're on the verge of heavy petting."

She giggled and put her fingertips to his lips before he could kiss her. "Go upstairs," she whispered. "Get ready for bed. Then come see me."

He held his breath as she leaned up and brushed her mouth over his—not quite a kiss, but he'd take it.

Then she ruined his excitement by whispering, "We have some things to talk about."

He sighed. "Rule number two…"

Kara laughed as she pulled away. "Hurry up, Harry. I'm tired."

She disappeared around the corner before he pushed himself upright. He hurried upstairs and readied for bed, yanking on a pair of house pants and a T-shirt before quietly easing back down the stairs. Kara had told him that Phil knew he'd been sleeping downstairs, but he didn't feel the need to advertise it. After knocking on her bedroom door, he entered when she called out to him.

His stomach tightened as he opened the door just in time to see her tug a tank top over her head. He flipped off the overhead light and crossed the room as she tied her hair back from her face. He tugged the blankets back and collapsed on the bed. She sat next to him, leaned against the headboard, and pulled her legs up to her chest. Disappointment rolled through him. She hadn't been kidding about talking.

He waited, but she didn't say anything. Finally, he asked, "Why did you go see my mother?"

"Why did you go see my parents?"

"Because I hated watching you torture yourself."

She winked at him, and he laughed quietly.

He ran his hand down her shin and rested it on the top of her foot. "How'd it go?"

"She fixed me chamomile tea and told me to sit down so we could talk civilly. Apparently she didn't appreciate my brooding, rot-in-hell look."

"You gave her the look?"

"Oh, you know I did. I cussed at her, too."

He laughed softly, imagining how the scene had played out. "You cussed at my mother?"

"I said the F-word."

He dragged his hand over his face. "The one and only time I said that in front of my mother, she dragged me to the bathroom to wash my mouth out." Elaine was a tiny thing, but she had some balls.

"She told me not to cuss at her. I told her not to lie to me. I also said her excuses were bullshit."

"And she said?"

"She pointed out I was cussing again. I told her to deal with it."

"I'm kind of sorry I missed this. There aren't many souls who dare defy Elaine Canton."

Kara sighed loudly. "Hopefully there aren't many souls who have suffered at her hand the way we have."

"So did you resolve anything other than releasing some pent-up anger?"

She nodded. "Your mother felt threatened by me, Harry."

He lifted his brows at her. "Please don't tell me you put her in a chokehold."

Kara giggled and entwined her fingers with his. "I mean back then. Apparently you talked about me quite a bit."

"I was infatuated."

"She thinks you still are."

He looked at their tangle of hands and rubbed his thumb over hers. "I might like you."

"Yeah? I might like you, too. I think she was afraid you'd be put in the position of choosing between me and her and that you would have chosen me."

"I would have." He untangled his fingers from hers and lightly ran them up her arm. "Even when I was a scared kid with no way to take care of you and a baby, I would have chosen you."

"Well, it seems she didn't want take that risk, so she cut out the competition. It's sad, really. She was so scared that she thought she had no choice but to manipulate her own child so she wasn't left alone."

"Don't feel too bad for her, Kare. She has friends and other family. She wasn't alone when my dad died."

"It's not the same as having the love and adoration of your only son. Trust me."

Harry scoffed. "She never had my adoration. Dog killer."

Kara snickered as she sank down under the covers until she could rest her head next to his. Her eyelids slid closed, and he considered how exhausted she must have been. She'd faced one emotional hurdle after another since waking up.

"She said they'd started the lie so you would stay in school, and when your father died, she was too scared to come clean. She thought about writing to me, asking me for help." She sneered. "Isn't that rich? She wanted me to tell you about Phil to get her off the hook for her lies."

"But she didn't."

"No. She didn't." She rolled onto her side to face him. "I told her I couldn't forgive her but I was going to let go of my resentment. I don't want to be angry anymore, Harry."

She traced her fingers along his jaw. He captured her hand and kissed the pads of her fingers.

"I want to move on," she whispered.

"I want that, too." He cupped her cheek with his palm and gave her a weak smile. Her eyes filled with concern, and he thought he could get lost in them. He traced his thumb over her lips, which he'd become obsessed with ever since giving in and kissing her on the swing set. "Heck of a day for you, huh?"

She closed her eyes. "I'm so tired."

"I bet." Reaching over, he turned off the light on the nightstand. He kissed her forehead as she snuggled against him. "I'm proud of you."

"For not killing her?"

"For everything. And I'm so glad you came home. I've missed you for a very long time." He pulled her closer to him, wrapped his arms around her, and held her as she fell asleep.

CHAPTER FOURTEEN

Kara turned from her easel when Harry walked into her room. She tried to read his expression, but he had on one hell of a poker face. "Well? How'd it go?"

"As well as could be expected." He crossed the room and kissed her head as he looked at the painting she'd started for the living room. Finally, his face cracked and he smiled. "I like this already."

She didn't respond to his compliment. She was far more interested in his evening with Elaine than his thoughts on her work. "Did you take her to dinner?"

"As I've done every year since Dad died."

"And?"

"I told her the same thing you did. I can't forgive her, but I'm letting go. I don't want our future to be tainted by the past anymore."

"How do you feel?"

He was quiet for a moment. "Relieved."

"Good." She focused on rinsing her brush. "I had breakfast with my parents, and then I called that woman, the one who was looking for help in her gallery."

His lifted his brows. "I assumed you weren't interested."

She shrugged. "I'm going to give it a try. I teach my first class Saturday."

He grabbed her hand and pulled her to her feet. Putting his palms on either side of her face, he searched her eyes. The seriousness on his face started to concern her. He looked so introspective, she couldn't read his reaction.

"Are you happy?" he asked after a moment.

"I am," she whispered. "Are you?"

He smiled. "More so than I think I've ever been. I know we've just found each other again, Kara, but I'm in love with you. I'm in love with you, and I need you to be happy with me."

Her heart melted. His words surprised her. She couldn't remember the last time a man had professed love to her, but she did know that it had likely struck a fear so deep in her heart that she had run away.

There was no running this time. Not from Harry.

Instead of terror at the thought of being emotionally tied down, a warmth spread through her, and she had a feeling of belonging that she wasn't sure she'd ever felt. "I love you," she whispered. She covered his hands with hers and nodded. "I always have."

Harry held her as he brought his mouth down on hers. She stepped back, taking him with her as she made her way to the bed. "Wait," she breathed, pulling away. She moved around him, locked the door, and made sure the curtain blocking the view from the hall was in place. Flipping the switch and leaving only the moonlight streaming in through her window, she walked back to Harry.

Putting her hand to his chest, she pushed him until he was on his back on the bed, as she'd done all those years ago. She tugged her ankle-length skirt up to her thighs, straddled his hips, and looked down at him, grinning with a mixture of amusement and excitement. "Try not to get me pregnant this time."

He chuckled. "I'll do my best to keep my reckless sperm under control."

"I'd appreciate it."

Leaning over him, she ran her fingers through his hair and skimmed her gaze over his face in the silver-blue light of the moon. "No more looking back."

"No more looking back."

He maneuvered his hands under her skirt and ran his palms up her thighs. She nearly melted into him. The heat of his skin made hers burn with desire.

She started working on the buttons of his shirt. As she parted the material to reveal the dark hair peppering his chest, he pushed her T-shirt up. They quickly traded tasks—she lifted her shirt over her head, and he took over tugging his free. Both were tossed aside, and Kara focused on his belt buckle while he tugged on the clasp on her bra.

He released his hold and stared at her breasts, sending a thrill through her. He trailed his thumbs over her nipples, the same way he constantly did to her lips, and the sensation caused her to gasp. Pulling her down to him, he grazed his teeth over her flesh, followed by a hot flick of his tongue.

She moaned and arched her back, encouraging him to continue while she reached inside his open zipper. She wrapped her hand around his erection and stroked as he ground up into her hold and moved his mouth to her other breast. Finally, he fell back, panting. She didn't give him a moment to catch his breath. Instead, she covered his mouth, running her tongue over his. He grasped her hips as he pressed his feet into the mattress, using the movement to roll her beneath him. He pushed his slacks down while she shimmied out of her skirt and panties.

He was between her legs before she even settled. She was half sitting, the mound of pillows piled against the headboard stopping her from lying all the way down. He didn't seem to notice, and if he did, he didn't care. His lips went to her breast again, sucking her nipple into his mouth, licking and fondling with his tongue. She rolled her head back as she fisted his hair.

"God, you're so much better at this now," she panted.

Harry laughed softly. "I'd hope so." Leaving her chest, he placed a path of hot kisses over her neck and then crushed her lips with his.

His hand moved up her thigh and between her legs, causing

her to make another contented sound. She closed her eyes and bit her lip as his fingers slid inside her and his thumb, which she'd decided was his secret weapon, moved over her clitoris. There was no build up, no slow rise to pleasure. Her orgasm simply slammed her hard and fast.

"Shh," Harry insisted as he put his mouth to hers.

She bit his lip in response, ignoring his hiss of what she assumed was pain. The ripples eased, and she released his lip and gasped for air.

"You should have warned me you were a screamer."

"I'm a screamer," she said breathlessly.

"Yeah, the neighbors and I just figured that out."

She giggled as he nestled his body between her legs, pushing her thighs apart as he prepared to love her.

As he held her gaze, his smile softened. "I never want to be without you again."

She put her fingers to his lips. "I'm not leaving, Harry."

"Promise."

"I promise," she whispered.

He slid his hips forward and entered her slowly. All the playfulness left them as they started moving together. He slowly thrust forward and then eased back, only to do it again, clearly making a statement, staking a claim on her heart, and using their bodies to express how he felt.

For the first time in her life, she understood the difference between sex and making love. She fell back on the pillows, moving with his slow strokes, accepting his sweet kisses, and responding in kind. He filled her in every way, and when he softly pressed his lips to hers, she was startled at how cherished she felt. She hadn't even known it was possible to feel so loved, so wanted.

"Harry," she whispered, surprised that his name caught in her throat. She didn't quite understand what was happening, but as he breathed her name in time to a slow and gentle thrust, a tear fell from her eye. He wiped it away and smiled down at her as he continued his leisurely rhythm. He put his lips to hers and ground into her, going as deep as their bodies would allow. She gasped, clung to him, and rolled her hips.

"It's okay," he whispered. "Let go."

A sob welled in her chest. His mouth on hers muffled the sound as more tears filled her eyes. Digging her hands into his hair, she wrapped her legs around him, clinging as he pulled back and thrust again. This time, instead of a slamming orgasm, the sensations rolled through her like the ripples on a pond. Her body tensed, and she trembled and cried out. In response, he grunted her name and then stilled deep inside her.

She sniffed as he finally relaxed and leaned back to look down at her. "Why am I crying?"

He grinned and dragged his thumbs across her cheeks. "Because we've been waiting for this moment our entire lives."

She inhaled a ragged breath. "That's no excuse."

He smiled and kissed her. "It's the perfect excuse."

Harry lightly ran his fingers over the curve of Kara's waist. She was breathing quietly, steadily, sleeping deeply. He, in turn, stared up at the stars, trying to get his mind around his life. He and his mother had shared a tense dinner, but at least they'd been somewhat civil to each other. He'd told Elaine he had decided to skip their dinner this year, but it was important to Kara to resolve the issues with their parents, at least enough to decrease the stress surrounding them. He wanted a life with Kara that was as free from turmoil as possible. They'd suffered enough secondary to what Elaine had done.

His mother accepted that they would likely never have a normal relationship again, at least what had passed as normal for them all his life. Elaine had been far from a nurturing, hands-on kind of mother, but Harry knew that she loved him in her own control-everything-for-everyone kind of way.

He had meant it when he told her he couldn't forgive her for what she'd done to Kara, but he'd also meant it when he said it was time to leave that in the past. He and Kara had a chance at the happiness that had been taken from them. He wasn't going to blow it being angry—even when those feelings were well deserved.

Things couldn't be going better for them now. Phil was enjoying his new job, or so he said. Jessica loved school and had made friends who seemed to truly accept her. Kara had made peace with her parents and seemed to be committing to a life there. And Harry had everything he'd always wanted—his family.

He smiled as he turned onto his side and wrapped his arm

around Kara. He hadn't meant to tell her that he was in love with her. The words had slipped out, but he hadn't regretted them. She'd clearly been shocked, but when she'd smiled, he knew she felt the same. Years may have gone by—a lifetime, really—but something had remained between them all that time, a bond that had easily been reconnected the moment he'd seen her at the gallery.

Starting tonight, starting where they'd left off thirty years ago, Harry was taking this life and making it right. He would have his woman, their son, their granddaughter. He would work with Phil to make their company the best it could be to give Phil and Jess the security they deserved. He would make certain Kara never felt alone again. He would provide for them all so she could concentrate on the things she needed to—Jessica, art, reestablishing a relationship with her parents. He would be the man he hadn't been able to be thirty years ago. He would give them—all of them—the life he hadn't been able to.

He kissed Kara's head to seal his silent vow. She shifted, moving against him and pressing her naked body to his. He put his lips her shoulder and ran his palm down her side, resting it on her hip. Then he nipped her ear.

"What time is it?" she mumbled in a sleep-thick voice.

He lifted his head and looked at the clock. "Almost three."

She sighed. "Why are you waking me up?"

He grinned. "I didn't mean to. I was just thinking."

She shifted, rolling onto her back, and then licked her lips and sighed heavily. "About what?"

"How happy you've made me."

Her eyes fluttered open. He grinned as he brushed her hair back and skimmed her face. The moonlight illuminated her face, and Harry couldn't resist running his fingers along her jawline. That gave way to the urge to kiss her gently, which gave way to licking and softly biting her lips.

"Oh, Harry," she breathed. "You're going me make me scream again, aren't you?"

"I certainly hope so."

CHAPTER FIFTEEN

Between the warm bath and the wine, Kara was quite certain her muscles were about to melt off her bones. She hadn't been so relaxed in a long time. She'd awakened with Harry wrapped around her, and the day had just gotten better from there. She'd never taught a group of giggly, wine-sipping women before, but her first class had proven to be much more fun than Kara thought it would be. She'd even connected with a few of them on a friendly level.

When she told them she'd just moved to Iowa, two of them had dragged her out to lunch. Making friends and local connections hadn't been a priority for her since coming home, but she couldn't deny the fun she'd had. She'd come home and sat in the backyard watching Phil and Jessica play while Harry sat next to her reading.

It had been the perfect Saturday. In fact, she didn't think her day could have possibly gotten better.

She looked up when the bathroom door opened and Harry slipped in, and she realized she had been wrong. Her day was about to get a lot better. He sat on the edge of the tub, sipped his wine, and smiled at her.

"What's on your mind, Harry?"

"Just wanted to see if you needed anything."

She lifted a washrag from the water and held it up for him.

His grin widened as he accepted it. Setting his glass aside, he dipped his hand into the water and gently grasped her ankle. Water ran down her calf as he lifted her leg up and rested it on his shoulder, apparently not giving a damn that she was drenching his T-shirt. He massaged the rag over her shin, down her calf, and over her inner thigh. He worked meticulously, not missing a spot before easing her leg back into the warm water. He followed the process with her other leg and then reached for her arm. When all her extremities were clean, he dropped the rag into the water, tugged his wet shirt over his head, and tossed it onto the floor along with his shorts.

She smiled and sat forward, releasing the plug to drain a bit of water and making room for him in the tub behind her. He settled in and went to work on washing her back.

"Good day?" he asked.

"Best day."

"So you're going to enjoy working at the gallery?"

"Well, I enjoyed the class. I haven't done anything else, but yes, I think I'll enjoy it."

He pulled her back against his chest and dragged the rag over her front. She arched when the material caressed her nipple. Exhaling slowly, she dropped her head onto his shoulder, letting him touch her however and wherever he wanted. His decision to abandon the washrag and resort to using his bare hands wasn't a disappointment. His fingertips alternated between light and deep massage, awakening every nerve. He rolled her nipple between his forefinger and thumb as his other hand sank between her legs. He licked her ear and whispered how much he wanted her.

A moan ripped from her, and Harry gently covered her mouth. Rivulets of water ran from his fingers and tickled her skin as she rolled her hips into his hand. He kissed her ear, her neck, and then gently bit down, and she lost control. Her body and mind came undone, leaving her panting as he wrapped his arms around her.

She wasn't done. She wasn't even close to done. Rolling over in the small space of the tub to face him, she pressed her tongue between his lips, instantly drawing him into a deep kiss as her hand roamed down his chest and grasped his erection. He fisted her hair as she stroked him, rubbing her thumb over the head of his shaft.

He made the same guttural sounds she had as she worked him into a frenzy. After several minutes, he gripped her hips and shifted her over him. Their position wasn't the most comfortable, but Kara barely noticed as she slid him into her body. Bracing herself against the walls of the tub, she ground her pelvis as he used his grip on her to help her move up and down.

Water sloshed and bubbles popped as he started moving

faster. Within minutes, her body was tense with the power of her orgasm as he shoved his body into hers. Breathless, he eased back and sank into the water. Leaning against his chest, she panted for a moment before tilting her head to kiss him.

"I love you so much," he said quietly.

She pulled his arms farther around her and rested her head on his chest. "I love you, too."

Harrison settled into a chair on the back porch of Kara's parents' house, a glass of lemonade in his hand and a smile on his face. Kara held her mother's hand as they walked around the perimeter of the yard, talking flowers and gardening while Phil taught Jessica how to play horseshoes.

They'd had a fantastic Sunday dinner with only a few hiccups. Kay and Charles didn't appreciate that Kara had opted out of prayer before the meal, so Kara reminded her parents that their deep devotion to their religion had made them disown her. Phil cursed under his breath, Jessica asked someone to pass the jelly, and Harry smoothed things over by offering a moment of silence rather than praising any specific deity.

Several tense moments passed before he steered the conversation to Jessica's first week of school, and the girl worked her magic by melting the hearts of everyone at the table. The tension faded until Kara started talking about her first class and

Charles pointed out that her affinity to the arts was to blame for leading her astray.

Kara responded that art had saved her—no one else was around to provide for her and her son. Phil again cursed under his breath, Jessica stuffed a roll into her mouth, and Harry smoothed things over, that time by directing the conversation to how Phil had picked up a thing or two from his mother. His designs were amazing, and the clients who had seen them were very impressed by his artistic abilities.

Kara had passed on dessert and instead took out some of her frustrations on the dishes. Phil had convinced Kay to let his mother clean up. While he and Harry understood she needed to release some anger, Kay had taken it as Kara's willingness to help. Kay finished her slice of pie, and peace was restored. At least for now.

Harry looked over his shoulder when the screen door slammed. He was about to stand to help Charles, but the older man waved his hand to dismiss the notion. Truly, Harry thought the man should have a walker—a cane, at least—but he seemed determined to walk on his own, slow as that may be. He sank into the chair next to Harry's and looked out over the yard.

After a minute he said, "She's still full of spit and vinegar, isn't she?"

Harry grinned. "Yes, sir."

"By the time she was Jessica's age, I realized nobody would ever be able to control her."

He nodded. "She certainly has a mind of her own."

"You seem to be able to handle her."

"Kara doesn't need handled, Charles. She just needs to be accepted."

"And you accept her?"

"I'd like to think so."

"You going to marry her?"

Kara bent and smelled a flower and then turned and looked at Jessica when the girl laughed. The smile that spread across her face warmed Harry all the way to his soul. He nodded without giving it too much consideration. "If she'll have me."

Charles reached into his pocket and withdrew a small band on the tip of his finger. He held it out to Harry. "This was my mother's wedding ring. She wanted Kara to have it. She's the only one of us who held on to the belief that she'd ever come home."

Harry took the small band topped with several diamonds surrounding a larger one. Even the large one wasn't huge. The stone was barely more than a chip, but it was beautiful.

"She'll love this," Harry said. "Thank you."

Charles focused on his daughter again. "Someone needs to take care of them when I'm gone. I'm putting that responsibility on you. You understand that, don't you?"

Harry rolled the ring Charles had given him between his fingers. "I understand."

"From what I've heard, Kara and Phil haven't had the easiest time. I expect you to take care of her from now on."

"I will."

"And make sure my grandson and great-granddaughter don't ever want for anything."

"They won't."

Charles nodded as if he'd said all he needed to.

Kara looked toward the porch, shielded her eyes from the sun, and offered Harrison a hesitant smile. He smiled in return and silently toasted her with his glass of lemonade. Her smile eased into a natural pull, and he sighed.

"You're sick, aren't you?" Harry asked.

Charles hesitated in answering. "Not much time now, according to the doctor."

"Why haven't you told her?"

"Because I want to have her back before I tell her she's going to lose me."

"As far as I can tell, you do have her back."

Charles sighed. "What kind of father says the things I said to her?"

"She'd dropped a bombshell on you. I'm sure it was the shock talking."

"That's no reason to disown your child. I paid the price. God knows I paid the price. We all did."

"That's behind us now."

"It's boiling below the surface. You wouldn't have spent half our dinner playing referee if it weren't. I just don't want anything to tear us apart again, especially when I won't be here much longer."

Kara and Kay stopped in the shade of an old oak tree and

applauded Jessica's horseshoe toss. The girl beamed at their appreciation, and a new sense of determination filled Harry.

"I swear to you, Charles, I won't let anything take our family from us again."

sh

Kara bit her tongue as long as she could, but as Harry drove them home, she asked, "What was that all about?"

"What?"

"You and Dad."

Harry cast a glance in her direction. "What about me and your dad?"

"Harrison."

"I noticed it, too," Phil offered from the back seat. "It was borderline conspiratorial."

Harry shook his head. "Such paranoia. Did you have fun, Jess?"

"Sure did, Harry."

He smiled. "What was the best part?"

"Beating Daddy at horseshoes."

"Hey, Punk," Phil teased, as if offended.

They giggled, and Kara looked back and smiled. Phil was sitting behind Harry with Jess snuggled up next to him, giving her a clear view of them both. She loved seeing how happy they were. It made all the stress of the last few months worth it. She hadn't wanted to come back to Iowa, but she wouldn't change a thing now that she had. She'd never felt such a sense of contentment. But then she looked at Harrison again and narrowed her eyes. "What were you talking about?"

"Might as well tell her," Phil said. "She won't let up until you do."

Harry shook his head. "Why do you think it was a conspiracy?"

"Because I can read you like a book," she said. "Even from across the yard and with the sun shining in my eyes."

Harry chuckled, but then his smile faded and he withdrew into his mind again.

"There you go," she said as he slowed to a stop for a red light. "You have that look again."

"What look?"

"Like you are plotting something. Your eyes glaze over. Your body is here, Harrison, but your mind is elsewhere."

"He made me promise to take care of you."

She caught his gaze when he glanced at her. Her heart sank. There was more. Much more. And he wasn't telling her. She closed her eyes. She wasn't stupid, and she wasn't in some kind of delusional world where she thought her parents would live forever.

"How much time does he have?" As soon as the words left her, it was like the air had been sucked from the car. Their tension was palpable.

She looked at Harry. "I could tell he was sick the first time I saw him. I just didn't ask how bad it was. So, tell me. How bad is it?"

"Let's talk about this when we get home." He put his hand on her knee, and she exhaled.

"That bad, huh?"

"What are they talking about, Daddy?"

Kara glanced back and gave Phil a slight smile. He looked as thrown as she felt. Just like Harry had done to her, Phil patted Jess's knee to soothe her.

Like father, like son.

Kara returned her attention to Harry. She covered his hand with hers and squeezed it as her heart swelled with love and pride just as much as it was overshadowed with sorrow that her suspicions had been confirmed. She was going to lose her father all over again. "Sure. We'll talk when we get home."

He pulled her hand up and kissed it as he glanced at her and offered her one of those sexy half smiles that never failed to melt her. The light turned green, and Harry returned his attention to driving. The rest of the ride home was silent. Even Jessica quit rambling as the apprehension in the car grew.

Kara carried in the leftovers her mother had sent and was putting them in the fridge when Harry walked in and leaned against the counter. He slid his arm around her waist and pulled her to him. He ran his hand over her hair, and her defenses broke. Tears filled her eyes and her lip trembled. "Is he dying?"

He offered her one slight nod, and she crumbled. Falling against his chest, she found as much comfort as he could offer.

He held her, stroking her hair and kissing her head every few minutes until she finally found her voice.

"Why would he tell you instead of me?"

Harry exhaled, debating his answer. "He doesn't want you to know. He was asking me to take care of you and your mother."

She lifted her head, trying not to look as offended as she felt. "I'm perfectly capable of taking care of my mother."

"Yes, I know. But he needed the peace of mind knowing that it wasn't going to be a burden on you. We men like to think we are needed, even when we aren't."

She relaxed a bit. "I do need you, Harry."

"Do you?" His voice was quiet, a bit introspective.

Putting her cheek to his chest, she buried herself as deep into his arms as possible. "Yes. I do."

He held her for a few moments before he straightened and took her hand. "Come with me." He led her to the swing set and sat on the child-sized seat he'd occupied the first night he kissed her, just a week before.

She sat next to him and stared at the grass. "I should have come home years ago."

"No looking back, remember?"

"Kind of hard not to when I wasted so much time being mad at him. Now he's dying."

"He has time, Kara. Make the most of that while you can."

She took a breath and nodded. "That kind of applies to everything, doesn't it? We've all lost so much time. All we can do now is make the most of what we have left."

"Do you believe that? That we should grab what time we have left and make the most of it?"

She creased her brow, and he reached into his pocket. Her gaze fell on a band on the tip of his forefinger as he held it out to her. She touched the diamonds. "Is that my grandmother's ring?"

"Your father gave it to me."

She focused on him, thoroughly confused. "Why would he give you his mother's wedding ring?" Her eyes widened as the answer to her question lit in her mind like a flashing neon sign. She looked at the ring again, recalling how she used to twist the band around her grandmother's finger. Nana had promised the ring would be hers one day, when she was old enough to be married. "Harry?"

"He asked if I planned to marry you. I told him I did, so he gave me this."

Her heart did a funny kind of flip in her chest, causing her breath to catch.

He slid from the swing onto his knee in front of her. "Will you marry me, Kara?"

She swallowed as she looked from the ring to his eyes, back to the ring, and then did it again. She was a grown woman with a grown child and a grandchild, and in all that time no one had ever proposed marriage to her. She'd never stuck around long enough to get close to that point. She wasn't even sure what marriage meant, besides an excruciatingly long commitment that she had no idea how to abide by. "Married?" she breathed.

Harry gave her half a smile. "We're making the most of the

time we have left, right? I would have married you a long time ago if I'd been given the chance. We have a lot of years to make up for."

"But this is… I didn't see this coming."

"Yeah. Me either. Not exactly. But you're not the only one who gets to be spontaneous."

She stared at the ring for what seemed like an eternity. "If you marry me, Harry, I'll drive you crazy. I'll paint the house without consulting you. I'll make you try new foods and learn about different cultures you have no interest in. I'll go from one thing to another so fast it will make your head spin. I'll… I'll drive you crazy, and you'll regret committing to me."

"There are a lot of things I regret in my life, Kara, but I'll never regret you. Ever."

"I'm nothing like that fantasy girl you created in high school."

"No. You're not. You're much better."

Damn. She couldn't have asked for a more perfect response. "You don't have to marry me."

"You don't have to marry me either. But I want you to."

"Are you sure?"

"I've never been more certain of anything."

She swallowed. "Okay."

"Okay?"

Holding her left hand out, she smiled. "Let's get married."

He gave her a brilliant smile as he pushed her grandmother's ring onto her finger, taking note of the excess room. "We're going to have to do something about that."

She curled her fingers so the too-big band wouldn't fall off. "I'll take it in tomorrow."

He kissed her hand, and she smiled.

"Harry?"

"Hmm?"

"We're engaged."

His bright smile returned. "Yes, we are."

Kara grinned as she slid off the swing in front of him. She put her arms around his neck and looked into his eyes. "Promise me something."

"Anything."

She bit her lip for a moment. "If there ever comes a time when I disappoint you—"

"Kara—"

"—you'll tell me so I can fix it."

"Kara."

She put her fingers to his lips. "I don't want you to resent me, Harry."

He pulled her hand down. "We just got engaged."

"I know."

"You haven't even kissed me yet."

She grinned as she leaned forward and put her lips on his. His arms went around her waist as he turned her until she was lying in the grass. She traced his jawline as he leaned back and looked down at her. "I love you, Harry."

"I love you, Kara."

"Grandma! Harry!"

Kara rolled her head and grinned. Phil had slowed to a stop, but Jess was running toward them. Harry sat back on his knees and opened his arms as she threw herself at him. He caught her just as Kara leaned up on her elbows.

"Sorry," Phil said as he finished crossing the yard.

"It's okay," Harry said. "Actually, it's good you're here."

"It is?"

Kara smiled and lifted her brows at Harry. "Your dad has something to tell you."

Harry brushed his hand over Jessica's hair as she sat on the grass next to him. "We are getting married."

Jess gasped as she put her hands to her mouth. "A wedding?"

Kara laughed. "Yes. A wedding."

"Do I get to be the flower girl?"

"Of course you do."

She bounced with excitement. "Can I have a pink dress?"

"You can have anything you want." Kara looked up at Phil, and her smile faded. He had that tight-lipped, disapproving stare he'd given her most of his adult life. "Hey, Punk, will you run in and grab my camera? I think you need to take a picture of Grandpa and me, don't you?"

Instead of responding, Jess jumped up and ran inside. She never failed to take an opportunity to use the camera.

"You're supposed to smile and say congratulations," Kara said.

"Harry, could you give Mom and me a few minutes?"

Kara looked at Harry. "This is the part where he lectures me about ruining his life."

"That's not it," Phil said.

"Then what is it? What can't you say in front of your father?" Kara huffed as she pushed herself to her feet. "I'm going to go check on Jessica."

"What's the problem?" Harry asked as she walked away.

She didn't hang around to hear Phil's response.

CHAPTER SIXTEEN

"He's right," Kara said as Harry came into her room.

He couldn't help but smile a bit. She hadn't turned from her canvas to even look at him, but she'd sensed him there. However, his smile fell as he realized she didn't even ask what Phil had said. She'd just assumed he had trashed her. How easily they all fell back into a cycle of mistreating each other.

Harry closed the door behind him. "Yeah. He probably is."

Kara turned, her brow creased, clearly confused as to why Harry was agreeing with her.

"As a matter of fact," Harry said as he threw up his hands, "he's absolutely right." He sat next on the stool next to her and held her gaze. He frowned as he wiped her cheek. "What's with the tears?"

She looked down at the ring on her hand. "You...you deserve better, Harry."

Something flashed through his gut. Anger perhaps. "Better than what?"

"Better than some irresponsible, flighty woman who has never even held down a job. What if…"

"What if what?"

"What if you grow tired of me? I won't change. I can't change. I don't know how to be anyone else."

"I would never ask you to be anyone else, Kara. I love everything about you."

She shook her head. "You don't know what you are saying, Harry. I'm full of crazy ideas and plans that I never follow through on. I'll never fit the mold of a suburban wife. I mean, I can't even commit to one style of art. How could I possibly commit to a lifelong relationship?"

"I know exactly what I'm saying. Your crazy ideas keep me alive. Your individuality reminds me that it's okay to live outside the box of normalcy. Without you, I'm just another man getting through life without any spark, any color. You are my color. You always have been. And you have already committed to two lifelong relationships. If it weren't for Phil and Jessica, you wouldn't be here, would you? As far as your art, who cares if you change projects and styles every other day? You do what makes you happy, and that's all that matters. I wouldn't ask you to change, Kara, because I want you just as you are. I'm not asking you to do anything other than become my wife without any expectations or demands. I just want you to love me."

"I do love you."

He stroked his hand over her hair. He'd never get enough of feeling her silky strands. "Would you like to know what Phil said?"

She closed her eyes and lowered her face. "He told you not to marry me."

"He told me he's never seen you this happy and I'd better not hurt you. He said if I made you run away, he'd never forgive me because he and Jessica need you here with them."

Kara exhaled as she looked at him. "You're lying."

"No. I'm not. He's afraid I'm jumping in too fast and will change my mind. He's worried you're going to get hurt, and that if you get hurt, you'll leave."

"He's worried about me?"

Harry wiped her cheek again. "Why is that so hard to believe?"

She cocked a brow, and he chuckled.

"Okay," he said, dropping his hands to hers. He clutched them and let his breath out slowly before meeting her gaze again. "If you have any doubts, Kara, that's okay. I know I sprang this on you out of nowhere, and I fully recognize that this is crazy. If you don't want to get married right now, I swear to you, I won't be upset. I won't even be hurt. We will wait as long as you need."

"Wait. Are you asking me to be the logical one?"

He grinned slightly. "Yeah. I guess I am."

"That's never happened before," she said with amazement. "I'm always the one people go to when they want confirmation that acting crazy is okay."

He rotated the ring on her finger. "I don't want you to feel pressured. I want you to do this because it is what you want, not because you feel like you have to."

She put her palm to his cheek, and he turned his face and kissed it. "Never, not even for a moment, did I feel like I had to. I just don't want you to go into this with some great expectation of me, Harry. I'm not very good at living up to expectations."

"Stop." He pulled her hand from his face. "Stop being so damned hard on yourself."

"I'm being real. And you need to be real, too. We don't really know each other that well. Some things are the same, but we're both completely different people than we were thirty years ago. The last two months, we've been very focused on our parents. What happens when all that is settled and we have nothing left to distract us?"

He smiled slowly. "Here's the thing, Kara. I've been playing it safe my whole life. The only time I ever did anything unexpected was graduation night. Even when I left for school, pretending I was getting away from my parents, I was doing what I was supposed to. I don't know how to be the person I want to be when I'm not with you. You're the only one who makes me feel safe enough to let go of all that. You make me the person I want to be, and I know this is scary for you, but I need you to know, you aren't tied here. Phil can run the business while we travel. We can go wherever you want, do what you want."

"But this isn't just about me. What do you want?"

"You. I just want you."

She smiled as she squeezed his hand. “Oh, Harry. You already have me.”

Kara cradled a cup of coffee in her hand as she sat across the tiny table from her father. “Why didn’t you tell me?”

“Because I didn’t want you to know.”

“Why?”

“You just came home. I didn’t want to ruin that. And I wouldn’t have told Harrison if I’d known he was going to blab about it to you.”

“He didn’t blab about anything. I’ve been thinking how sick you look since I first saw you. He just didn’t lie when I asked him. You’re pale. Too thin. It’s obvious you are sick.”

Charles sipped his drink. “I’m old, Kara. That’s what happens when you get old.”

“You should have told me.”

Reaching across the table, he put his hand on her wrist. “I want to see your wedding. When will it be?”

“We just got reacquainted a few months ago, Dad. The fact that we are engaged is insane enough. We’ve agreed not to rush into a wedding date.”

“I won’t be here forever,” he said quietly. A wistful smile played at his lips. “I want to walk you down the aisle. Give you away.”

She flashed back to the night he'd kicked her out, and bitter sarcasm rose to the surface. Somehow she held it back.

She swallowed and stared into her cup. Her drink was suddenly far too bitter.

"What is it?" Charles asked. "Why aren't you more excited?"

She sighed. "Nothing."

"You've never been good at hiding your emotions. Something is bugging you."

Kara pushed down the anger that suddenly surged at her father. "Even though he keeps telling me I won't…I'm going to disappoint him."

"Why do you think that?"

"Because I disappoint everyone. I always have. It's what I do."

"Everyone lets someone down sometime. That's life."

"Some of us are just better at it than others." Pushing herself up, she dumped her coffee into the sink and rinsed the mug so her father couldn't see the tears threatening to fall from her eyes.

"Do you love him?"

She looked out the window at the tree in the backyard. Fall was creeping in, making the leaves change colors. Her mother was in the garden gathering the last of the vegetables. "Yes, I love him. I've always loved him in some deep, dark, dysfunctional way."

"Does he love you?"

"He seems to."

"Do you make each other happy?"

"I suppose."

"Then what's the problem?"

Kara turned and faced him, no longer able to hold her tongue. "How can I trust that he won't leave me the first time I do the wrong thing? I'm sure you remember I am very good at doing the wrong thing."

He pushed his cup away. "What your mother and I did all those years ago was a mistake. It was *our* mistake. It wasn't yours. He's a good man. Don't lose him because you're afraid."

"I'm going to see if Mom needs help."

"Kara—"

The screen door slammed before she had to listen to any more lectures from her father. She didn't need him analyzing her faults. She smiled as Kay looked up. "How's it going, Mom?"

"Wonderful. You and your father get everything straightened out?"

"Sure."

Kay held her hand out and let Kara help her stand. "Sure?"

"I don't appreciate him going to Harry instead of just telling me himself."

"Your father didn't want to upset you."

Kara started toward the house. "I've seen some hard truths in my life thanks to you two. Sugarcoating things to protect me now is pointless."

Kay held her gaze for a long moment. "We'll try to refrain from being considerate in the future."

Kara opened her mouth but stopped herself from engaging in an argument. They walked inside in silence. Kara set the wicker basket of tomatoes on the counter as Kay washed her hands.

Her mother turned the water off and patted her hands dry on a towel as tension filled the room. “If you hadn’t run into Harrison in Seattle, would you have ever come home?”

Kara swallowed hard. “No.”

“Why? Why would you hold one mistake against us for so long?”

She gawked at her mother. “You told me not to come back. You and Dad both told me to *never* come back.”

“We were hurting.”

“And I wasn’t? I was terrified.”

“If you’d come home, we could have settled things.”

“So it’s my fault you were shitty parents?”

“Hey,” Charles warned from the door where he’d reentered the kitchen. “I don’t care how old you are. You will not speak to your mother that way.”

“Or what? You’ll kick me out?” Kara’s shoulders sagged as soon as the words left her. She should apologize for lashing out, she knew she should, but she couldn’t. She didn’t want to. Instead, she snatched her purse off the table. “I have some errands to run,” she said quietly. “I’ll see you later.”

Kara stormed from the house and into Phil’s car. Slamming the door behind her, she finally exhaled. She looked up at the house, and a mountain of pain collapsed onto her chest. Her parents had apologized over and over that first day she’d come home. She'd thought she'd let go of some of anger, but clearly it was still there. She was going to have to deal with it.

She grabbed the door handle but didn't pull it. After a moment, she reached for her seat belt and started the car. She drove aimlessly, hating how she was surrounded by buildings and traffic. This place was like a plague on her serenity, but she couldn't quite figure out why.

She had her parents back. They had, for the most part, put things behind them. Phil and Jessica were happy. Harry loved her. She even had, to some extent, come to a truce with Elaine. She couldn't ask to be in a better place in her life. She couldn't ask for things to have worked out better.

But there was a fear creeping in on her. How long would Harry be happy with her? How long until she screwed it up? And her parents—how long until she lost them? This time forever?

And when everything crumbled, as it tended to do, where did that leave her?

She looked up at the clouds, as if they could somehow answer her. "What am I doing?"

Harry watched Kara staring at her easel. "You're a million miles away."

She faced him and lifted her brows in question. "Hmm?"

"How's the painting going?"

She sighed and looked at the canvas again. "I can't seem to focus."

"Something on your mind?"

She looked at the engagement ring she was wearing on her middle finger—the only one it fit securely—turning it side to side.

His heart started pounding in his chest. "I thought you were going to take that in to get it sized," he said in a desperate attempt to defer her from what he suspected she was thinking—regret over getting engaged.

"I will."

"I don't want you to lose it."

"Are you sure?"

He knew what she meant, but he didn't acknowledge her unspoken words. "Of course. Why would I want you to lose it?"

She closed her eyes. "Are you sure you want to marry me?"

"Yes."

She looked at him again. "Tomorrow?"

He thought his heart might stop. So much for his fear that she was going to break things off with him. "I thought you were going to be rational and make us wait."

"I'm not so good at being rational, Harry. You should know that by now."

He held her gaze, trying to read her mind, but he couldn't. "There's a three-day waiting period after we get the license."

"Fine. We'll go tomorrow and get married Friday."

"What's the point of having a wedding on Friday when we can have it Saturday?"

"Okay. Saturday."

"What about a dress?"

"I can make a dress by Saturday, and Jess can wear the pink sundress I made for her."

"Guests?"

"Just family."

"Food?"

"I'll roast a few chickens and make a salad."

"Cake?"

"There's an organic bakery across town."

Harry narrowed his eyes at her. "Photographer?"

"I can barter with the best of them."

Harry smiled. "I'm beginning to realize that." Crossing the room, he kneeled in front of her. "What's the rush, Kara?"

"Asks the man who proposed after ten weeks of living together."

"Talk to me."

She sighed. "I'm tired of being so scared, Harry. I've been so scared for so long."

"Scared of what?"

"Of not being enough. If I'm your wife, then…then maybe I'll be enough. I know that sounds stupid—"

He cut her off by putting his fingers to her lips. "You've always been enough. I'm sorry I wasn't there to tell you that, but you have always been enough. And it isn't stupid. We all have fears. I'm scared, too. What if I'm not enough for you?"

"You? You're perfect."

"Hardly."

She looked down and sighed. "I'm being irrational. I know that. I can't seem to help myself."

"What happened?"

She frowned so deeply, he felt his own heart break. "I went to see my parents this morning. Managed to piss them off before I stormed out. I haven't talked to them since." She picked up a brush and then put it down again. "After leaving Mom and Dad's house, I started driving. I just wanted to get away. Clear my head."

"Run."

She blinked but couldn't stop the tears. "Yeah. I wanted to run."

"Why?"

"Because it's so much easier than all this…pain and doubt. Does everyone go through life being so scared?"

"Yes. Life is a frightening thing. We're happy today. But who knows what tomorrow will bring? All we can do is make the best of what we are given, and we've been given a second chance. We don't have to get married Saturday. We can get married a year from now or ten years from now or not at all. But you have to stop running, Kara. You have to face life, even when it hurts."

"We brushed so much under the rug when I came home. I finally went to them, and they apologized. I wanted that to be enough. But I just can't let this anger go." She exhaled as she wiped her face. "Dad wants to give me away at the wedding. Isn't that ironic? He threw me away all those years ago, and now he thinks he has the right to give me away. Like I'm some *thing*. I've always just been a thing to them."

He brushed away a tear that she'd missed. "Is that what you fought about?"

She laughed humorlessly. "Oh, no." Standing up, she stepped around him. "I said some pretty terrible things. Mom asked if I ever would have come home if it weren't for you. I told her no. She, of course, was beside herself with how I could hold a grudge for so long. I reminded her they'd told me I wasn't allowed to ever come home. Then I told them they were shitty parents."

Harry followed her across the room, put his hands on her shoulders, and kissed her head. "They were shitty parents for what they did. But we've all grown since then."

"I know that. I know they're sorry. I know they regret kicking me out. I know I have to let it go. Yet, I can't stop spewing venom when I'm around them. They'll be gone soon. They'll be dead, and I'll regret every hateful thing that has popped out of my mouth. I'll regret the years gone by and not being able to let go. I know this, Harry. I know all of it, but I can't stop being angry."

"It hasn't been that long, and the wound runs deep." He slid his arms around her shoulders. "Getting married isn't going to change that. It won't make this particular pain lessen. But, if you want to get married Saturday, we'll make it happen."

"Do you want to get married Saturday?"

"I'd marry you right now if I could. Under one condition. You never run from me."

Turning in his arms, she met his gaze. He ached at the sorrow in her eyes.

"Maybe you should run from me, Harry."

"I can't."

"Why?"

"Because I love you too much." He used his thumbs to brush her cheeks.

"Good answer," she whispered before falling into his embrace.

Harry closed the door behind him after walking into his mother's house. "The door is unlocked again!"

She poked her head out of the living room, clearly surprised to see him. "It's the middle of the afternoon. Why aren't you at work?"

He smiled. "I took the day off."

Her brows lifted. "And you aren't deathly ill?"

"Kara and I went to the courthouse to get a marriage license."

Elaine didn't respond.

"We went shopping, and she found some old lace she's going to use to make a wedding dress." He beamed with pride. "I swear, she can make anything. She's amazing with a needle and thread. I just dropped her off so she could pick up Jessica from school."

He waited, but she didn't respond. He nodded curtly. "For some reason, she didn't want to be here when I told you our big news. I told her you'd have the decency to congratulate us. So. Congratulate me."

She sighed. "This is what I was afraid of all those years ago. She's cornered you into marriage."

Harry's breath caught for a moment. He opened his mouth but closed it before the anger her words had stirred flowed as freely as it would from Kara. Instead, he shook his head slightly. "I asked her to marry me. She's the one who was hesitant."

"She makes you careless, Harry."

"She makes me feel alive. I haven't been this happy in years." He frowned when she didn't respond. "Mother, I'll give you two choices right now. Be excited for Kara and me, or consider yourself officially expelled from my family."

Elaine held her posture rigid for a few moments, clearly waiting for him to back down. He didn't. Finally, her shoulders relaxed a bit. "This is the influence she has over you?"

"Yes." Crossing the entryway, he kissed her cheek. "I love her, Mom. I've always loved her, and I'm getting exactly what I've always wanted. I'd like you to be there, to be happy for us, but if you can't, then you need to not be part of my life right now. That's all there is to it."

"She's probably going to have you dancing naked under the moon."

Harry laughed. "I wouldn't be surprised if she suggested it. Nothing she does surprises me, but at the same time, I'm always shocked at what she says and does. My life will never be dull with her around."

Elaine squeezed his arm for a moment before moving past him to the kitchen. "Will Phil and Jessica be there?"

"Of course. Sit," he instructed as she lifted her teapot off the burner with a shaking hand. He took it from her and started filling it. It was the middle of the day. She'd have one more Earl Grey before she switched to something more soothing. It was the same ritual she'd had for years, but it had been several months since he'd partaken in it. "Would you like to have dinner with us tonight? The three of us."

"Kara's still too angry to break bread with me?"

"She'll be working. She's teaching art classes."

"Well, that's better than living off you."

Harry set the pot on the burner and looked at her. "Even if she were, she's earned it. I don't need to remind you that she raised my child all by herself. I more than owe her a place to live and a little spending cash if she wanted it. But, for your information, she doesn't. She's perfectly capable of taking care of herself, and she does."

He continued his task, pulling out teacups and saucers. He also took a few cookies from a container. "It's going to be a small ceremony. Just family. The kicker is we're doing it Saturday."

"Saturday?" She gasped. "*This* Saturday? Harrison!"

"Mom," he said, his voice a combination of soothing and dire warning. "Be happy for me."

She exhaled, and he returned to the cabinet, looking for the right teabags.

"If Kara asks for help," he said, "I expect you to step up and nicely give her whatever she needs."

"The sun will fall from the sky before she asks me for help."

"She's working very hard to put the past behind her. However, I know her well enough to understand that if does she ask you to help, it will probably be to do something that goes completely against your sensibilities. If that's the case—"

"I'll accept it as my comeuppance."

He smiled. "Good to hear. Now, about dinner tonight. I think you should meet your grandson and great-granddaughter before the wedding, don't you?"

She sat back and nodded. "That would be lovely."

CHAPTER SEVENTEEN

Planning a wedding, even a simple one, turned out to be more than Kara had expected, but Saturday came, and with it, she was pronounced Harry's wife. Much to Elaine's dismay, the bride had put her soon-to-be-mother-in-law in charge of finding an ordained minister from a universal church, as she wanted a completely secular ceremony. Surprisingly, Elaine had taken on the task without the slightest amount of fuss, though Kara was certain she could hear the disapproval in Elaine's stretch of silence before agreeing.

Rather than white, she wore layers of antique cream lace and wild flowers in her hair as she walked barefoot across the grass with Jess, in her pink dress and fairy wings—which the girl had decided she needed—leading the way, depositing birdseed instead of petals.

All the men wore suits without ties while Elaine and Kay wore skirts and blazers, leaving Kara as the most casually dressed attendee at her own wedding. She didn't think she'd have it any other way.

Kara had loved everything about the scene. Charles and Phil walked her to her groom, since they both felt it was their responsibility. The minister didn't ask who was giving her away, however. Kara didn't need anyone to give permission for this day. Instead, she and Harry said their vows without any query if there were objections or any input from anyone else. Then they slipped handcrafted wedding rings that Kara had bartered for onto each other's fingers.

It was perfect.

Until they sat down for dinner.

Kara realized a bit too late that perhaps their parents should have had time to hash out their own anger toward each other before putting them at the same picnic table. Elaine's spine straightened as she took a breath while Kay pointed out that had Elaine not manipulated Kara, the girl would have gone home instead of disappearing. Elaine pointed out that had Kay not kicked her daughter out, Harry's parents wouldn't have had to make a rash decision on what to do about the pregnancy. Charles added his two cents: Kara wouldn't have gotten pregnant if his parents had raised a respectable son who didn't take advantage of innocent girls.

As that jab lingered in the air, Phil announced it was time for a toast and stood with his glass of punch. "To the bride and groom. I've been waiting for this day for a very long time. I couldn't be happier that it finally came. I hope the rest of your lives are filled with peace, happiness, and as much spontaneity as Harry can handle."

Harry and Kara laughed, but their parents were still too tense.

"Toast, Punk," Kara said.

Jessica stood, wings still attached to her dress, and held her cup up. "To Grandma and Grandpa—and I can call him Grandpa now—happy ever after. And unicorns."

Laughter again eluded their parents.

"Lovely toast," Harry said, "and you most definitely get to call me Grandpa."

Kara ran her hand over his back. He didn't have to tell her that was the best part of his day, and she didn't blame him for feeling that way. She kissed him and sighed as she leaned away.

"If I don't see more smiles at this table, a few of you are going to be dismissed before cake," she said.

"Is it time for cake?" Jess asked.

Kara nodded. "Take Daddy inside and get some plates ready, please."

Jess darted off with Phil following behind.

Once they were gone, Kara looked at Harry and smirked. "I didn't even start it this time."

"I'm proud of you. As for the rest you, today's not the day for hashing out your differences. There's plenty of blame, and even more anger, to go around for what happened," he said, "but it's our wedding day. We invited you to share in our happiness. If for any reason you can't do that, please leave."

No one stood.

"Okay," Harry continued. "You are free to point fingers and try to out-blame each other another time. Right now, we're going to eat cake and be happy."

Finally, Elaine cleared her throat. "Kara, Harry tells me that you are working at an art gallery now."

Kara very nearly laughed. The poor woman looked as uncomfortable making small talk as Kara thought Queen Elizabeth would look sitting on a chair made of nails. "Yes. I am. I'm mainly teaching group lessons. It's different, but I like it."

Elaine nodded. "And what of your own art?"

"The owner of the gallery has agreed to put a few of my pieces out, but really, I prefer to trade my art. It makes it more valuable."

Elaine's brow shot up. "How is bartering more valuable than money?"

Harry groaned, but Kara ignored him.

"Our rings were crafted by a local artist in exchange for a painting. It cost me a couple hours of time and some materials I already had on hand. We both got what we needed without exchanging a penny. And our rings were crafted to a design we agreed on. They're personalized."

"That's nice," Elaine said, but her tone was condescending.

"It is nice," Harry interjected.

Kara ignored his attempt at keeping the peace. "Why does everything have to be bought? Why do I need a diamond some poor child in Africa was forced to mine to prove that I'm loved?"

"Don't do this," Harry whispered.

"Don't do what?" Kara snapped.

"We all know you had to go through life trading for the necessities."

His words, much like Phil's chastising comments, stung. "I'm sorry?"

"Just…not right now."

She lifted her brow as she looked away from him and stared down her new mother-in-law. "When I was a young, *single* mother, Elaine, I didn't have the skills to get a full-time job. You see, I wasn't able to attend college, so I had to make do with what I had, which, in my case, was my art. I often traded my skills for things like diapers and a place to live. I've grown to appreciate the value of bartering."

At some point, Harry had lowered his face and closed his eyes.

"I sent you money," Elaine said, her voice tight.

"Yes," Kara said sarcastically. "That was so very considerate of you. Too bad that wasn't the equivalent of having a partner to help me raise my child." She looked at her husband, the man she'd married less than an hour before. "I think I'll go see about that cake I *purchased* from a store."

She stormed toward the house, slamming the door behind her. Phil stopped filling a glass with water and looked at her.

"You okay, Mom?"

"We should have eloped."

He laughed quietly, but the sound was cut off as the back

door slammed again. She turned to Harry, and her heart sank. She'd never seen him angry before, but he clearly was now.

His dark eyes narrowed, making him look ominous. "What the hell was that, Kara?"

"Excuse me?"

"Hey," Phil intervened quietly, "Jessica is in the bathroom."

Harry pointed to the other room. "Upstairs. Now. *Please,*" he added when Kara didn't move.

She turned and marched through the house and up the stairs to his room.

He closed the door behind them. "Was it too much to ask that you not instigate a fight with my mother today, of all days?"

"I didn't instigate anything, Harrison. She asked me a question. I answered it."

"By twisting a knife in her gut."

"You mean the knife she put in my back thirty years ago?"

He rolled his head back. "Jesus Christ, Kara. One day. That's all I wanted. One *fucking* day of not dealing with this pity party that you refuse to give up."

Kara straightened her back as she widened her eyes at him. "What did you just say?"

He shook his head. "Nothing. I didn't mean it."

"Oh, for God's sake, Harry. For once in your life just stand by what comes out of your mouth. If you said it, you meant it. You think I'm living some kind of pity party? Me? Why would I be having a pity party? I lived my life, Harrison. I did something with my life. I gave birth to our son. I raised him. I provided for him. I did it all on my own, and I even managed to see and do some amazing things. I've had a pretty great life, as a matter of fact. What about you? Huh? What did you do with yourself all these years? Besides buy a cookie-cutter house and sit behind a desk every goddamned day."

"At least my life wasn't selfish, Kara. You were so busy running, you never stopped long enough to think about anyone else. You could have come home. You could have made sure I knew I had a son."

"Your mother—"

"Sent you away. Yes, I know. You've made that clear."

"Fuck you," she screamed as she started around him.

Harry grabbed her arm. She struggled against his hold, but he pushed her to the door and put his hands to her face.

"Stop," he whispered when she tried to pull away. "Please stop."

She held herself rigid but quit fighting him.

"What are we doing?" he breathed. "Jesus, what are we doing?"

She blinked, but she couldn't stop herself from sobbing. "We…We shouldn't have gotten married."

"Don't."

She shook her head. "It's not too late. We can call the priest and ask him not to mail in the signed license. This won't be legal. We won't be married."

"*Stop*. We're going to fight. We're going to push each other's buttons. It's what couples do. But we're never giving up on each other and definitely not on the first day."

She swallowed hard as the world closed in on her. "I don't want you to hate me."

He sighed as he pulled her from the door and wrapped his arms around her. "I could never hate you. I just wanted today to be perfect. I overreacted when it went to hell. I wanted us to look back on today and remember it as the day we brought our families together."

She laughed through her tears. "Well, we'll remember something."

He pulled her with him to the bed and snagged several tissues from the nightstand to wipe her face.

"I'm sorry," she whispered. "What I said about your life. I didn't mean it. You've built something amazing. Something Phil always wanted and needed. What you've done is important."

He wrapped his arm around her shoulder and kissed her head. "And I understand why you never came home. I honestly do. I don't blame you. I could never blame you."

"I didn't mean to start a fight."

"You didn't. I did."

She sighed and looked at him. "Don't do that, Harry."

"Do what?"

"Take the blame for what I did. Elaine hit a nerve, and I responded. I knew I was picking at wounds, and I did it anyway. That's what I tried to tell you. I can't stop myself. Not with my parents, and apparently not with yours. I guess I'm just not ready for this happy family façade I'm trying to pull off. And it's not a pity party."

"I know." He ran his hand over her back. "This is a hell of a situation."

She fell back on the bed and looked up at the ceiling. "I ruined our wedding day."

He dropped back beside her. "No. You just made it more memorable."

Kara exhaled a shaky breath. "You know how I like to run away from my problems?"

"Yeah?"

"You want to run away with me?"

His lip curved. "Now?"

"Right now."

"What about our cake?"

Kara grinned. "I'd rather have ice cream. Just so happens, I know this great place."

"Let's go." He pulled her to her feet but stopped her when she headed for the door.

Putting his palm to her face, he brushed his thumb over her lips and smiled slowly. He dipped down and kissed her tenderly. When passion started to slip into the kiss, she leaned back and shook her head at him.

"You're just going to have to wait for that."

"Damn," he whispered. Draping his arm over her shoulder, he guided her from the room.

They'd just reached the first floor when Charles stepped out of the living room. The sorrow on his face immediately dampened Kara's spirits.

"Leaving?" he asked.

She nodded.

"May I have just a minute? Please?"

She drew a deep breath as Harry kissed her temple and headed toward the kitchen.

Charles gestured toward the living room. "Sit with me. Please."

She eased down onto the sofa, and he sat next to her.

"You remind me so much of my mother. Have I ever told you that?"

"Yeah. When I was younger."

"Right." He smiled. "She was so strong and brave."

Kara scoffed. "I'm not brave."

"You are. You couldn't have done everything you had to do if you weren't. I know we've said this already—I've apologized and you've accepted—but maybe…maybe you need to hear it again."

"Dad—"

"I never knew how to be a father to you, Kara. From the day you were born, you were so strong-willed."

"Stubborn."

"Determined. You were determined to be independent. To be your own person. To color outside the lines every chance you got. I didn't know how to handle that. You were never a bad child. You were just so *strong*. How could I be a father to you when you didn't need me?"

"I needed you."

"No, you didn't. You allowed me to be there, but you never needed me. You never needed anyone. And you've proven that in the way you raised Phil. You had that same grit growing up. You could take on anything, and you did it alone. Honestly, Kara, I don't see how you could have raised him any other way. You've always been on your own, even when you were a kid. I guess, maybe that's why I reacted the way I did when you told us you were pregnant. If I'd known how to parent you better, maybe I could have prevented that. Maybe I could have kept you on the right track."

She lowered her face and sighed. "Dad, I was a hormonal teenager infatuated by a very handsome boy. Nothing you could have done would have prevented me from being with him. The fact that I was so independent, as you call it, is probably the only reason I didn't get pregnant sooner. I was terrified to talk to him, let alone do anything else. But graduation night, you know, I suddenly thought I was a grown-up. You didn't raise me wrong. You didn't fail me. You were a great dad."

"No, honey, I wasn't. After you disappeared, we hired someone to find you. He came to the house with a list of questions. Where did you like to hang out? Who were your friends? Who was the father of the baby? Was there someplace that you always wanted to live? Did you know people in other areas of the state or the country that you would turn to? We couldn't answer any of that. Because we didn't know. Because we never bothered to know you. We just tried to...keep you coloring in the lines, and you just kept pushing back, and we didn't try harder." He smiled sadly. "Which leads us to me apologizing again."

"I don't need any more apologies."

"We're still on shaky ground, Kara."

"Apologies aren't going to fix that."

"What will?"

She inhaled deeply. "I don't know. I don't want to be angry. I want to just forgive and move on. But there are parts of me that are still very angry. I think I'm better, and then something sets me off. I try to control it, but—"

"That never was your strong suit." He chuckled. "You do tend to say what you feel."

She closed her eyes and attempted to push away the urge to cry. "I'm trying, Dad. I am. I'm sure sometimes it doesn't feel that way."

"You've had a long time to stew over things."

"Yeah. And believe me, I did. Whenever life settled down and things got quiet, the past replayed over and over in my mind. That's why I never stopped moving. Because I didn't want to have to think and feel. But I've stopped. My life is settled, and things are quiet. And all the things I've been running from are catching up to me, and sometimes I feel like they are tearing me apart inside. I wish I could make it stop. I don't want to feel like this anymore." She lowered her face as tears filled her eyes. "Harry is giving me this brand-new start. And I don't want it tainted by the past. But I can't pretend I'm over the hurt, because denying it only seems to make it worse."

"So how do we move forward?"

She swallowed down the urge to cry. "Harry and I are going to take some time. We're going to stop worrying about you and Mom and Elaine, and we're going to focus on us now."

"Kara—"

"I know. You're sick." She couldn't stop the sob this time. "I don't want—" Wiping her cheeks, she took a deep breath and exhaled it slowly. "Daddy, I'm afraid of ruining what little time we have left."

He gripped her hand and nodded. "I understand. I do. You think I'm not terrified of saying or doing the wrong thing? I missed so much of your life. I just don't want to miss a minute more."

"I don't want that either."

"You were about to walk out on your wedding."

She lifted her finger and grinned. "Yes, but I was taking my groom with me."

Charles chuckled.

"Harry has this calming effect on me. I don't know what it is, but he's always had it. Being with him makes all this feel less overwhelming. I don't do well with feeling overwhelmed."

"You never did." Leaning over, he kissed her temple and slid his arm around her shoulders. "I need you to know that even though I didn't always make the right choices, I was always proud of you."

"Dad," she whispered as the emotion in her chest bubbled up again.

"And I've always, *always* loved you." He kissed her head one more time. "Go find your husband. Let him bring back that sense of peace we stole during your dinner."

She sighed heavily. "I love you, Dad." She was slipping her feet into a pair of sandals when Harry poked his head from the kitchen.

"We going?"

She smiled. "Yes. We're going." She held her hand out to him and tugged him closer when he slid his palm against hers.

"You okay?"

"I'll be better when *my husband* gets me some ice cream."

He smiled about as wide as she'd ever seen. "Then I'd better get *my wife* some ice cream."

CHAPTER EIGHTEEN

Harry smiled as Kara pulled her hair back and used the elastic band she'd been holding between her teeth to secure the mass in place. He couldn't think of a time she'd looked more nervous—not even on their wedding day.

"I can't believe you are making me do this," she said.

Harry kissed the back of her freshly exposed neck. The way a shiver always rolled through her when he pressed his lips there had made it his favorite spot. "It's just dinner."

"With that prick Mitch Friedman."

"He actually just goes by Mitch Friedman now."

She stopped fixing her hair and smirked at him in the mirror. "I think you're developing a Kara Martinson-approved sense of sarcasm."

"Canton. Kara Canton-approved sense of sarcasm." He swatted her behind. "Hurry up. I don't want to be late." He left her to finish getting ready, whistling as he walked out of the bathroom and sat on the bed to put his shoes on.

"I can't believe I'm doing this," she called a few minutes later.

He'd lost count of how many times she'd said that since he informed her of their plans. "Consider it part of our plan to let go of the past."

She crossed the room and pushed him back on the bed. "Are you sure you wouldn't rather stay home?"

He ran his hands up her thighs as she straddled his hips. "Don't tempt me."

"Oh, I am tempting you." She reached for his belt buckle, but he grabbed her hand.

"Dianna wants to meet you. Apparently she got quite a kick out of the story about how you squirted paint on her husband."

"I'm not sure I want to meet her. What kind of woman marries a man who treats his girl like an ornament?"

"That was almost thirty years ago, Kara. He's grown up since then. And please don't call Dianna his girl. I don't think she'd appreciate it. He'd likely be amused, though."

She pushed herself off him. "I'm sure."

He leaned up, watching as she shrugged into a sweater. "He invited us to dinner to celebrate our marriage. Quite frankly, I'm glad someone besides our son is excited for us. And Dianna is a very sweet woman. Give her a chance. You may actually make a friend."

"I can't imagine that I could possibly have anything in common with Mitch's wife."

"She's from Oregon." He smiled when Kara stopped reaching for her earrings and looked at him. "Born and raised in the northwest according to Mitch."

"Well," Kara said, "maybe she won't be so bad after all."

Kara hated that her old high school nemesis could still raise her blood pressure. This time, however, it wasn't his commentary on Frieda Kahlo's eyebrows that had Kara riled up. Damn near every time a woman walked by, his gaze was wandering. Dianna, who turned out to be far too sweet for the rat, was oblivious to her husband's interest in every female around but her. Kara, on the other hand, was ready to rip his head off.

"I would love to take a class," Dianna said.

Kara blinked a few times and refocused. "I'm sorry?"

"A class. With you. Painting. I never could get the hang of art."

Dianna smiled, and Kara felt her frustration grow. She wanted to scoop this woman up and rescue her from the vulture who couldn't stop looking at their server's breasts.

"Mitch says you play piano," Harry offered.

Mitch returned his attention to the conversation. "Oh. She used to. Not much anymore." He reached over and patted Dianna's shoulder like she were a dog. "All she cares about these days are what the kids are into."

Dianna's smile faltered a bit at his dismissal.

"I love the piano," Kara said. "How long have you played?" She saw a guarded light in Dianna's eyes. She'd been there—in that place where everyone treated her art as a hobby. Hell, she'd grown up there. Her parents still seemed to think she'd eventually outgrow her craft. Leaning closer, Kara pushed Mitch from her mind and focused on subtly rebuilding the woman he probably didn't even know he was tearing down.

They talked about art, music, theater, anything that brought a spark to Dianna's face. By the time their meal ended, they had established a long list of shared interests, and Kara genuinely liked her. She wanted to spend more time getting to know her, but when Mitch suggested drinks, Kara insisted she was ready to go home.

She was moments from being free of Mitch when he nabbed her into a hug. It wasn't overly friendly, but it made her skin crawl.

"It was good to see you again, Kara," he said in her ear.

She leaned back and held his gaze. She wanted to tell him she was on to him and his sleazy ways, but she forced a smile instead. Turning to Dianna, she took the woman's hand and squeezed it. "It was wonderful to meet you."

"You, too. It's not often I get to talk about music."

"Me neither. Let's get together for lunch soon and do it again." She put her arm through Harry's and walked with him out of the restaurant.

"That wasn't so bad," he announced.

She pulled him to a stop and looked directly into his eyes. "Are you kidding me?"

His brow creased with confusion. "You looked like you were having fun."

She exhaled and her frown deepened. "Don't pretend that you didn't notice him looking at every woman in that place like she was on the menu while his wife was sitting right there."

Harry sagged a bit. "Yeah. He does that."

"It was horrible. She doesn't deserve that. I don't even know her, and I know she doesn't deserve that. I'm not a fool, Harry, and I'm certainly not a prude. I know men look, but don't you ever act like that when I'm right there."

"I wouldn't."

She exhaled and looked back at the restaurant. "She puts on a good front, but she's so sad. I could see it in her eyes." She pulled from him and started for the car.

They were buckling their seat belts before he asked, "What's going on in that mind of yours, Kara?"

"Nothing."

"It's something."

"All my adult life, I've been around women with that same look in their eyes. Women who'd had their spirits trampled in one way or another. They never saw it coming. They were all so blind. We were all so blind. I won't be again."

Harry frowned. "Don't lump me in with those people who hurt you, Kara."

"I'm not."

"You are. You think I don't hear what you're saying? You're warning me not to hurt you, as if I've done it before. But I haven't. I was betrayed, too. I just didn't realize it until much later."

She put her hand on his. "I know. I'm sorry. I can't help but feel solidarity with women like that."

"Like what?"

"Broken. She's broken, Harry. And it hurts my soul because I was broken, too. I want to help her. She needs someone."

He looked down for a moment before meeting her gaze. "Just make sure you are doing it for her."

She creased her brow. "Why else would I do it?"

"Because fixing her problems is just another way to avoid yours." He reached for the ignition. "Don't even try to deny it."

She huffed as he backed out of the parking spot. "You sound just like your son."

"Are you sure about this?" Harry asked as he taped a box shut.

"Positive," Phil said, doing the same.

"Your mom isn't happy."

"That I'm moving out or that I'm taking Jessica with me?"

Harry laughed. "Both. But mostly the latter."

"Jess isn't thrilled either, but she'll be okay. She can come over anytime she wants. We're not going to be that far away.

And she can have plenty of sleepovers at Grandma and Grandpa's house."

Harry nodded. "I like the sound of that." Leaning on the box, he bit his lip for a moment before saying what had been on his mind for a long time. "What's it going to take for you to start calling me Dad?"

Phil stopped for a moment before shrugging. "I don't know. I hadn't considered it much, I guess. Do you want me to call you Dad?"

"Yeah."

"Okay. Dad."

In that moment, Harry could have sworn it was Kara standing before him. She had that same kind of logic that was so basic it was almost illogical. Harry wanted him to call him Dad so he would, like it was no big deal, yet he probably never would have done so if Harry hadn't asked. Now that he had, it was settled. Simple as that.

"You know"—Harry reached for another box and started assembling it—"she's not the only one who isn't ready for you to move out. I just got you back."

Phil nodded. "I know, but it's time." He dropped the tape he'd been using and sat on the edge of Jessica's bed. "I don't have to tell you that Mom and I have this crazy back-and-forth relationship."

Harry laughed. "No. I figured that out pretty quickly."

"But under it all, Harry...Dad...Mom is my rock. It kills me to know how unhappy she's been for so long. I always thought she was so carefree. I hate that I couldn't see through her act."

"Hey," Harry said firmly, "you were the kid, Phil. Your mom's happiness wasn't on you."

"But it was. Because she didn't have anyone else. And I'm not trying to twist a knife here, Dad. I know you kick yourself over that. I'm not throwing it in your face. I'm just pointing out the facts. It was Mom and me. Always. And I should have known she was so sad. I shouldn't have added to it by being such a little jerk all the time. Even after we got here and I could see the change in her, see that she was balancing out, it didn't really sink in how miserable she'd been all these years until you two got together and I saw her happy. For the first time in my life, my mom is happy, and I'm not exaggerating about that. And I'm happy for her, but you know what else?"

"Hmm?"

"I feel like I can take some of that burden I've always carried and pass it on to you. I've always felt like I had to look after her. You know how she can be. She just dives in, and so many times I felt like I had to rein her in for her own sake. I had to stop her from doing something too insane. That's on you now. And I can breathe a little easier knowing she has you to be there for her."

Harry nodded. "You shouldn't have had to take that role, Phil, but I'm glad she had you."

The younger man nodded and pushed himself up. "I'm glad we have you now. It feels right, you know?"

"Yes, it does." He knew that more than he thought Phil could possibly understand. "Do you still think it's crazy that we got married so quickly?"

Phil chuckled. "Yes. But that's Mom."

"Well, this one was on me."

"That's Mom's influence, then. She has a way of making people want to let go and just jump into things."

"She does. I love that about her."

"I love that you keep her somewhat more grounded, so, you know… Let her have the corner on the insanity market."

Harry laughed as he watched Phil wrap up a few of the knickknacks that sat on Jessica's dresser. "What about you? Are you happy here? In Stonehill?"

Phil nodded. "Yes, I am." He looked up at Harry. "I love working with you. I love that whole following-in-my-father's-footsteps thing. It's kind of cliché," he said, shrugging when his cheeks turned red, "but as a kid who didn't have you around growing up, I like that we're so close now."

Harry's heart warmed, and he damn near wanted to cry. "You feel like we're close?"

Phil lifted his gaze, and hints of Kara's insecurity played in his eyes. "Don't you?"

"Yeah. Yes," he said more firmly. "Yes. But I…I like hearing it from you."

Phil smiled and turned his attention back to packing. "I imagine Punk and I will be here a lot, but you and Mom should have your own space. You need that as much as we do. I've relied on Mom to help me for a long time. I need to get that independence back. We all do."

Harry nodded his agreement, and they finished packing in silence.

"Okay." Harry sealed the last box. "Is that it?"

"Yup. That's it."

They carried the boxes down to Phil's car. Harry was giving him the bedroom furniture he'd purchased for Phil and Jessica before they had moved in. Kara had found a living room set and kitchen table for them, all traded, nothing bought. It never ceased to amaze Harry what she could accomplish when she put her mind to it.

They'd spent Sunday getting Phil and Jessica settled in. Now, their first quiet evening alone on the sofa, she dug out a needle and spool of thread while he skimmed the paper he had set aside that morning in favor of packing. The moment was so basic, so every day, that it made his heart feel full. Watching her—his wife—sew on a button was the most perfect thing in the world.

"I love you," he said.

She glanced up over her glasses and smiled. "I love you, too."

"No," he said, causing her lips to fall. "I love you. With everything that I am."

She lowered his shirt and pulled her glasses off. Her eyes filled with concern as she met his gaze. "What's wrong, Harry?"

"Nothing is wrong. That's the point. In this moment, there is absolutely nothing wrong. Everything is right."

She stared at him for a few seconds before her eyes softened and her lips curved again. "Yes. Everything is right."

He nodded and returned to the paper in his hand. Once she was sewing again, he peered over the pages and watched her, thinking how his life couldn't get more complete. The feeling was disrupted by the ringing of her cell phone. She looked at the screen and scrunched up her nose at him.

"Hi, Mom," she practically sang, looking at him.

As Harry watched, her face went from a sarcastic smile to colorless and slack. Her mouth fell open.

He moved to her side. "What is it?"

She didn't answer, so he took the phone from her.

"Hello?"

"Harrison, it's Kay. Charles is in the hospital. He collapsed this morning and..."

"This morning? Kay, it's almost nine o'clock at night. Why are you just calling?"

"They were running some tests. I didn't know what to tell you."

"We would have come over."

She was silent for a moment. "It would appear my daughter is avoiding me again. I thought it best to respect that."

Harry sighed and ran his hand over his hair. Kara certainly came by her stubbornness naturally. He looked at his wife, saw that same old hurt written all over her face. Putting his hand on hers, he got as much detail about Charles's condition as he could pry from Kay before hanging up the phone.

"What's wrong with my father?"

"They don't know yet, but he's slipped into a coma. We should go."

She shook her head. "She doesn't want me there."

"Stop," he insisted. "Listen to me. Everything you say and do over the next few days are going to stay with you for the rest of your life. You do not want to live with the guilt of not being with her right now. Despite the past, despite everything she's done to hurt you, you need each other right now."

"I don't know how to do this. How to act like a daughter."

He turned her face so he could look into her eyes. "You aren't acting, Kara. You are her daughter. Come on. We'll call Phil on the way."

CHAPTER NINETEEN

Kara had never liked funerals. She had wanted to skip the entire circus, insisting she would say goodbye to her father in her own way, but Harry and Phil convinced her to go. If for no other reason, they said, then so Kay wasn't any more upset than she was already. Not that she seemed to even care that Kara was there. She'd stood next to her mother for the first few minutes, but she was quickly edged out by people she didn't know and who her mother failed to introduce her to. They offered Kay hugs and shared memories that Kara had no tie to. She didn't know the people or the stories, and Kay was too distracted to try to include her.

Harry had gone to find her coffee, and Phil had been pulled into a conversation with some of Kara's extended family. She'd given up trying to reconnect with them after the third time she overheard a whispered profession that she at least had enough respect to come home for the funeral.

She found a chair near a window and collapsed into it so she could look out at the heavy, gray clouds.

"Ignore them, Kare-bear. You know how they are. Gotta look down their nose at someone. Those of us who matter know why you pulled a Houdini."

Kara grinned as she turned to the woman who had dropped into the chair beside her. Before today, she hadn't seen her younger cousin Becky since they were kids.

"I hear congratulations are in order. Not on this..." Becky gestured around the room. "You got married, right?"

"Eight days ago."

Becky creased her brow. "And then Uncle Charles passed. I'm sorry."

"Thanks."

"When Aunt Kay called to say you came home, I couldn't believe it. I didn't think we'd ever see you again." She put her hand on Kara's. "I remember when you disappeared. They were terrified. They searched for you everywhere."

"I didn't exactly disappear. I was sent away."

"You know they didn't mean that, Kara."

"I was physically dragged out of the house and told not to return. I sat on the porch for hours waiting for them to calm down and let me in. They didn't. Trust me, Beck, they meant it."

She gave Kara an exaggerated frown. "You always did take things too far. I'm glad you got to see Charles, though. We all wished you'd come home sooner. Grandma Martinson especially. She asked for you every day when she was sick. It was so sad. We were constantly reminding her that you were still gone. Why didn't you just come home?"

Kara looked at her cousin, and her feeling of comradery faded. The blame always came back to her, didn't it? They all asked the same question: why hadn't she just come home?

But nobody asked why her parents hadn't simply hugged her, dried her tears, and promised her things would be okay instead of screaming ugly words at her and kicking her out.

While everyone else was sharing stories about how Charles was always there for them, she was stuck with the memory of his face red with anger as he told her she had never been anything but a disappointment.

"You're not going to break your poor mother's heart anymore! Get out, Kara Jane. Get out of my house and don't ever come back."

She swallowed a sob before pushing herself up.

"Hey, I didn't mean to upset you," Becky called, but Kara didn't stop walking.

She pushed open the doors of the funeral home, and the cold autumn evening compressed around her, stinging almost as much as her memories.

Why hadn't she just come home?

When she took a breath, the cold filled her lungs, nearly choking her. The feeling was so symbolic. That suffocating sensation. She shook her head, trying to dislodge the panic rising inside her. She knew this feeling well—this overwhelming need to escape. Being here hurt too much. This place hurt her back then, and it was hurting her now. She needed to leave. No place else in the world had betrayed her like Stonehill.

Logically, she understood it was the people, not the place, hurting her. But when had Kara Martinson ever been logical?

Canton. Kara Canton.

"Mom?" Phil called.

A moment later, his suit coat was over her shoulders and she was looking up at him.

His concern faded into clear disenchantment. It had been weeks since he'd looked at her like she was letting him down, but it was there now. That look she knew far too well. "You can't run, Mom. Not now."

She swallowed hard. "I can't stay here."

"What about Dad?"

Her lip trembled. How long had her son wanted to call someone Dad? All his life. Now he had that. He had his father. The father he'd always wanted. She put her hand to Phil's face. "He has you now. He'll be okay."

"No, he won't."

"All those years, I was so alone and so afraid, but I would look at you and you would somehow make me feel better. You were this little miracle, this little bit of proof that I'd done something right. When Harry looks at you, he feels the same. He'll be okay because he'll have you."

"He loves you."

"I love him, too. Very much. Would you tell him that, please?"

Phil shook his head. "You can't just walk away. What am I going to tell Jessica?"

Kara lowered her face as she pictured her granddaughter. Her shoulders shook with the strength of the emotion forcing its way out of her. Phil hugged her to him as what felt like a lifetime of pain ripped through her body and left in the form of body-wracking sobs.

A moment later, a hand pulled her from Phil and she was cocooned in Harry's arms. For some reason, that only made things worse. She wanted to run, needed to get out of this place, but how could she when he was hugging her so tightly?

"Get the car," he told Phil as he held her more tightly.

Kara took several shuddering breaths and leaned back, looking up at him. "I need to go home."

"Phil's getting the car. We're going to take you home."

She shook her head. "No. I need to go home."

Her heart broke even more as her meaning dawned on him.

"No."

"Please. You don't understand. I can't be here."

"Kara. You're upset. You just lost your father. Things are overwhelming right now. But you can't leave. You can't."

"I can't stay."

He held her gaze. The hurt in his eyes ripped another cry from her.

"I can't stay," she said again.

Instead of responding, he nodded toward the curb. "There's Phil."

Kara took a breath, but he gave her a slight push toward the car, cutting her off. He helped her into the back seat and then slammed the door behind her. She spent the short ride home trying to pull herself together. Phil had barely parked the car before she was climbing out. She rushed to the door and unlocked it as quickly as she could. She was on the second-floor landing before Harry made it into the house.

He called out to her, but she ignored him. She needed to leave, and she needed to go now, before he gave her that brokenhearted look and stole her last ounce of strength. She dug into his closet, the closet he was now sharing with her, and found her old duffel bag. She shoved several sweaters inside and was pulling her sock and underwear drawer open when Harry barged into the room.

He grabbed for her bag, but she pulled away from him, ignoring the few articles of clothing that fell onto the floor.

"You're not leaving me," Harry said.

She shook her head. "I'm not staying. I can't." She grabbed an extra bra, a few T-shirts, and then headed for the bathroom, not bothering to close the drawers. They were slammed shut as she packed her toothbrush and a bottle of shampoo. Conditioner was a luxury her bag didn't have room for.

She left the bathroom and shook her head at Harry as he blocked her way. Panic was closing in on her, making it nearly impossible to breathe. "Move. Please."

He grabbed the bag, yanking it from her hands so hard the friction burned her palms. He threw the bag across the room and glared at her with that angry, ominous stare she'd only seen one other time—on their wedding day. Too bad sneaking off for ice cream wouldn't make this particular problem go away.

"You. Are. Not. Leaving. Me."

She tried to push around him, but he stood firm.

"Goddamn it!" she screamed. "Don't you understand? I can't be here. This place is killing me." She turned her back on him, taking several breaths to try to stop herself from completely breaking down.

What seemed to her like an eternity passed before he wrapped her in a bear hug. "I don't want to lose you."

"I know. I don't want to lose you either."

"So don't run."

She slowly turned in his arms. "If you want a divorce—"

"Jesus, do ever listen? I'm all but begging you not to go. I don't want a divorce, Kara. I want you to stay and face this. Face it with me. I'm right here. You're not alone anymore."

She shook her head. "I never should have come here. I just...I didn't want to be away from Phil and Jess. I knew this was going to end badly. I just didn't... I never wanted to hurt you, Harry. Please know that."

"So don't hurt me."

Tears ran down her cheeks as she stepped around him. This time he let her. She grabbed her bag.

"At least...change into something more comfortable. And let me take you...wherever."

"It's better if I just call a cab," she said flatly.

He lowered his head. “Will you call me?”

“You’ll know where I am.”

He finally turned to face her, and the pain in his eyes shattered what was left of her heart. “I need to know that you are okay.”

“You will.”

“I love you, Kara Canton.”

Her lips curved into a slight smile. “I love you, Harrison Canton. With everything that I am. But I’m in a place you can’t reach right now. I wish you could, but I have to find my way back on my own.”

“I won’t wait another twenty-seven years.”

“I know.”

“She’s gone,” Harry said, walking into the kitchen.

Phil sat at the table, looking out the window, a cup of hot tea cradled in his hands. “Where’s she going?”

“I don’t know.” He laughed angrily as he pulled a bottle of beer from the fridge—a local brewery Kara had insisted they support even if the ale tasted like shit. He put the bottle back and slammed the door. “Jesus Christ. I just put my wife in a taxi without a clue where she’s going.”

“She’ll end up on the West Coast. I can make some calls to people in the area. They’ll let me know if they hear from her.”

Harry looked out the window and shook his head. How had things fallen apart so damned fast?

"Are you okay?" Phil asked.

Harry sat across from him. "Yeah." He let out a long, loud breath. "No."

"What are you going to do?"

"I don't know. I love her. But I'm not going to chase her."

"She doesn't want to be chased, Dad."

"Well, what the hell does she want?"

"This is what she does. This is how she copes. She runs as fast and as far from her pain as she can, and when it catches up to her, she runs again."

He shook his head. "Goddamn it. That isn't a healthy coping skill. Running doesn't solve anything. She should know that by now."

"I think it's finally caught up to her. I've never seen her so upset before."

Rubbing his fingers into his eyes, Harry tried to free them from the grit of exhaustion, but they only felt worse. Dropping his hands back onto the table, he looked at his son. "How do I help her?"

"You don't."

"So I let her leave me?"

"She isn't leaving *you*. Did you see the way people were looking at her? Like she didn't deserve to be there. Some of the people were whispering about how much she'd disappointed Charles. I'm sure she heard it, too."

Harry nodded. "Kay has barely talked to her the last few days. She's been so busy planning for the funeral with her sister and friends. She didn't even ask Kara for help. Kara didn't want to insert herself where she wasn't wanted. They're never going to get past this thing between them if they don't just deal with it."

"Dealing with problems isn't Mom's strong suit. She'd rather run away and immerse herself in something else."

"What if she doesn't come back?"

"She will."

"How do you know?"

Phil smiled. "Because we're here. I hate to leave you, but I promised Jess I'd be home to tuck her in. Let me know if you hear anything, and I'll do the same."

Harry nodded. "Phil," he called as his son started out of the room. Pushing himself up, Harry crossed the kitchen and hugged him. It was the first time he'd done that since they had arrived from Seattle. He should have done it more, but he'd thought it would be awkward. He decided to put that notion out of his head. He'd missed out on too many years of being allowed to hug his kid. "I love you."

"Love you too, Dad."

He walked Phil out and locked the door behind him. Trudging upstairs, he collapsed on the bed. He lay there thinking as the hours ticked by while he considered the last few months. They'd been a roller coaster for everyone. So many ups and downs. So many emotions pulling in so many directions. And now Charles's death had multiplied everything Kara was going through. No wonder she was at the breaking point. He just wished she'd let him help her. He wished he knew *how* to help her.

This...letting her go...wasn't right. It didn't feel right. Nothing about letting her go through this alone felt right. She'd gone through too much alone, and he wasn't going to just stand back and allow her to continue her destructive cycle.

The sun was just beginning to illuminate the bedroom when he rolled out of bed. He dragged a backpack out of his closet and followed the same routine Kara had, only slightly less frantically. He grabbed several shirts, pairs of jeans, and some underclothes before heading downstairs to make himself a coffee. It was just after seven thirty, but he only debated a moment before calling Phil.

"What's up?" he asked.

"Is this a bad time?"

"Just getting Jess out the door for school."

"I'm going after her."

Phil was quiet. "We don't know where she is yet."

"I know. But I'm going to find her."

"What do you need me to do?"

"Make those calls and see if you can get a lead on where she is. Look after things at the office. Check on the house. And I guess you should wish me luck."

"I'd bet money she'll end up going back to the commune where I was born. She always considered that her first real home.

Fly into Eugene. I'll see what I can do about having someone there to meet you."

"Thanks, Phil."

"Hey, Dad?"

Harry smiled. "Yeah, son?"

"I know she doesn't make it easy sometimes, but don't give up on her, okay?"

"I won't." Harry hung up just as his coffee finished brewing. Sitting at the table, he opened his laptop and started searching for the next flight to Oregon.

CHAPTER TWENTY

Kara inhaled deeply as soon as she stepped off the bus. The air was filled with the scents of salt and sea. She was home. She tossed her bag over her shoulder and made her way through the crowd. She'd called one of her oldest friends in the world, the same woman who had picked her up from the bus stop the first time she'd arrived from Iowa.

The ride had been long and hard—and not because of the travel. Kara went from wanting to go back and beg Harry to forgive her to wanting the bus to go faster and put more distance between her and her heartache. Every time she closed her eyes, she saw his face, the way he looked at her. He hadn't been surprised. He'd just been sad. Hurt. The one thing she swore to herself she wouldn't do, she'd done in abundance. She'd hurt Harry.

Shaking the thought from her mind, she put on her hand

over her eyes to shield them from the sun as she started looking for Teri. She stopped scanning when her gaze landed on Harry. But it couldn't be Harry. She almost had herself convinced she was imagining him when he gave her that sexy half grin that always drove her crazy. Her heart sank. She had to force herself to take a breath as he started toward her.

"Hi," she said when he stopped in front of her.

"Hi."

"What—What are you doing here?"

"We didn't have a honeymoon."

Kara creased her forehead. "Honeymoon?"

"That's what people do after getting married. But we never did. So, I thought, hey, why not go to the West Coast? My bride loves the West Coast."

She wanted to smile at his joke, but her mouth wouldn't cooperate. She couldn't stop staring at him.

He sighed. "I abandoned you once, Kara. I'm not doing it again."

"You didn't abandon me."

"I did. I abandoned you by leaving without a word. I'm not going to do it again." He caressed her cheek. "When I found you in Seattle, I pushed pretty hard to get you and Phil to go to Iowa. I didn't concern myself too much about what you were going to have to deal with. I knew facing your parents wasn't going to be easy for you, but I just kept telling myself that we could do this, we could get through it and go on. And you tried. But that's not how you get through things. I see that now. I promised I would never try to fit you into a mold, but that's exactly what I did. I wanted this life so much that I pushed you to process your feelings in a way that best suited me. That wasn't fair to you."

"Don't blame yourself for me being so messed up, Harry. I've always been a disaster."

He smiled. "But you are the most beautiful and amazing disaster I've ever seen."

"Sometimes I think you're more disturbed than I am."

"That is possible."

She laughed softly. "I don't know what I'm doing. I don't know where I'm going. I just know that I can't be there right now."

He nodded. "So let's not be there right now."

"What about your business?"

"I've got this kid now. He's going to look after things for his old man." He brushed his thumb over her cheek. "I promised him I wouldn't give up on you."

She lowered her face. "Maybe you should."

"I went to the community where you and Phil lived. It was like visiting a piece of history that I'd heard about but never fully grasped. As Teri was showing me around, I realized there's a big part of you that I don't even know. But I want to. I understand you need to be in this place to reconnect to whatever it is that keeps you going. I'd like to be there with you. If you'll let me."

"You want to stay with me at a community for pregnant teens and single mothers?"

"Yeah. I do."

She laughed softly, not really sure why she was surprised he would react this way. She blinked her tears back and took a breath. "I didn't want you to follow me."

"I know."

"But I'm glad you did." Looking up, she held his gaze. "Nobody has ever cared about me enough to follow me."

Smiling, he put his hand to her cheek. "I care about you enough. More than enough. I'd follow you anywhere."

Leaning into him, she sighed as his arms went around her. "Thank you."

"For what?"

"For loving me."

sh

Harry cursed as the hammer he was using crushed down on his thumb. He sucked at the wound for a moment before shaking his hand out. He wasn't exactly useless with tools, but less than a few hours into his first community living experience was showing him he wasn't as handy as he thought.

Kara smirked. "You'd probably hit more nail heads than fingers if you'd quit looking at me while hammering."

"I can't help it." He adjusted the row of shingles he was working on. "You are so sexy."

She laughed, and he thought he'd never seen her more at peace.

When they'd arrived at the commune, they were welcomed with opened arms and smiles. Kara had spent a few minutes introducing Harry to the women in charge. Then Teri had walked them to a little one-room house to stay in right before she handed them a long list of repairs that needed to be made to it. Kara hadn't batted an eye, but Harry had watched Teri leave, feeling a bit confused. The woman had shown him great hospitality the night before, giving him a room at the big house by the entry to the community. Now she expected him to stay in a tiny house with a leaky roof. It wasn't even a tiny house, really. There was no kitchen or bathroom. Just a twin-sized bed, a crib, and a scratched-up table in the middle.

"We better get to it," Kara had said as she dropped her bag on the dusty table. "It won't be daylight much longer, and I don't want to get rained on."

Within twenty minutes of arriving, they were on the roof, and he had a growing admiration for her roofing skills. And a sore thumb.

Returning his attention to the shingles, he focused on the nails and hammer more than his wife until the project was complete.

He hoped they'd get a reprieve, but as soon as they climbed off the roof, Kara handed him a broom. They dusted and swept out the inside and tossed clean blankets on the bed.

They'd barely done that when the ringing of a bell filled the community.

"Come on. Let's go help with dinner."

And just like that, Harry—as exhausted as he was from a day of hard labor—was standing at a table with a peeler in his hand. The assembly line of people, mostly women far younger than Phil, was passing vegetables along to be peeled, washed, and chopped until the food landed in a pot to be carried to the stove.

Kara was standing next to him, catching Teri up on Jessica and Phil, telling her about her art classes, talking about everything except her parents. Harry realized Teri didn't miss out on that fact any more than he had.

"But did you mend fences before your father died?" she asked.

Kara sighed loudly. "No. Not exactly. I mean, we were talking, but there was still a lot of anger."

"I'm sorry, Kara." The older woman gave his wife a knowing look.

"Don't be. It was more than I thought I'd ever get." Kara's honesty made Harry glad he'd forced the issue with her parents.

"I'm glad you went home. I know it's been difficult for you."

Harry smiled when the woman next to him gave him a nudge. He hadn't realized he'd stopped peeling. He went back to work on the carrot as the subject changed to their wedding. Teri thought it was amusing that they'd left, and Harry was beginning to see this woman had had a big influence on Kara's life—probably bigger than anyone else. It was almost as if Teri had been the mother figure Kara had never gotten from Kay.

As they sat down to dinner, Harry noticed a young woman who looked almost as out of place as he felt. She was shy, but everyone made it a point of speaking to her, including her, trying to make her feel part of the group. The mashed potatoes hadn't even made it around the table before he realized, despite being far enough along into her pregnancy to look like she could give birth any moment, she was new to the community.

She was clearly in the same situation Kara had been in when she'd come here—pregnant and alone. The girl had a deer-in-the-headlights quality about her, and he pictured his wife in her shoes. Putting his hand on Kara's knee, he squeezed it. A silent reminder to himself that he was there for her now.

Harry thought dinner would be the end of their day, but after cleaning up, the group settled into a big room with enough chairs, couches, and beanbags for everyone to sit somewhere. Teri started the meeting by welcoming Kara, along with her new husband, home and introducing Molly, the young girl who'd looked so frightened at dinner. She had arrived just that morning and had spent the day settling in.

"She's going to need a partner," Teri said. Several hands shot up, but Teri nodded at Kara. "Molly, Kara and Harry are already working on getting your house ready. Might was well team up with her. She'll help you out the first few days, make sure you get what you need, and you can do what you can to help them out so your place is ready before the baby comes."

Harry sat a little straighter. Kara hadn't told him they were fixing up the small house for someone specific. He thought they were just doing general repairs on the rundown place. Suddenly he wished he'd put more effort into fixing the roof. Kara had looked like she was working with a purpose. Now he understood she was.

He also thought maybe he understood why she'd started to feel like she was floundering in Iowa. She'd spent so much of her time in these places, where everything she did had a deeper meaning. She hadn't had that in Stonehill. Sure, he needed her, and Jessica and Phil depended on her, but not like this.

The meeting adjourned, and he stood back while Kara talked to Molly. His wife looked so damned maternal, so protective, as she alternated between holding hands and hugging the girl. He was certain she'd even wiped a few of her tears away. Kara had the same look she'd had with Dianna as they'd said their goodbyes after dinner. She had the need to take this girl in and make her life better. It was the same desire she'd told him she had felt for Mitch's unhappy wife.

He took Kara's hand as they walked back to the little house. "You're amazing."

She chuckled. "No, I'm not."

"I watched you with that girl. You're amazing."

"I just know what she's going through and want to make it easier for her, the way Teri made it easier for me."

"Did you live in a house like the one we're fixing up?"

"Yes. Until Phil was five. I guess that's when the running started. After I mailed your last letter."

"I get it now, you know. I get why you needed to come back to this place."

"It's my home, Harry."

"It's more than that. It makes you feel like you're part of something."

"I guess."

He thought for a moment. "You're a part of something with me, too, you know? Maybe not on this scale, but I need you. So do Phil and Jessica."

"I know."

"Have you ever considered becoming a midwife?"

She laughed. "Yeah, actually. I have."

"You should. You have a lot to offer these girls."

She sighed. "I don't know how much those services would be needed in Stonehill."

"We could look into it, if you want."

"Maybe."

He kissed her hand. "We can't stay here forever, Kara. We have a life in Iowa. We have responsibilities. I want to be near our family. I lost too much time with my son not to be with him now. But maybe..."

"What?"

"Maybe we should make this a regular thing. I think being here is good for both of us. We could plan a few trips a year and stay for a few weeks—help out as much as we can while we're here."

She stopped walking and looked at up at him. "You'd do that?"

"Why wouldn't I? Being here makes you happy, doesn't it?"

A slow smile spread across her face. "Yes. Being here makes

me very happy." She threw her arms around his neck. "I don't think I could possibly love you more."

"I couldn't love you more, either." He put his arm around her shoulders as they started walking again. "I heard Molly telling one of the other girls that yellow is her favorite color. I think we should paint the inside of the house yellow. What do you think?"

"I think that would be perfect."

CHAPTER TWENTY-ONE

Kara and Harry stayed in Oregon until Molly and her newborn son were settled into the little house they'd repaired for her. Harry had gone a bit overboard as far as Kara was concerned, but Molly had genuinely appreciated all the improvements. He also had dragged Kara to a bulk shopping center and had her help him buy supplies that could be used at the community. Teri was grateful for the additional baby clothes and cloth diapers that would be distributed as needed.

They returned to Stonehill the week after Thanksgiving. She and Harry had arranged with Phil to have their big feast late because Molly wasn't quite ready to be on her own. Phil, of course, had understood, and while she thought Harry was a bit disappointed to miss his first big holiday with his son, he had agreed it was best for Molly for them to stay.

Being in Oregon with Harry, seeing her life through his eyes, had soothed the rough edges of Kara's anger. She had never considered how the chain of events put her in the position where she was—to help so many girls over the years find their own place in the world. She'd always focused on her pain instead of what she'd gained from it. Living her life, even just for a few weeks, with Harry had given her a sense of peace she'd never had before.

She'd sat with Molly as the girl had given birth, as she'd done with a dozen other girls. With Molly, however, the situation touched Kara on a deeper level. Perhaps because Harry had convinced her to check into becoming a midwife. Maybe because he was sitting next to her, looking terrified and amazed at the same time. Or maybe because she finally understood that her life meant something and helping Molly meant something.

She couldn't blame her mother anymore. She could no longer resent the things that led her to this place. Things came together for Kara in that birthing room. The stars finally aligned for her and the pieces finally fit. After Molly got settled in and Kara and Harry could finally breathe easy, she told him she was ready to go home. He booked them a flight the next day.

There was only one...maybe two...things Kara had to do.

She knocked on the front door to her mother's house and smiled tentatively when Kay opened it, looking angry.

Kara couldn't blame her. She hadn't spoken to her mother since the funeral. Phil had told her that Kara left. He'd looked after his grandmother while his mother was in Oregon. But Kara hadn't reached out herself, and that was wrong.

"I'm sorry," she said. "I needed to get my head on straight, and I couldn't do that here."

Kay stepped aside and let her daughter in. "Phil told me you went back to the place where that woman sent you."

Kara looked around the house. The vibe was different. Sadder. Her father was dead. Sitting in a chair, she waited for her mother to do the same. "That place is my home, Mom."

"Kara—"

"No. You need to hear me. You need to know me. Dad said at my wedding that you guys never knew me. He was right. You don't know anything about me, Mom. Dad is gone. I can't fix things with him. I wish I'd had the guts to tell him the things I'm going to tell you, but I didn't, and now he's gone. But you are going to hear me, and then we are going to put this behind us because I don't want to blame you anymore."

Kay sighed. "I was going to apologize. For the funeral. I should have included you. I was angry. And I didn't want to deal with it, so I dug into what needed to be done, and I didn't consider that you were hurting, too." She smiled faintly. "Seems I have a bad habit of not taking your feelings into consideration. I'm sorry for that."

Kara nodded. "I understand. It's okay. I went to Oregon, back to the community where Elaine sent me. I always end up back there somehow."

Kay nodded. "Well, if it's what you consider to be your home..."

"It is. Because they took me in and gave me a safe place in the world. A place where I finally felt I belonged. I thought it was a temporary solution. I thought once Harry finished school and could afford Phil and me, he was going to send for us and we'd come back here and be a family. But Elaine hadn't told him about Phil. He didn't know I was waiting for him, so he never came. When I finally accepted he wasn't coming, I felt like..."

"An awful lot like you must have felt when Dad and I said you weren't welcome in our home."

Kara nodded. "I was angry and hurt. So I took Phil, and we moved to another community. And when the anger and hurt caught up to me, I moved again. And again. And I never looked back because all that was behind me was rejection. But sometimes, things would get to be too much and I'd end up back at that first community. They'd always welcome me. It did become my home, Mom. It became my safe place.

"When Harry found me in Seattle and brought us here, I tried to keep going forward, but I couldn't. The past was pulling at me. Whenever I was around you and Dad, I would start feeling this anger boiling below the surface because I had never dealt with the hurt and the rejection. When Dad died, everything just fell in on me. It became too much, and I had to leave. I had to go home and recover so I could keep going."

"Did you?"

Kara nodded. "I'm at peace with the past now. I wasn't before, and there was no way I could forgive you and Dad when I hadn't made peace with it. I'm very sorry that I couldn't make things right with Dad before he died, but I'd really, really like it if you would give me another chance to make things right with you."

Kay pulled a tissue from her pocket and dabbed at her eyes. "You aren't the one who has to make things right, Kara. You never should have had to find another home. You never should have had to make a family for yourself out of strangers. We should have been there for you and Phil. Your father never stopped regretting what he said to you that night. I want you to know that. He did love you. Very much. And he understood your anger. As much as he wanted to put things behind us, he understood. So do I. I'm the one who needs to be asking for a second chance. You never needed one."

Kara smiled through her tears. "We're having Thanksgiving next week since Harry and I weren't here. I know you had Phil and Jessica over, but I'd really like it if you'd join us for our family dinner. Will you come?"

"Of course."

"Good." Standing, Kara crossed the room and hugged Kay tightly. Leaning back, she took a deep breath. "Now, I need to go see my mother-in-law."

Kay laughed humorlessly. "She's not pleased with you. Just so you know."

"She hasn't been pleased with me since Harry told her he liked me thirty years ago."

Kay ran her hands over Kara's hair. "I'm sorry we ruined your wedding."

"You know what? You didn't. Harry and I said what we needed to. That's all that matters."

"I'm proud of you, Kara Jane. It takes a strong woman to survive the things you have."

"Thanks, Mama." She kissed her mother's cheek and left to extend one more olive branch. She just hoped her visit with Elaine would go as well.

sh

Harry looked around the kitchen, amazed at what he saw. Happiness. Peace. And, the most shocking of all, tranquility. Kara, Kay, and Elaine were working together to prepare their belated Thanksgiving meal while Jessica sat at the table decorating cookies. This was the first time he'd seen all the women in his life in the same room at once and there was no fear of someone snapping.

Kay and Elaine were comparing piecrust recipes when Kara noticed him watching. Her face lit with excitement. She reached for a towel as Molly walked in behind Harry, carrying a bundle wrapped in blue blankets. Kara wiped her hands as she rushed around the counter to embrace the girl. "I'm so glad you're here."

"Are you sure it's okay for us to stay here?"

"Of course."

"I told her that a hundred times already," Harry said, "and the airport is only twenty minutes away."

Kara put her hands on the girl's face. "You can stay here as long as you want. Now, give me this little guy. I've missed him."

Molly eased the baby into Kara's arms. "I know I wasn't there long, Kara, but I just didn't fit in."

"It's okay," Kara assured her. "Community living isn't for everyone."

"I thought about going home, but..."

Kara caressed her cheek again. "You'll know when it's time."

"I'll get a job and find us a place as soon as I can."

Harry put his arm around Molly's shoulder. "We talked about this, too. Take some time to breathe, kiddo. Having you here to help Kara out is payment enough."

Kara smiled and nodded her agreement. The minute the girl called Kara crying, not wanting to stay at the community, Kara had extended an offer to take her in. She hadn't even consulted Harry first, but he didn't bat an eye. In fact, he'd insisted—for the safety of the baby—the crib be bought not bartered for, and then he'd come home with one the next day, as well as a car seat, cloth diapers, and a stack of new clothes.

He and Kara had given fair warning to the other two women in the room. They were going to make Molly and Caleb a part of this family for as long as it took to get the girl on her feet, and they weren't going to say a single negative word about their decision to open their home.

Surprisingly, Elaine was the one who stepped up and took Molly's hand, pulling her from Harry. "I'm sure you're tired from the trip." She guided Molly farther into the kitchen. "Just take a seat and relax. Dinner will be ready soon. Would you like some hot tea?"

Kara lifted her brows at Harry. He shrugged. His mother had never been maternal, but she was trying. Sometimes it still took him by surprise.

"Let me see, Grandma," Jessica said.

Kara bent down, and Jess carefully tugged a blanket back to see the scrunched-up little face.

Kara smiled, and warmth spread through Harry's chest as he watched his family. *His family.*

"This is Caleb," Kara said softly.

Jessica stared at him for a moment. "He's the baby staying in my room?"

"Yes, he is."

She eyed Kara suspiciously and tilted her head as if pondering. "Are you going to paint my room blue?"

"Oh, no. I wouldn't dare cover up those unicorns."

Jess stared at the baby for a minute before looking back up. "You're still my grandma. And Grandpa is still my grandpa."

Kara smiled and hugged her. "Always."

Phil came into the crowded kitchen, rubbing his hands together. "Okay. I got all your stuff upstairs."

"Thank you, but I would have done that," Molly said.

He dismissed her with a wave of his hand. "It's not a problem."

"Molly," Kay said, "help me set the table, please."

The women trailed out, each carrying dishes. Phil followed

with a pot of potatoes in his hands. When Caleb let out a little cry, Kara started gently bouncing and soothing him while stroking Jessica's head at the same time, silently reassuring the girl of her place. It reminded Harry of the day he'd watched Kara talking to Jess about her new school.

Harry's heart filled to bursting as Phil came back in for the organically fed, free-range turkey. "You guys better hurry before we eat it all."

"Better not, Daddy." Jess darted out of the kitchen.

Kara laughed as she walked to where her husband had been taking in the scene. "What's on your mind, Harry?"

Reaching out, he stroked his hand over her hair. "Our mothers are getting along."

"Yes."

"I'm married to the love of my life."

Her smiled widened. "Yes."

"We have a wonderful son and an amazingly beautiful granddaughter."

"Yes."

"We have a chance to help Molly and Caleb the same way you were helped so long ago."

She nodded. "Yes."

"This is it, Kara. This is the happiest day of my life."

Kara sighed as he moved in and kissed her sweetly. "Mine too, Harry."

CONTINUE STONEHILL SERIES WITH FRIENDS WITHOUT BENEFITS

STONEHILL BOOK TWO

AVAILABLE NOW.

Keep reading for an excerpt.

STONEHILL SERIES BOOK TWO

FRIENDS WITHOUT BENEFITS

The stress of the judge's decision hit her again. "Um…not well, actually. I don't know how I'm going to…" She gestured lamely at the room around her. "Our oldest son Jason is away at college and Sam is a high school senior, so the judge didn't feel that Mitch owed me anything. I've been a housewife since we got married. I'm not sure how I'm going to…you know…" She pushed herself up from her seat when a sob started building in her. "When I get stressed, I bake. Would you like some cookies?" She didn't wait for him to respond. She grabbed a container off the counter. "I made oatmeal and chocolate chip. Sam ate most of the chocolate chip ones as soon as they were out of the oven, but there's plenty of oatmeal left." She put the container on the table and sat down. "Please. I don't need to eat all those myself."

He hesitated for a moment but then grabbed a cookie. The silence returned as he took small, measured bites. She watched until she noticed the light glimmering off his wedding band.

"He wasn't wearing his ring," she said before she could stop herself.

Paul lifted his brow in question. "I'm sorry?"

"This morning. At the hearing. It's the first time since we were married that I've seen Mitch without his wedding ring."

Paul nodded, as if he understood exactly how much that had hurt her. He took the last bite from his cookie and carefully brushed the crumbs from his hands onto a napkin, which he folded and used to wipe the table clean. He chased the bite with a sip of coffee. "Look, there's never going to be a good time for me to ask this, but I was wondering..."

"What?"

"I, um, I'm so sorry, but... When Michelle told me she was leaving me, I asked her what she was going to do when this *great guy* she was seeing decided he didn't want to leave his wife. She said that wasn't going to be a problem because you had caught them together. Is that true?"

Her mind again flashed to the night she'd walked in on Mitch and Michelle having sex in his office. He had her bent over his desk as he gripped her hips and thrust into her. Those sounds returned—skin smacking against skin, soft moans. Michelle's black skirt was hiked up onto her back as she clung to the edge of Mitch's desk, and his face was tense as he neared release—a look Dianna knew all too well.

She winced. The painful memory still struck her like a slap across the face. "Yes, it's true."

Paul's cheeks lost a few shades of color, as if she'd

confirmed something he was trying to deny. "Well, now she's trying to say that her relationship with your husband wasn't sexual."

Dianna laughed bitterly. "Oh, it was sexual, all right."

The muscles in his jaw tightened, and she had the sudden urge to reach out and stroke his face to help ease his tension. Her hand was several inches off the table before she realized what she was doing and stopped herself.

"I know it can't be easy for you," he said quietly, "especially having just gone through your hearing, and I swear to you I wouldn't ask if there were any other way, but would you be willing to testify on my behalf? About when you caught them together."

Dianna exhaled slowly. She'd give anything not to have to think about her husband's affair ever again. She didn't want to remember how completely unexpected catching Mitch cheating had been. Or how she'd walked into the room, as she'd done a hundred times before, carrying his still-warm dinner. How the Tupperware container fell to the floor. How the sound of plastic crashing onto the tiles pulled the lovers from their passion as shock rolled through her, numbing her mind and freezing her body. She didn't want to remember how Mitch gasped out *her* name or how the woman he was screwing lifted her face off his desk to smirk.

Dianna closed her eyes, and hot tears slid down her cheeks. She didn't try to hide them. Her pain overpowered her dignity, as it had so many times in the last six months. How could she care that this stranger was seeing her cry when her heart hurt so much?

"Please, Mrs. Friedman—"

"Dianna," she spat. "I *really* hate the Friedman part right now."

"Please, Dianna. She doesn't deserve alimony."

She scoffed. "God. Wouldn't that be something? I was informed that *I* don't deserve alimony because I am capable of work. Yet you think *she'll* get alimony when she's got my husband to support her."

"I think she's got a hell of a better attorney than you had."

"Yeah, well, I couldn't afford to pay the bills, support our children, *and* pay for a top-notch attorney, could I?"

He didn't respond.

"Sorry," she whispered as her angry words lingered between them. "That wasn't directed at you."

"I know. I have no right to ask you to go through this again, but she will get alimony if I don't stop her."

"Well, that hardly seems fair. To either of us."

"So, you'll testify?"

Those damned memories flashed through her mind again, bringing with them the familiar stinging and crushing of her soul. She reached into the container sitting between them and grabbed a cookie. She'd likely eaten a dozen the night before, but that didn't stop her from biting into another as she debated.

"Yes," she said, finding a conviction that she hadn't felt for a long time. "Yes, I will testify."

ALSO BY MARCI BOLDEN

STONEHILL SERIES:

The Road Leads Back

Friends Without Benefits

The Forgotten Path

Jessica's Wish

This Old Cafe

Forever Yours (coming soon)

OTHER TITLES:

Unforgettable You (coming soon)

A Life Without Water (coming soon)

ACKNOWLEDGMENTS

When I initially wrote *The Road Leads Back,* I wanted to be respectful in my presentation of Jessica and Down syndrome. I reached out to Mark Priceman of National Down Syndrome Society who was kind enough to read and assist in areas where I had concerns. To learn more about Down syndrome, please visit: www.ndss.org

ABOUT THE AUTHOR

As a teen, Marci Bolden skipped over young adult books and jumped right into reading romance novels. She never left.

Marci lives in the Midwest with her husband, kiddos, and numerous rescue pets. If she had an ounce of willpower, Marci would embrace healthy living, but until cupcakes and wine are no longer available at the local market, she will appease her guilt by reading self-help books and promising to join a gym "soon."

Visit her here:

www.marcibolden.com

facebook.com/MarciBoldenAuthor

twitter.com/BoldenMarci

instagram.com/marciboldenauthor

CPSIA information can be obtained
at www.ICGtesting.com
Printed in the USA
LVHW011620300720
661977LV00002B/198

9 781950 348008